PRAISE

The Half Wives

"Part historical fiction, part heartbreaking romance, and part bildungs-
roman, this book takes readers on a journey rich with detail and darkness. Told over the period of just one day, the book reminds us that our
lives are filled with so much, and, if we'd only slow down, we'd have so
much more to see . . . *The Half Wives* is the kind of book that makes
you want to hold your loved ones a little closer and say prayers of thanks
for the blessings of each day."
— *Seattle Book Review*

"The developing San Francisco of the 1890s becomes a rich background
for these three as they play out their messy, somber, and intertwined
fates."
— *New York Times Book Review*

"Gorgeous details . . . Rivets the reader's attention to the last humbling
page."
— Historical Novel Society

"[A] finely tuned novel about grief, interpersonal connections, and
the long journey toward independence . . . The novel moves smoothly
. . . between present-day events and people's memories about their moments of happiness and heartache. Pelletier provides poignant insight
into the odd, dependent relationship between Lucy and Marilyn that
directs their lives, even though they've never met, and Marilyn doesn't
know of Lucy's existence."
— *Reading the Past*

"Pelletier sketches [her] characters in great detail to create a moving
story of hope and loss."
— *Booklist Online*

"Pelletier's writing is moving and enthralling and conveys the conflict at the heart of the book . . . [she] keeps readers hooked right up to the book's satisfying conclusion."
— *Publishers Weekly*

"Pelletier's second novel unfolds a complex story in the span of 24 hours . . . [The author] expertly fills in the back story — introspection and memories mingle smoothly with the present . . . Well-crafted characters struggling alone with shared grief furnishes a coursing river on which this intriguing story effortlessly flows. Tough to put down."
— *Kirkus Reviews*

"*The Half Wives* is a profoundly hypnotic and mesmerizing work. The characters do not capture you as much as claim you, as the writing — languid, heartbreaking, and hopeful — pulls you deep into their world. The backdrop of Old San Francisco comes gloriously alive, as though the mist of the city itself rose from every page."
— Kathy Hepinstall, author of *Blue Asylum*

"Stacia Pelletier's *The Half Wives* is set in the past, but it is a story for any time: a poignant, sometimes heart-rending, beautifully crafted, always gripping tale of loss and love, and the human need to try to set things right. A great read."
— Kevin Baker, author of *The Big Crowd*

The Half Wives

The
Half Wives

STACIA PELLETIER

Mariner Books
Houghton Mifflin Harcourt
BOSTON   NEW YORK

First Mariner Books edition 2018

Copyright © 2017 by Stacia Pelletier

Reading Group Guide copyright © 2018 by Houghton
Mifflin Harcourt Publishing Company

Q&A with Author copyright © 2018 by Stacia Pelletier

For information about permission to reproduce selections from this book, write
to trade.permissions@hmhco.com or to Permissions, Houghton Mifflin Harcourt
Publishing Company, 3 Park Avenue, 19th Floor, New York, New York 10016.

hmhco.com

Library of Congress Cataloging-in-Publication Data
Names: Pelletier, Stacia, author.
Title: The half wives / Stacia Pelletier.
Description: Boston : Houghton Mifflin Harcourt, 2017.
Identifiers: LCCN 2016034890 (print) | LCCN 2016046882 (ebook) |
ISBN 9780547491165 (hardback) | ISBN 9781328915412 (paperback) |
ISBN 9780547519463 (ebook)
Subjects: LCSH: Ex-clergy—Fiction. | Wives—Fiction. | Parent
and child—Fiction. | Family secrets—Fiction. | Life change
events—Fiction. | San Francisco (Calif.)—Fiction. | Domestic
fiction. | BISAC: FICTION / Historical. | FICTION / General.
Classification: LCC PS3602.R722885 H35 2017 (print) |
LCC PS3602.R722885 (ebook) | DDC 813/.6—dc23
LC record available at https://lccn.loc.gov/2016034890

Book design by Kelly Dubeau Smydra

Printed in the United States of America
DOC 10 9 8 7 6 5 4 3 2 1

Cemeteries, like people, must move onward to make room for those pressing behind.

—*San Francisco Call*, 1902

Preface

—BLUE? WHERE'D YOU RUN OFF TO?

The wind carries Ma's voice. She's outside the pump station.

—I'm in *here*.

My reply isn't loud enough. Overhead, gray city glares through the broken skylight.

I kick again, until I'm floating on my back. How deep does this cistern go? Deep enough. I'm half floating, half paddling, glad now for those wretched swimming lessons she made me take.

—Blue!

The water in this well is moving. It gurgles and foams. It tugs at my shoes and skirt and sailor jacket. A man's voice reaches my ears:

—Hear something again. Swear I do.

—I'm here, I call again.

Ma'll have to pay for that broken skylight. She'll have to stop her work, march me home, tell me to change out of my wet clothes and put on something *presentable,* and that will make her late. If I cause her to fall behind whatever she's trying to do today, whatever task she's trying to accomplish, she'll grow not angry but sad, which is the worser of the two.

—This is a day to remember, Blue, she said while serving my oatmeal this morning. She set the bowl down so hard, the oats slopped.

—It's a day for the record books. Your mother is finally going to be brave.

Then she turned and wrung out the dishtowel, wrung it until it was drier than dry, until her hands reddened.

Saturday, May 22, 1897

9:00 a.m.

Henry

WAKING IS NOT THE MOST ACCURATE way to describe your current state. You're leaving your bed. That's it. That's a fairer phrasing. Leaving this mattress, this flea trap, after eight hours.

The last fellow to stay here left behind a maroon robe. You're now wearing it. You're not proud. You're cold. You're cold, and you feel old. The robe ties with a sash around the waist. You're still wearing last night's suit beneath it. The robe turns you into a velveteen sultan. You're double-dressed now.

Stand; pace the cell; that's right—get the blood flowing. That's the trick. The robe is too short, and your legs are too long. The police dragged you here last night. You're in the park lodge, otherwise known as the Golden Gate Park police station. They arrested you after the so-called mass meeting.

If by *mass meeting* they mean fifty people, all right, fair enough. But Hubbs did not achieve a higher head count than that. Neighborhood consensus be damned. That's what they tried to claim—consensus.

Not one soul except the officers of the cemetery associations has lifted a voice against it.

That was Hubbs's line, Hubbs the attorney, leader of the Richmond Property Owners Protective Association. He spoke last night to the assembly at Simon's Hall. *Over three hundred thousand citizens of San Francisco are in favor of the removal of the graveyards.* And again, in the same speech, stroking his handlebar mustache: *You can't make money and be successful alongside of a graveyard.* And again, in conclusion: *What use could a dead man have for a view?*

So it's Henry Plageman against three hundred thousand, then. Henry Plageman presently being held in the police station. Your odds could be better. That's nothing new. The neighbors don't know what to do with you. The improvement associations have declined to let you serve on their boards. You're the thorn in their flesh, the pebble in their shoe, the cliché they overuse. *He's against progress. He's against property ownership.*

—I *am* a property owner, you reminded them.

When you took the stand at the front of Simon's Hall, towering over the podium to say your two-minute piece, for a moment there, you felt on fire, suffused with that old sensation of arresting an audience. Then the members of the Point Lobos Improvement Club started whispering, and their wives started smirking. You lost your temper, banged your fist on the podium like an idiot, like a politician.

—Have some respect for the dead, you said. —Of which I am not yet one.

Now you're the sole occupant of this holding pen across from Golden Gate Park, this rat hole that shares a wall with the local sanatorium. A threadbare sheet covers your mattress. This police lodge serves the entire Richmond district, all of the Outside Lands. And it's May 22, a day that comes but once a year and, when it comes, lasts as long as a year. Your timing couldn't be worse. That's nothing new either.

If your mind wanders toward the Cliff, toward the occupants of the black-and-white-tiled kitchen inside the cottage at Sutro Heights, pull on the reins and tell yourself: Stop.

Your watch has to be somewhere. It's in your coat, the old Prince Albert slung over the chair next to your hat. Your head's pounding. The policeman blessed you with his billy club last night. Your watch: nine o'clock. Christ. You slept later in this pen than you do in your own bed. You need to be long gone before this day takes over. Be ready, in place, prepared. Your small family has followed the drill for fourteen years, has perfected it. May 22. Marilyn's day; your wife's day. It will swing you from the rafters; it will wrap its limbs around your neck. This day will force you to carry it. You'll do whatever it commands.

The police arrested a second man last night. He must be locked away in a backroom.

Thomas Kerr has to be close to seventy. Thomas Kerr, foreman of Odd Fellows' Cemetery, arrested, like you, for disturbing the peace.

You don't care for the cemetery foremen, not as a rule. But they're your only allies left in this fight. They're salesmen; they sell peace after death. They trade in burial plots, coffins short and long. They drive hearses, hire gravediggers, maintain grounds, chase vagrants off private property.

When you told them you couldn't let the proposal to close the cemeteries reach the board of supervisors, when you declared you needed to kill the proposition before anyone called a vote, the foremen agreed to help.

The cemetery men want to protect the Big Four: Laurel Hill, Masonic, Odd Fellows', and Calvary Cemeteries. All these reside within spitting distance of one another, blocking the Inner Richmond, with Odd Fellows' touching the district boundary.

Your attention falls farther west. The city cemetery, also known as the Clement Street or Golden Gate Cemetery, contains the finest land in San Francisco, in all of California, if by *finest* one means wild terrain overlooking the Golden Gate strait, a windy hinterland with views of Mount Diablo and Mount Tamalpais across the waters, desolate gravesites surrounded by dunes and topped by native scrubs, pansy flowers, poison oak, berries.

The cemetery men regard you with interest and pity. They don't disagree with your cause. It's one for all and all for one at this point.

But the city cemetery is the largest and poorest, the most dilapidated. It's a potter's field, a burial ground for the immigrant, the indigent, the homeless, the nameless, the outsider. It's filled with Chinese and Italians, Jews, forgotten mariners, wanderers of obscure Scandinavian and Germanic origin. It also holds the benevolent associations, members of the Knights of Pythias, charity cases from the St. Andrew's Benevolent Society. It's an underground metropolis. Here and there someone has tried to tend a grave, has left behind an offering or artifact: a bracelet, glass beads, a pair of eyeglasses. The Chinese leave clothing.

You have to find a way out of this police station. Does Marilyn know you're here? She thinks you're still home, sleeping. Your wife never comes to your bedroom anymore. She respects your privacy too much.

She'll be out the door early herself. Marilyn will survive today, survive May 22, by staying in motion, by moving ceaselessly. She will not slow down once. Not until, say, eight o'clock tonight, at which point she'll go to pieces. You'll be there when that happens. Your wife needs you. She doesn't want you, but she needs you. You understand this. Oh, do you. You can't help her; your presence does not console her. But to leave would cause harm, so you stay. You are not a physician, but you strive to live by the oath a physician is required to take. It's the one law, the one principle you still retain; in common parlance, *first, do no harm.* This is easier lived than explained.

So you will stay and sit with her through the night after cramming the stove with coke, the stove you will light even though it's May, especially because it's May. And if Marilyn permits, you'll hold her, guide her head until it rests against your chest, gather her in. Wrap a blanket around her. Not a quilt. Never a quilt.

—No, she'll say.—No blanket. Get it off me, Henry. I'm burning up.

—You're freezing.

—Take it away.

Then you'll hold her again, and when it becomes time to sleep, you'll ask to lie down beside her, to visit her room and sleep with her in your arms. Some years she will say yes, and other years, most years, she will rise and drift out of the parlor without uttering a word. As if the question did not hover there between the two of you year after year, as if the man who asked the question never existed. Maybe that's accurate. Either way, the rule remains the same: Wait to fall apart until the last gasp of the day. Don't collapse too soon. She cannot hold her burden and yours too.

Marilyn retired early last night. She didn't accompany you to the neighborhood meeting. She can't stand the words the debaters use. *Disinter. Exhume. Remove.* Right about now she'll be arriving at the Maria Kip Orphanage for the grand opening of its new facility. Orphans are her latest cause. Last year it was the San Francisco Nursery for Homeless Children. The year before that, it was the Home for the Aged Poor of the Little Sisters of the Poor, on Fourth and Lake.

This station has to have a telephone. No—you can't ask for Marilyn's help this morning. Any diversion from the day's plan will unravel her. You're off schedule as it is. You'll have to find a way out of this station on your own.

There's time, but not much. Nearly a full day's labor awaits.

What supplies are needed? A trowel. A rake or shovel. Pruning shears.

What plants? Roses? No. You tried them once. Disaster. Calla lilies are better. That's what you ordered.

And if your mind wanders outside, bounds again toward the tin-roofed cottage at Sutro Heights, the modest lean-to overlooking the ocean, then haul your thoughts back the same way you'd haul your dog, Richard, away from a stray cat and tell your thoughts: Sit. Stay. Let her be. Let Lucy Christensen find the way on her own.

Your name is Henry Plageman, and you are forty-nine years old, too tall for your own good, six feet three inches, more tree than man; you shed pieces of yourself every time the wind moves. You used to be a Lutheran. You used to be a minister. You have a wife. You have two children, one living. You have a lover, or you used to. What counts as success in this life increasingly troubles you. By now you have come to grips with the fact that becoming a great man is not going to happen to you. You'd settle at this point for being a good man. This, too, is proving impossible. Of late you have picked your battles with exceeding care. Often, you lose.

The light down the station corridor flickers on and off, a lone incandescent bulb suspended from the ceiling with twine. The front door creaks open. A desk sergeant, shirt stained and untucked, shuffles inside. He reeks of stale beer. Noticing you in the lockup, he rubs his eyes. He has the look of a man who would rather be someplace else. You know the feeling.

—Good morning, you say.—I hope you slept well. Now please get me the hell out of here.

Marilyn

YOU ARE THE WIFE IN THIS TALE; you are the one people will call faithful.

You are also the volunteer, the decorator, the baker, and the breakfast maker. You're the butler, the accountant, the lawyer, and the tailor. You're the mother, the woman who has lost something. And you slept as long as you could this morning—which was not very—because May 22 never fails to ground you, never fails to rip off a chunk of wing. You can't imagine where you'd fly even if you could.

Maybe this is your problem. Maybe it's time to exercise some imagination.

Richard roused you at half past six when he began whining to be let out. He should have stayed put. He should have remained curled at your side, his mucosal eyes meeting yours; in that predawn moment you saw that the only way to survive today was through Richard alone, geriatric basset hound Richard, who never says a word, who tottered into your world with his thumping tail one year after your life stopped, who has followed ever since, wordless, patient, cold-nosed, nudging you outside, sniffing your hands, observing you, observing Henry, canine head cocked, measuring your conversations. *I'm still here,* you told him—told Richard, that is—quietly, so your husband wouldn't hear. Your dog understands what Henry has failed to comprehend: you dwell in purgatory.

Henry tells you he lives there too, but if that's the case, why can't you find your husband beside you anymore; why can't you feel him near you? Two people in limbo should be able to glimpse each other, to call out across the canyon. At the very least, one should hear an echo. On the surface, you remain Lutheran; underneath lurks a good old-fashioned Romanist. You yearn for miracles, signs and wonders, prayers for the dead, indulgences, confession to a living person. What good is a sin confessed to the air, admitted without consequences? The only good confession is one that hurts.

You are Marilyn McLarty Plageman, forty-one years old; you never thought you would be this old in your life. You are still beautiful. And today is Jack's day. You hate it; you are wedded to it. This day is here when everyone else fails you. It never fades and never changes. It never implores, never broods, never disappears for hours in the study, then reemerges in a cloud of exhaled cigar smoke to send Richard outside to do his duty. This day prostrates itself on the sandy beach and spreads its limbs in frantic love of you. This is your day, your submission. You would leave it all behind if you could.

That's not true. You could leave it all behind if you wanted. But you've borne enough; you've earned the right not to move, not ever again if you don't choose to.

You do want to move, sometimes. You do and don't, both.

The news is buried on page 14. You didn't learn about it until you finished hanging the streamers and haggling over the placement of bunting along the balcony and stairway landing. You wouldn't have picked up the newspaper at all if Catherine Wood hadn't just forced it on you, her finger pointed, charged with jubilation.

—Look, Mrs. Plageman. Isn't that your husband?

RICHMOND PROTESTS LOUDLY read the headline. Beneath, five sentences summed up last night's situation:

Big Meeting of Property-Owners to Voice Their Will. Potter's Field Must Be Removed. No Obstacles to the Progress of the District Will Be Tolerated. Sanitary and Other Reasons Urged. Gravediggers from the Cemeteries Attempt to Break Up the Meeting, but in Vain.

The full article followed, two columns laid out above an advertisement for a dermatologic ointment promising "sleep for skin-tortured babies."

Mrs. Wood jabs again.

—See? That paragraph, there. Read it. That's your husband, isn't it?

About fifty unfriendly persons packed a meeting of the Richmond District Improvement Association last night in Simon's Hall and caused a disturbance that for a while threatened to break up the meeting. Order was restored by the vigorous action of Policeman Schafer, who arrested Mr. Thomas Kerr and Mr. Henry Plageman for disturbing a public meeting.

Her bow-shaped mouth parts slightly. Her straw boater bears a mauve ribbon.

You hand the newspaper back to her.

—It's a mistake.

—Are you sure?

—Of course I'm sure. My husband went to that meeting last night, but he wasn't arrested. Don't be silly.

You're not about to let Mrs. Catherine Wood, incoming vice president of the board of managers for the Maria Kip Orphanage, know the truth. You're not about to tell her you didn't bother to check if Henry returned home last night. Didn't wait up for him, didn't fix him a nightcap as a good wife should. Didn't cook him breakfast after awakening this morning in your bedroom. You sailed out the door alone.

—Are you *quite* sure he's all right? It sounds serious.

—Of course I'm sure.

—If you say so.

—I do say so. Do you think I'd be here if my husband had been arrested? If that article contained any truth, Mrs. Wood, I'd be down at the police station this minute.

—I guess you would be, she acknowledges.

Now you've done it. Now you can't duck out to retrieve him from the park station. You'll have to fake that everything's fine; you'll have to stay here with your hardheadedness and let Henry handle things himself.

That's all right. Henry's fine. He takes care of things on his own. Besides, he landed himself in this mess. He can haul himself out. You're not being harsh. This is how one has to deal with him, or one will be dragged into the quagmire that is Henry Plageman. Bad things happen to your husband. He's brilliant and outspoken and unlucky. People misread him; he misreads people. He resists help. He hates being corrected. He scowls when he should grin and grins when he should scowl. He's so tall, he has to stoop, bend from the waist. This turns him into a leaning tower.

He's obsessed with the cemeteries.

When he returns in the evenings from his store, he sits on the front porch in his dilapidated wicker rocker and smokes a thin cigar; he reads and thinks and broods. If you stand in the bay window, you can observe him without interruption. To get his attention, all you have to do is rap. He twists around, rocking, still smoking, considering one ponderous thought after another, surrounded by potted and hanging ferns, plants you ordered from the nursery, anything to relieve the desolation of a street populated by weeds and sage. He calls to you through the glass pane:

—What do you need, Marilyn?

You don't always have an answer. Just because you ask for him, does that mean you have to have a reason? Can't a wife issue the summons for no other purpose than the desire to summon?

—At least the cemeteries make me interesting in my old age, in my dotage, he said recently.

—That's not the word I'd choose, you replied from the open door; you had stepped outside to see if rain was coming. It wasn't.

—What word? *Dotage*?

—No. *Interesting*.

Ten years ago he quit his parish. He left his pulpit for no good reason that you could see and opened a hardware store in the middle of nowhere, trading the catechism for the Sears catalog. And so you had to move to the middle of nowhere too, meaning from the Western Addition to the Richmond district, where Henry bought a wood-frame house with ten groaning steps leading up to a slanted front porch. Behind the house, a windmill and a tank supply fresh water. Yours is one of only two homes on the block, a few streets from the city cemetery. You have two neighbors, an elderly couple, former parishioners. When Henry left his pulpit, the Chamberses followed.

—Best thing about church was the sermons, Mr. Chambers said. —With Reverend Plageman gone, we saw no need to continue.

Selling dry goods is more rewarding than pastoring, Henry sometimes says. It's more practical. The results of mercantilism can be measured, tallied. At Plageman's Hardware and General Merchandise, Luther's bondaged will doesn't matter.

Your husband employs one clerk, Stevens, whom you adore. Stevens lives in the flat above the store. A couple of times a year, when Henry heads on his business trips to Portland, Stevens takes over. Both men keep permitting their customers to purchase items on credit. Then they forget to send the bills.

When Stevens does it, you find the forgetfulness endearing. When Henry does it, you find the same oversight exasperating.

You offered yourself as a solution.

—I could bill them, you told Henry. I could collect the payments on your behalf.

He searched your face.—Whatever for?

—Someone has to do it.

—You never forget a debt, Marilyn, do you?

—No, you said.—Not until it's paid.

He should have stayed a minister.

Today is a big day for the orphans. The grand-opening celebration of this brand-new three-story facility on Seventh and Lake starts in two hours. The waxed floors shine. The windows squeak to the touch. Donated chromos decorate the walls. In one corner hangs a lithograph of pointer dogs at the start of a hunt, and in another, a portrait of children with cherubic faces. No real child ever had a face that round.

The local women's guilds have sponsored the dormitory rooms and named them after saints. A girl can sleep in St. Agatha's room, St. Cecilia's, or St. Ursula's. There's no such thing as a Saint Marilyn. You've checked.

Yes, today is fully scheduled, packed to the gills from now until midafternoon. You'll deal with Henry at two o'clock and not a moment sooner. Ticket sales are expected to be strong for this afternoon's benefit concert. Where is the twine for that bunting? There's nothing wrong. You're fine. You've figured out a way to get through, to endure another May 22. Perfectly fine, thank you.

—I'm glad to hear it, dear . . .

As Mrs. Wood speaks, she delivers a curious glance. You must have said that last bit out loud.

A woman who lives in the Outside Lands can be identified by her ruddy cheeks, burned not from sun but wind. This effect now appears in your own mirror. You've developed crow's-feet squinting against the wind, and your cheeks—you will never need a pot of rouge. That, too, is Henry's doing.

Mrs. Wood has gathered her volunteers around the staircase to deliver her final instructions.

—Thirty of the best orphans are on their way. One hundred little inmates will reside here come June, but for today we're bringing thirty. A representative sampling.

She pauses to sip her tea, swallows, and replaces the cup in its saucer.

—And we're expecting a hundred and forty guests as well, not including the band. Does everyone have her assignation?

Assignment. She should use the right word. Someone needs to correct this woman's way of speaking. Henry would. He corrects people's grammar like he's brushing lint off a sweater. He thinks he's doing the person a favor. But you've learned to step away and let your husband sort out his missteps in private, let him repair his own mistakes. One has to let Henry Plageman sew his own arm back on or he'll grow agitated and say you're interrupting him.

The volunteers circle around Mrs. Wood, anxious and a bit the worse for wear, women of a certain age, sallying forth to do good works. To contribute.

—Are our stations ready for the guests?

That's Mrs. Wood again, running down her checklist.

—Mrs. Plageman, which station are you covering?

—The buffet.

It's supposed to be a secret, Henry fixing up Jack's garden each year. It's supposed to help. And you cannot bring yourself to dash his hopes.

It's good that he tries. He tries in all the wrong ways. But *that* he tries —that's something.

And when you arrive at the graveyard this afternoon, he'll regard you with eyes you cannot bear. He'll pin you with a pleading expression, a softness, a pliancy lingering around his mouth. He'll scrutinize you, waiting for you to compliment the garden, yearning for some quality in you, some essential spark of the Marilyn he once knew. He seeks some litheness, a forgotten curvature of your soul.

You do not have what he seeks. Or if you do have it, there's not enough to go around. You do not possess enough to cover yourself and him too.

You've tried to tell him, but he fails to listen. Either that, or he listens but you haven't told him. It's growing harder to distinguish between the two.

Mrs. Wood calls the volunteers to join her in a prayer. The piano tuner has arrived; the band of the Third Artillery from Angel Island is expected momentarily. She addresses the group, ten earnest women behind the scenes, a circle of bustles and sashes and plumed hats, heads ducking in unison.

—Dear Father—

As she prays, you squeeze your eyes shut.

—We thank You for this opportunity, for this blessing, for this day.

Now open your eyes. Now shut them again, until the redness imprints itself behind your lids, until all you see is darkness interrupted by redness, silence by light.

Jack Plageman would have turned sixteen today.

—Thank You for Your mercifulness and Your power.

Mercy. Mrs. Wood should have said *mercy* instead of *mercifulness.*

You squeeze harder and harder until you feel like your eyelids might never open again. You no longer believe in a powerful God. You no longer believe in your husband. You hold on to both. They are necessary. They are handholds in the rock.

Henry

THE CITY CEMETERY OFFERS few distinguishing markers. Paupers' coffins, constructed of rough-hewn boards, have sunk and shifted over time. Broken slats doubling as headstones burrow sideways, wandering out of place. It's easy to step where firm soil used to be, to twist an ankle. Abandoned corners and rotting fences greet the visitor. The dead are spread wide. They march all the way to the Golden Gate.

Jack Plageman is buried with the master mariners at one of the highest elevations in the city cemetery. The mariners overlook the strait and the bay. Ships pass through the Golden Gate as the headstones keep watch.

Your neighbor Chambers belongs to the mariners' group. Chambers acquired the plot on your behalf; he obtained permission for your son to be buried there. You're not a mariner. You've never sailed a day in your life. But you wanted Jack to be able to see the coast.

When you asked Chambers to speak to the mariners, to request the favor, he didn't hesitate.

—How much space does he need? the mariners wanted to know.

—No space at all, really, Chambers said.

—What size coffin?

—Small.

—Small?

—Small. Chambers nodded. —For a two-year-old.

Them's mariners, you overheard a gravedigger telling his dog when you visited once at sundown. The old man stood leaning on his shovel as the dog nosed a coffin rope. *They're put there so's they can see the ships come in.*

Burials in the city cemetery require patience. Sand seals off any open holes wherever the wind blows. Dig a hole an hour before an interment, and, if the wind kicks up, the hole will vanish by the time the coffin is lowered, driven sand filling the earth's cavity.

That's what happened in Jack's case. The ground didn't want to take him. You had to borrow a shovel and enlist Chambers's help to reopen the hole your parishioners had dug out of the goodness of their hearts the day before.

Fingers blistered, lips chapped, the two of you rolled your sleeves past your elbows and attacked the earth, sand flying, swallowing sand. Marilyn sat, countenance ashen, in the funeral carriage. Her eyes stayed on the waters of the strait.

When it came time to lower the coffin into the ground, you went to her, opened the carriage door, and held out your hand to help her down. The sun burned high overhead, rankled and acrid.

—Sweetheart, it's time, you said.

She sank to the floor of the carriage. A smothered cry expelled itself. She would not allow you to help her.

A few days after the funeral, you paid your first solo visit to the cemetery, and the rain poured so hard it nearly blinded you. Finding Jack's grave proved difficult. You blundered up and out of a shallow ditch, and a half-buried plank, driftwood, snagged your trousers, causing you to fall, palms scraping gravel, the particles sharp with minerals, dried salt crystals.

Regaining your footing, you faced north. Beach sagewort spotted the path, pale twigs stretching toward a fallen sky. You could not ask anyone for directions. It was raining; this was the city cemetery; no one visited the city cemetery in the rain.

Besides, a father should not have to ask for directions. A father is supposed to be good at directions. He should be able to find his child. He should know where his child is at all times.

But you lost Jack that day. You forgot where you'd buried him. You had laid him to rest among paupers and seamen instead of in one of the better cemeteries because you used to believe the Gospel when it said *blessed are the poor.* You used to believe Luther when he wrote *every town should support its own poor.*

Once you finally found the grave, you couldn't leave, or you might not find it again. The fog pulled back, replaced by a howling night wind. The temperatures plummeted. The skies swept themselves bare. The strait vanished into blackness. You spread your overcoat on the sand, on top of where Jack lay; you rested your coat on the top of your son's grave, and then you couldn't remove the coat, because to move it would mean leaving him exposed. So you sat there and couldn't head home, because if you rose to leave now, you would have to don your coat, and if you donned your coat, then Jack wouldn't have it, and nothing would lie between your child and the night but wind and darkness; he would be marooned out here in the wasteland with nothing but sand to cover him. You couldn't stay, couldn't leave. You sat, blinkered. Your knees locked up.

At last you remembered the living and staggered up, reaching for your coat. You retraced your steps to the entrance on Thirty-Fourth and Clement. Losing your bearings, you missed the last streetcar of the night. You walked home. At the time, you and Marilyn still lived in the Western Addition; the walk took two hours. You returned to a wife beside herself, saying she could not afford to lose anyone else, saying this was what she deserved, she knew it, all her life she had been waiting for God to punish her, and now look. You were too spent to pull her into your arms; you went ahead and pulled her into your arms. Sand had caked your neck, filtered into your coat, invaded the pockets and stitching. It funneled downward, sifted to the floor. Sand from Jack's resting place dusted the redwood boards.

In the morning, on your way to the kitchen in your stockings, you slipped. Tiny grains ground underfoot for days. No amount of sweeping would remove them.

The desk sergeant has disappeared down the corridor. He returns with the cane stumper himself, Odd Fellows' foreman Thomas Kerr. The sergeant shuts the older man in the holding cell with you and stomps away, the stink of drink lingering.

— He's in worse shape than I am, Kerr says once the sergeant's out of earshot. — And that's saying something.

One look at the old foreman and you can tell he slept poorly. He's hoary and cragged and weathered. He grips the ivory handle of his cane and bends over it, low and searching, like the old woman in Luke's parable who loses a coin and has to comb the floorboards for it.

— Some night, you say. — Some meeting.

Kerr nods. — Least it's over.

— I'm not sure it is.

— It is. They'll forget us by tomorrow.

When the foreman smiles, he reveals two rows of crooked yellowing teeth.

— Tomorrow's not what I'm worried about, you say.

Today is the problem. You have to make it to the cemetery today. Before two o'clock. Well before. Preferably right now.

Marilyn will make it through this day if the ritual stays unchanged. If it doesn't move a muscle.

Marilyn

AT TWO O'CLOCK YOU WILL MEET Henry in the cemetery. What if he's late? He'll find a way. He'll resolve whatever argument led to last night's arrest. The officers will treat it as a misunderstanding, a dispute among neighbors.

Probably he's negotiated his release by now and is headed to the mariners, striding with those skinny legs of his, that hitching gait. He never takes the streetcar or rides Bailey when he can walk instead.

—I think when I walk, he once explained.

—Why can't you think when you ride? you asked.

—They're not the same.

As for you, well, you think all the time, walking or riding, standing or sitting. Your mind won't shut off. Meanwhile, your husband spends an increasing number of hours outside, braving the elements to chase his thoughts, to catch up with his conscience.

You have done your utmost to dodge this business with the cemeteries. You don't want to know what Henry's doing about them, what he's quarrelling about now.

—Don't tell me, you say whenever he introduces the subject.—I can't hear it. Don't tell me. Just handle it, Henry.

There was that time he went on a tear about an injunction.

—The associations want a city order, he announced, setting aside the newspaper he'd been reading.

He was out on the porch again in that wicker chair you can't abide. He poured a tumbler of whiskey as you wandered in and out the front door, trying to decide if you could stand to listen to him.

—Marilyn, are you hearing me? They want an order to prevent new burials inside the Big Four.

—What does that have to do with us? you said.

It was late. Henry had worked late on Wednesdays for years.

—It sets a precedent.

—For what?

—If they succeed in passing a statute for the Big Four, they could apply the same statute back to the city cemetery.

—Meaning what?

—When you and I die, they won't let us be buried beside him.

You retreated into the house, leaving the wind to sweep the porch. How dare he. How dare he speak these things while you were trying to digest supper. Unthinking, unfeeling, heartless, foul-mouthed Henry. Your philosopher. Your husband. Mr. Head in the Clouds. Your one and only Henry, who must not change.

He's lost weight in recent weeks. He didn't have much to spare in the first place. He'd better not be ill. You've tried to take care of him, have made every effort to act the part of a good wife. You eat supper together every night that you don't volunteer. True, you volunteer three nights a week, but that still leaves the other four, and Henry, to his credit, rarely complains about your absence.

The other volunteers at Maria Kip sometimes ask if you need to head home at a certain hour. They ask if your husband is expecting his supper.

—Does Mr. Plageman need you? they say.

—An excellent question, you reply, and you continue folding the girls' linens and uniforms.

You miss living closer to downtown; you miss civilization. You miss streets that don't dissolve into mud every time it rains.

You were nineteen, living with your parents and sister in Gettysburg, when you first met him. You remember having to tilt your head up to meet his gaze.

He was twenty-seven years old, two weeks free of seminary. He could not stop looking at you; he placed you under observation, a current of curiosity, dry heat, a hint of alarm emanating from him. He had spent too many months reading books. He did not know what to do with you. He had forgotten *woman* existed outside the written word, outside Luther's pronouncements about Eve, marriage, the Virgin. When he smiled at you, warmth cascaded through the tunnels of your body.

We cannot seem to keep away from each other, you wrote your sister shortly after you and Henry had married.

Penny wrote back: *How long does that part last?*

Henry used to unbutton your dress, unfasten your laces, and remove your undergarments in a painstaking process that took longer than the act itself did. He'd had no experience with the layers a woman wears. He needed instruction. And practice. You gave him so much practice, he could have become a tailor. Then the bishopric transferred him from Gettysburg to San Francisco, which you hated. And then came years of waiting before Jack arrived, and with Jack two astonishing years of tranquillity and quiet, two impossibly short-lived years of believing you might actually take root out here, this planet of sand and mist and rock.

When two people lose a child, the ground beneath their feet opens. A crack in the earth swallows them. How they climb out is no one's business. How long it takes is no one's business either.

You and Henry didn't have to discuss the day's plan. At one o'clock, you will set down whatever saucers or plates you're stacking, break away from the orphanage's grand-opening festivities, board the streetcar west, and disembark at Thirty-Third and Clement. Henry will be waiting at two. He'll meet you at the entrance on Thirty-Fourth across from the caretaker's hut, hat in hand. He'll take your arm, if you allow it, and together you'll hike the curving path due north, past the other burial grounds. You'll make your way to the mariners' graves.

Then, after: Home, choke down a fried egg, swallow some bouillon, read and reread the same page of your dime novel a dozen times without absorbing a word, the ceiling lower than on any other day of the year, the ceiling crushing you both. At eight or nine, rise, murmur:

—Think I'll turn in.

Henry will incline his head, set down his tumbler, extinguish the lamp, and follow you into the dark. This is the one night of the year he will ask if he can share your bedroom. He has given up asking the other

364 days of the year. Usually you refuse. It's not that you don't want him in the room. It's that *you're* not in the room. So if you were to let him inside, he'd swiftly realize he was alone; he'd see that you are, fundamentally, not at home. Marriage is a series of carefully managed letdowns.

If you do allow him to come in, and once in a great while you will, he'll sit beside you on the bed, wrap his arms around you, and hug you so tightly, cup his hand so firmly against the back of your head that your hairpins will poke your scalp. He won't notice. They're not jabbing *his* head. He will hold you and hold some more. There's nothing else he can do. There is no mutual comfort on this night, no crossing from his world to yours.

When did you start being the mother and stop being the wife? When did you start being the wife and stop being the woman? Wait; all wives and mothers are women, but not all women are wives or mothers. It's best to distinguish phylum from class, order from family, genus from species. The more particular identification ought to be the more prized one; the specificity of love ought to win.

Your neighbor Mrs. Chambers says you need to talk more with your husband, to spend more time with him. You maintain a different view. Of late you have seen Henry too much. Familiarity doth not make the heart grow fonder.

Last week you told him you might become a suffragist if you grew any angrier.

—You're angry? he asked, leaning forward to stub out his cigar.

You tried to explain what you meant, but you tripped over your words, and his eyes clouded. He stood and prepared to head inside.

—You don't have to tell me if you don't want to tell me, Marilyn. It's all right.

He spoke as if you needed a reprieve, as if you wanted time alone. That was the wrong response. Henry is supposed to *make* you talk; he's supposed to force you to say what can't be said, to articulate the unspeakable, to scrape out the bottom of the pot. How else are you going to improve? You're not getting better. You're getting worse. Not in any overt sense. You are not an unwell person. But you are missing some vital piece of information about the world and how it works. You're certain of this. If you weren't missing anything, your life would make sense. Wouldn't it?

The thought causes you to drop a plate. It shatters. Mrs. Wood bustles over, bosom like the prow of a ship.

—Are you faint, Mrs. Plageman?

No. But it's early.

Henry

FOREMAN KERR LOWERS HIMSELF to the iron cot in the corner of the holding pen and sits heavily. The mattress groans. He crosses one leg over the other, knuckles gripping the handle of his cane.

—Wouldn't turn down a spot of coffee, he says, and then coughs like he means it. He coughs for a solid half minute.

That hacking hasn't helped your case. The Richmond Property Owners Protective Association has taken to arguing that the cemeteries spread disease, that the dead infect the living. A cemetery foreman with persistent phlegm does little to counter this claim.

Last night, Kerr stumped into Simon's Hall coughing so hard he nearly capsized, and attorney Hubbs, seated on the dais, stroked his salmon-colored necktie and whispered to the officer on his right.

The first quarter-hour proceeded uneventfully. The executive committee passed a resolution asking for mail to be delivered to the outside district. They passed another approving the "firm stance" taken by the streets committee concerning the grading of California between Central and First Avenues.

Then Hubbs read a letter from Mayor Phelan supporting the group's campaign to rid the district of the cemeteries.

Personally, Phelan wrote, *I am in favor of forbidding interments within the City and County of San Francisco and the ultimate removal of the large cemeteries.*

Hubbs looked up.

—Shall we bring this to a vote?

Your hand shot up.

—Sounds to me as if the mayor's forbidding the *removal* of the cemeteries.

—I'm not sure how you heard that in what I just read.

—Look at the structure of the sentence.

Beside you, Kerr hung his head. He'd been in meetings with you before.

—"I am in favor of forbidding"—that's the main clause. Then follows not one but two direct objects, "interments" and "the ultimate removal of the large cemeteries." So, really, it technically means that the mayor is in favor of forbidding *both* interments *and* the removal of the cemeteries.

Hubbs frowned.—Plageman, what's your point?

—The mayor *doesn't* favor the removal of the cemeteries. If he'd wanted to say that, he would have written, "I am in favor of forbidding interments and *of removing* the cemeteries." It's basic grammar.

—I see, the attorney said acerbically. Chuckles arose from the audience.

You pressed: So, while the mayor might want to stop *new* burials in the cemeteries, he doesn't approve of removing the *existing* deceased from their current resting places. I think that can be accepted as obvious.

In the back of your mind, with every argument, every useless thrust, a refrain repeated itself: *Don't let them move Jack. Marilyn will not survive it.*

Hubbs crossed his arms.—Thank you for that comment. I suggest we move on to a vote.

He read the proposed resolution aloud:

—"The district lying between Golden Gate Park and the Presidio and west of Central Avenue has made enormous strides in its rapid growth and development. With the exception, that is, of the blight on the district known as the City Cemetery, which is the burying-place of paupers and all Chinese"—he briefly glanced up from his reading—"many of whom die of loathsome diseases. This blight, as you all know, is situated just west of the settled portion of the Richmond district, over which the ocean winds blow direct from this potter's field and carry with them microbes and other invisible messengers of death and disease, thereby imperiling the lives of many of our citizens."

He paused again.

— It appears death is contagious, you called out.

Kerr laughed, and when the foreman laughs, of course, he coughs. You shouldn't have said what you did, but you couldn't help it. These neighborhood groups have been the bane of your existence for two years. *We need to remove the cemeteries because they block the way to Ocean Beach,* they say one month. *We need to remove the cemeteries because they create pestilence,* they say the next. Or: *We need to remove the city cemetery, but not the Big Four.* Or: *the Big Four, but not the city cemetery. Think of the parks we could build. Think of the children. The tourists!* Or: *Hold on, let's use the land for civic purposes. We want the bodies removed. They stink. The Chinese scrape flesh off the bones of their dead and ship those bones in boxes to Shanghai. Take them all away; we don't want to see them. We don't want to live next door to the dead. Especially not someone else's dead. Take them to San Mateo County. Cart them to Colma.*

Hubbs read on:

— "Now, it just so happens that the city cemetery occupies the most beautiful western spot of the peninsula. It lies in close proximity to the world-famed Cliff House, Seal Rocks, and Sutro Heights. Boards of health, both state and local, have declared that the cemeteries are dangerous to public health."

Kerr dug around in his pocket for a peppermint, found two, offered you one. You motioned it away.

— Now, gentlemen, are we ready to call for a vote? Hubbs said.

Kerr popped both peppermints in his mouth and rapidly stood.

— No, no, no!

You rose to stand beside him. He linked his arm through yours. With his other hand, he thumped his cane.

— No! he repeated.

— Only property owners in this neighborhood can vote, Hubbs warned. — You, sir, are not a property owner.

— The hell I'm not, he roared. — I'm foreman of Odd Fellows'. That's more property than the rest of you gentlemen have put together.

You joined in. — People would never know there was a cemetery here in the first place if it wasn't for you, Hubbs.

— Plageman, you don't have the floor. You're out of order.

But what you'd said was true. The Richmond residents didn't care about the cemetery, hadn't fretted about it one damned second until Hubbs started his petition, knocking on people's doors, telling them the dead were going to come out of their graves and spread infection.

— Poverty killed half the souls in the city cemetery, you said. — Is destitution transmissible too?

A heavyset man in the first row lumbered to his feet.

— If you don't like this meeting, gentlemen, I suggest you go away and hold a meeting for yourselves, one that you do like.

— No vote is going to happen tonight, you fired back.

— Amen, Kerr trumpeted.

Hubbs, stern as a schoolmaster: — The health of our citizens is paramount. And it must and shall be protected by the removal of the cemetery.

Remove a cemetery? How does one remove a cemetery?

Marilyn asked this question when you first told her about the neighborhood's plan. Barefoot, in her nightgown, black hair unbound, your wife bit her thumbnail till the quick sprang red. She didn't look her age. She looked fatigued, but, in that astonishing way some women have, her exhaustion rendered her lovelier, more finely wrought, than she was when rested.

She lowered her hand and warily eyed you.

You told her not to worry; you told her you would take care of things. *Jack will be safe. Jack will never be touched.*

You should not have promised that. Never promise a wife something you're not one hundred percent certain you can deliver. Possibly one hundred and thirty. She's taught you that without uttering a word.

Marilyn does not want any native plants in Jack's garden. She prefers eastern flowers; she wants imports. She wants to pretend she's in Gettysburg, where she still dwells in dreams. Marilyn Plageman has resided in San Francisco more than twenty years, and she still wakes up each morning hoping Pennsylvania lies outside her window. She misses the trees.

Courting, you sent her flowers, cut flowers; that's how she developed her fondness for them. You remember the first time you caught the lav-

ender scent of Marilyn McLarty's black hair, thick as a rope when she
unwound the braid from its coil.

To the mission field, the Lutheran bishopric announced shortly after
you married. *To California.* When you told her the news, she looked at
you as if you'd dragged home a dead horse and settled the carcass in the
parlor. More cut flowers followed, as did a journey west, a hand-carved
bed, nights spent listening to the wind moaning while memorizing her
young body, her pliancy, the pulse visible in her neck, the homesickness
she tried to disguise as quietness. With Marilyn, you felt as if the sun
were shining on your face for the first time. The sun did not last.

And she cried last year when you told her the neighborhood men
wanted to shut down the cemetery.

—What about Jack? she kept saying.—Are they going to move our
Jack?

—What about the land? you added; it was the wrong thing to say.

—Who cares about the land out here? For God's sake, Henry.

She disappeared, fled to her bedroom, before you could explain.
Jack *is* the land. He's been there fourteen years. His body has settled in,
sunken down, dissolved to sand. As has your marriage.

Hubbs finished his speech.

—Here are the procedures for the vote. Only property owners will
be allowed to participate.

You glanced at the back of Simon's Hall, and there was Lucy Christensen.

She stood holding a notation book in one hand and Blue's hand in
the other. Eight-year-old Blue had come to the neighborhood meeting. The two of them hid in the rear, behind the last row of chairs,
which held the reporters, men sporting bowler hats, brandishing pen-
cils, clutching papers.

You blinked, forgot your next line of argument. Lucy had shown up
where your wife could not. Lucy, whom you hadn't seen in almost four
months.

Her fair hair was pulled away from her face. She wore her old black
dress, the faded one. Her square jaw was set. She had strong shoulders, a

sturdy, compact form. A steady gaze. Calm. Careworn. As you watched Blue looking up at her, admiring her mother, your thoughts seized up.

Ten years, Henry. Ten years. Fool.

You mailed her another letter last week. She hasn't written you back. Each time you compose a new epistle, you tell yourself: *This is the last one; I will not send any more; I will give her up. There. See? I have relinquished her.*

Then you return to your desk, Richard staring longingly up at your lap, and write another:

> *We see most clearly in others what is truest of ourselves. But I paid no heed to my own advice.*
>
> *It is no small testament to the extraordinary quality of your person that in the blistering heat of our final conversations, you held your ground, refusing to let me use my narrative to force from you what you can give only in your own voice, not mine. And only from that very space of rupture in my speech — indeed of its cessation — can the gift beneath find its own space that alters speech.*

Probably she thinks you've lost your mind. Probably she sat there with your letter, curled up with her legs tucked under her at the kitchen table, the same table you bought for her, her brow knit as she read your effortful words, saying to herself: *What in the world is he talking about now?*

She should know. She's been with you almost half your married life.

Several of Kerr's friends from the other cemeteries showed up at the meeting then, bringing with them their gravediggers, a cast of rougher characters, *muckers,* Kerr called them, who kept their distance from the police officers in attendance. People started shouting. Over the crowds, over the speechifying heads, you and Lucy spoke soundlessly to each other.

Lucy: *How long has it been?*

You: *Three months. Three months and nineteen days, to be exact.*

Lucy: *Feels longer.*

You: *Yes.*

Lucy: *How've you been?*

You: *Bearing up.*

Lucy: *Still miss me?*

You: *Every goddamn centimeter.*

You might have played a small part in the fight that subsequently broke out. You had drunk a bottle of beer, possibly three, before the meeting. Consuming several drinks remains the only way you can propel yourself into Simon's Hall, the only way you can keep tackling this cemetery fight. Each time, it pulls the teeth out of you. This close to Jack's birthday, it pulls the eyeteeth. And seeing Lucy and Blue upended you.

People started leaving their seats as the argument worsened. The crush of foot traffic blocked your exit. You glimpsed Lucy steering Blue toward the door, leading her outside to safety. She didn't stay. She didn't wait to speak with you.

Back up front, someone demanded that the police officers arrest the cemetery foremen. The older of the two officers shook his head.

— Far as I can see, this is still a discussion. Arguments ain't illegal.

But then Hubbs started shouting, and the women in the front rose from their seats, terrified and disgusted; they wanted no part of this nonsense. Hubbs demanded the police take charge. Kerr left his row and approached the dais, pushing past the crowd. Kerr was a mighty old man, Neptune with his trident, when he chose. He banged his cane and shouted *Amen* and *Amen* as Hubbs demanded the officers return the room to order.

— Amen, damn it! Kerr hollered again.

The two officers strode over and arrested him for disturbing the peace.

You lost your calm.

— How dare you, you said. — If you take Kerr to jail, I'm going with him. He hasn't done anything.

You glanced back at the door — no Blue and no Lucy.

— Glad you can join us, Plageman, the younger officer said, and he brought out a second pair of handcuffs.

That was when you shoved Chairman Hubbs with your shoulder,

but only because you were frustrated, only because he was bobbing and weaving in your face, demanding that the officers arrest you this red-hot second, as if a policeman required any encouragement, all the while continuing to spew bunk about the need for order and quiet, about how all the Richmond needed was peace and order and quiet.

And Lucy and Blue were gone. Vanished. Out the door. Your hands would not stop shaking. The older officer rapped you with his club, though he apologized as soon as he'd leveled the blow. Your hands shook so much, the younger officer had a hard time putting on your cuffs.

—It's a cemetery, you shouted as the police pulled you outside into the night.—It's a goddamn cemetery. How much quieter do you want?

Inside the cell, Kerr picks at his unevenly spaced teeth. It's nearly half past nine.

—I say we rustle ourselves up some breakfast. What do you say, Plageman?

—I doubt they serve it here.

—Not here. Outside. There's a diner on Point Lobos.

—We seem fairly tied up, you point out.

—I ate there once, Kerr says.—Finest fried potatoes a man'll ever get.

He pushes up from the cot and hobbles to the door. Gripping the bars, he peers out, a lord surveying his estate.

—Ham bits and all, he adds wistfully.

—We're not going anywhere until we're released.

Kerr shakes his head.—You've got a lot to learn.

9:30 a.m.

Lucy

YOU ALMOST WALKED UP to him last night. Almost marched right up to the front of Simon's Hall. You couldn't stay away. The urge to see him compelled you.

Reporting on street conditions requires attendance at those meetings, so you had an excuse. But the cemeteries would dominate the agenda. And where discussions of the cemeteries are found, there Henry can be found too. You knew that heading into it. A guaranteed opportunity to run into him.

You needed to do it, to test yourself. To find out if you were over him yet, if your body was over him. Your mind too. You needed to learn if the sight of Henry Plageman had lost its power.

It hasn't.

Your name is Lucy Christensen, and you generally triumph in your head more than you do in real life. You are careful, rash, generous, penny-pinching, wise, foolish, and private. You avoid using certain words: *suffer, trouble, swoon.*

Henry understands this difficulty. Henry steers around certain words too. He used to think so hard about finding the right words and avoiding the wrong ones that he'd halt outside your cottage, stop short, mid-search, the sea in his sightline, much like Richard will hesitate outside Henry's front door, in limbo, unable to trot in or out, torn between mistress and master, two competing goods. You have not actually met Richard in person. Henry has talked about him. If you were to see him on the street, observe his flopping ears, his belly that grazes the earth, you would recognize Henry's dog immediately, but Henry's dog would not recognize you.

Today's another test. Today's the real one. Saturday morning, the Outside Lands. Henry's day, but you're still in it. A person can put an end to something, but that doesn't make it stop. Catch a wolf in a trap, and the wolf doesn't die. It's just trapped. Its eyes stay fast on you.

To keep away from Henry today, you'll recite self-admonitions. You used to have a fair number, but in the past months you've whittled them down to two:

1. Stop being who you're not.
2. Start being who you are.

But being who you are isn't something God guarantees. It's not a right; it's not a law of self-preservation.

A woman can't be two things, your mother once wrote. *She can't be irresistible and unmarriageable too.*

It appears she can, you wrote back. But you never mailed the letter.

You've been reading about rights and responsibilities as part of Blue's American government assignments. Yesterday the two of you tackled the Declaration of Independence. You worked your way through the pages of your daughter's reader, sitting at the kitchen table beside the glow of the lamp; you bit your nails, looking at her fine hair shining in the thrown light.

After Blue read the part where the Founders insisted on the right to seek happiness, she pointed out that they hadn't mentioned how many people found it.

Maybe that was wise of them. Maybe people are better off not knowing.

Your name, your full name, is Lucinda Anna Christensen, and you do not think your age is relevant—but it is thirty-two. Your appearance is not relevant either. You're a reader. *My literary interlocutor,* Henry once called you; you rose and left the room. You thought he'd meant *interloper;* sometimes he uses words unfamiliar to you. But you're catching up. An entire Sunday morning can pass while you browse volumes in

Adolph Sutro's library. You can lose a Sunday morning *and* afternoon if you don't keep track of time.

You don't like keeping track of time. At this point in your life, time ought to be keeping track of you. That's the least it could do.

Right now, you're backed against the brick exterior of the Olympic Salt Water Company pumping station. The station supervisor leans in, his sun-filled face close, the scent of tobacco and yesterday's sunshine radiating from his skin. Behind the pump station sprawls the Great Highway, and west of the highway lies the ocean.

—By damn. You're a curious one, he says.

He crosses his arms over his jacket. Spilling from his overall pockets are sections of lead pipe and pairs of pliers. At his feet, in the sand, rests a pasteboard lunch basket painted to imitate leather.

You try again, raising your voice to be heard over the sound of crashing waves: I'm reporting on the pipe repairs. Aren't you the supervisor for this station?

—By golly, you're a busy one. Quite the interrogator.

Gracefully he expectorates into the sand, taking care to aim away from your shoes. Then he directs a level stare at you. His eyelashes are long and full; his hair's a ginger hue. You're only a couple of inches shorter than this man. You're not used to that. Henry's almost a full foot taller.

—That's not what I meant, Mr. . . .

You've forgotten his name.

—Stone. J. B. Stone, at your service. For anything a woman needs except playing twenty questions. Sandwich?

He bends and retrieves his lunch basket, offers its contents.

—It's too early for a sandwich, you say.

He shrugs, producing a roll of bread separated by a slice of ham. —Suit yourself, he says, and proceeds to tear into it without once taking his eyes off you.

The two of you are about as far west as a person can travel without standing in the ocean. Most maps don't include the Outside Lands of the city and county of San Francisco. Adventurers find their way here, as do loners, misanthropes, missionaries, women of a certain ilk. Mud and sand pave the streets. This far out, the city has erected telephone lines but not streetlamps, has installed water pipes but not sewer clean-outs. It's half neighborhood, half dune. Perfect for not being asked what your life has turned into.

—The steeper the street grade, the better, you'd told Blue before her eighth birthday, back in February.—If I could live on top of a mountain, I would. Like Moses.

You added that last part for Henry's benefit.

Your daughter, hair mussed from the day's outdoor explorations, was tucking into split-pea soup at the table. Henry was putting on his coat.

Blue lifted her head.

—I thought Moses lived in the desert. And if we lived on a mountain, where would Pa live?

Henry started to reply, but you interrupted from your station by the stove.

—Wherever he wants.

Then you took a knife to two heads of lettuce still on their stalks and decapitated them. Henry rubbed his temples. He left for his house soon after.

—Mr. Stone, you say again.—If you can't tell me about the pipe-repair delays, I'll find someone who can.

—Will you, now. He nods, wipes his mouth on the back of his hand.

—Sure hate to be replaced. Sure do love being peppered with questions.

He studies you before returning his lunch basket to the sand.

—I'm out of time, you say.—I have to get this into the *Banner* before deadline.

That second sentence is a bald lie. The first—that's another story. Out of time? What woman isn't?

The truth: You don't work for the Richmond newspaper. You're not a reporter. You're a taxidermist's assistant. You make the dead lifelike. But you do *hope* to be a reporter. You'll write about one subject only; you'll cover just one beat: the city beneath the streets. You'll deliver tales of bitumen paving, describing the engineering and taming of the Richmond district: Here lie the subterranean avenues, the ancient springs, the cesspools and gas lines and clean-outs, the metropolis beneath our feet. Here lies the world everyone walks on and no one sees.

Stone slides an arm up the station's brick wall. This close, he's younger than you thought. He might be several years your junior.

—Surprised I haven't seen you before, he says.—You live close by? I would've remembered you.

He straightens.—Hear that?

Stepping away from the brick, he raises a hand. You don't hear anything unusual. Then again, your hearing isn't infallible.

—Where's your girl? That kid you brought? She didn't sneak inside the pump station, did she? The engine room.

—She's too smart to do that. She's smarter than I am. Blue?

The only reply to your query is the constant sound of waves plowing into sand. Where did your child go roaming? Why in God's name did you allow her? To the north lies a ramshackle strip of simple concessions hardly anyone visits: a beer hall of splintered wood, a photography booth, a shabby play palace, a shuttered shooting gallery. She could be almost anywhere. Here it is, May 22, and you've bungled things already by trying to steal an hour before the day settles in, a few minutes of feeling like a reporter. It seemed important, even today, especially today, to drive a stake in some territory that's still yours. To face forward, not sideways and not backward. To keep away from Henry for the duration.

The corners of Stone's mouth turn down with concentration.

—I hear something. Swear I do. Someone calling.

—She does this. She wanders. She knows the coastline.

—What's her name again?

—Blue.

—Blue. What sorta name's that?

—Her real name's Anna, but it never took.

He nods and looks around, so intent you start searching too. Your daughter's scrappy. She'll outthink, outtalk, outrun anything. She's gunpowder. Combustible. And she sees more than she should.

The Olympic Salt Water Company uses steam power and an underwater pipe to suck the ocean past the Great Highway and into a well encircled by the pump station. From there, with the help of gravity and more steam, the water travels underground, through pipes headed east. Its destination is the Olympic Club downtown, which provides heated salt water and a steam room for businessmen to swim in and then sweat out the previous night's indulgences.

—There it is! Heard—

The supervisor wheels around, sentence unfinished.

—Blue?

The wind drags your call across the highway. Mist is sliding in from the ocean. It will erase the saloon, the tintype booth, the gallery. Behind the station hulks an engine room with a tall stacked chimney. Stone tilts his head at the building.

—Repaired it right before you came. Engines'll be back up soon. Pipes were leaking in a couple places. Not enough to conk out. They'll be swimming in the deep end downtown today.

Steam plumes from the waking engines. Vapor streams from the brick chimney and dissipates into the morning air. You shake your head. Something's not right.

—My daughter.

—Right. Right. Let's check inside. Make sure she didn't wind up someplace she's too smart to enter.

He's teasing you, or trying to. He retrieves a corduroy cap from his pocket and shoves it low on his forehead before testing the handle to the station door. It sticks. He tugs, intent on his task.

—Stand back, lady. Need to get it open.

He shoulders the door, hard. He's wiry, bristling with energy. Humidity and damp have swollen it shut.

—Rot, he mutters.—Might take a minute.

You're used to waiting. You're good at it.

Another letter arrived from Henry last week. The longer this separation has ground on, the more impenetrable his sentences have become. He's waiting for the separation to stop. You're waiting for it to stop feeling like separation.

I used to believe that one could live fully having seen a magnificent sunset. I was wrong.

It is customary to observe a period of protracted, complete silence out of respect for the departed. God knows if or when a space may open within which words might again pass between us.

Did you write him back? No. There's no safe place to mail it to.

You're having difficulty breathing, so you unhook the top of your dress's collar. That's better. When it comes to a choice between decorum and breathing, you'll take breathing. Every time. Though that can lead to problems.

Stone backs up. Again he throws his shoulder into the door. It flies open, sending him stumbling forward. He recovers his footing, and you both peer in. The sound is like three steam dummies colliding in a wind tunnel.

Inside, a cornice and firewall skirt a cistern. Overhead, a broken skylight provides the only illumination.

—Hold on, he says, raising one hand. —I see something.

Here in the dark, he stands awfully near, so close you catch the scent of his skin again: bread baked in sunlight. Henry's skin never absorbed the sun's scent. Your mouth is drier than dry.

Over the past ten years, you've grown used to missing someone, grown accustomed to it. If you didn't miss anyone, if your life brimmed over, brimmed full, if the one you loved stayed by your side, in grasping reach at all times, you have no idea what you would do. Is an ordinary life even what you wanted?

No, Henry would say. *Yet still you went from me.*

Stone again: By damn. Look.

He grasps for a metal skimming pole and points with his free hand at the well. In the water, you see a flash of open mouth, two white eyes, your child's eyes, just breaking the surface. The pump screams into high gear.

—By damn, Stone says again, and you both move.

Blue

FALLING THROUGH THAT SKYLIGHT was an accident. Anyone could have done it. I took a bad step, that's all. I slipped while climbing on top of the pump station, while climbing against the rules, because what else is there to do when Ma's too busy playing reporter to pay attention to me?

Someone has hooked a ladder over the lip of this well. My left foot searches underwater for a rung. The top of the ladder seesaws away. It's loose. It smacks my nose and scrapes my wrist. It disappears into the water. I touch my nose; still there, still attached, though when I draw my hand away, two fingers come back bloody. I keep swimming. The ladder has failed me. My mother has failed me too. Her job is not to live as she pleases. Her job is to take care of *me,* her daughter, her only beloved, eight years old as of February 2.

Blue Christensen is my name, and I am old enough to know better. Or to know more. *Old enough to be told,* Ma said when she thought I was outside organizing seashells.

It's not my fault I fell. Ma was standing outside the pump station pelting a redheaded man with questions, which she loves to ask and hates to answer. She was taking too long, so I made tracks and went exploring. I passed the folding table where Johnny the Birdman and his parakeets and lovebirds hold their show. My shoes crunched over old sunflower seeds. Johnny's birds weren't up this early. I passed the saloon and the shooting gallery; they were closed too. The pump station's rounded top called me back. It said: *Climb me.* Ma didn't notice. She didn't turn around. I climbed all the way to the top. My hands planted themselves on a glass skylight sticky with bird droppings. My knees found the pane too, my knees and hands both. Then the skylight cracked. And then it shattered. I fell through. I fell into the gaping mouth of this well that holds the ocean.

Now my skirt has snagged on something. I'm caught. Can't kick, can't push, can't swim. Someone bangs on the door leading inside.

—Ma!

I reach down underwater and find where my skirt's caught. Something jagged grabbed it. A nail, maybe. When I pull, my skirt rips free. The hem's shredded. Ma'll have to sew it back together. That's all right. She's used to it. Every day she sews up dead animals for tourists to view. When she talks to me about those animals, how they stay stuck for all time in their glass cases, her shoulders go stiff and she looks older than she should.

Or maybe her shoulders have started doing that because Pa hardly ever comes over anymore. Since February, since my birthday, he has come by just twice. And both times Ma left before he visited. I asked her about it afterward.

—I had business downtown, she said.

—Mother, I was not born yesterday, I told her.

—Yes, you were, she replied, and she grabbed my knuckles and kissed them, twice.

This cistern is slimy. My hand flies out, pats for something to grab. I need something to hold, a bolt, a hook. Anything. A pole. A skimming pole. There! Some loon has hooked it too high up the wall for a girl to reach.

—*Ma,* I shout again.

Paddle on. Kick. Stay afloat! Think. Recite those lines from school: *When in the course of human events, it becomes necessary for one people to dissolve the political bands which have connected them with another . . .*

I can recite those words better than my classmates. I put true thought into them. My school meets in a former saloon. Some of the teachers complain, but the saloon part doesn't bother me. I've seen people truly bad off, truly in the soup. One time I saw a man take his life at Lands End. He took a running leap and hurled himself off the edge of the cliff.

It took him three tries. On his first two, he skidded to a halt and leaned over with his hands on his knees. He gasped at the water. His third try worked. He leaped into the fog. He fell fifty feet. He never made it to the ocean. The rocks took him. Later I found out the man was Ma's cousin.

The door bangs again. My name's being called. Finally! Time for her to rescue me. Time for her to do her job. Hopefully she hasn't forgotten how.

And here it comes: suction, full strength, pulling at my feet. This well is a giant's windpipe. It wants to inhale me. I'm up to my eyes in ocean. My whacked nose is leaking. I tilt my head back, and my ears go under. She'd better hurry up. The suction pulls my legs. Two shadows hover above me that move like a man and a woman. It's hard to see.

—Blue, one of the shadows calls.

—By damn, the other shadow says.

Ma's voice is high and thin. I try to shout, but I take in sea instead. The ocean pours into me. Cough it out. Cough, gag, spit. And cough some more.

She yells my name again. She's going to be mad as a March hare when all this is done and over.

—I'm here! Ma—

The shadowy man is interesting. But I can't pay attention to him. This is a giant washtub, and I'm circling the drain. This water is headed downtown.

Hold your breath. Hold it and wait.

I can wait a minute or more. I timed it once, thinking about Pa; when the picture of my Ostrich with his long legs and long face crossed my mind, I took a breath and held it as long as I could, testing for something, I don't know what, until I almost fainted, and Ma came flying, her hair loosed from its pins, her fingers stained with ink. She slapped me awake. She left a black ink handprint on my cheek.

I can taste metal. Far above, shining through the moving water, Ma calls out again. She bends over her boots.

—I'm heading in, she says.

—No, ma'am. I'll do it, says the man.

—She's my daughter.

—Stay back.

The man pushes her away. He has the skimming pole I spied but couldn't reach. He's calling out again: *I'll do it.*

He leans toward the well, toward the water's surface, hands holding the pole out. He has red hair. The skimming pole is long. *But not long enough,* I think. Only I don't think it, I say it. And the sea comes with it.

Lucy

STONE GRIPS THE SKIMMING POLE in one hand and slides his free arm around your waist. The saltwater pump whistles and clangs. His ribs press against yours; his mouth is to your ear.

—Listen, he calls out. —Behind the well's the engine room. Pull the second lever. Pull all the way. That'll stop the pump, and I'll fish her out.

You extract yourself from his grip, bend forward, and begin to remove your boots.

—Lady, don't. Just shut it off. I can't fish your girl out till it's off.

He points at the engine room as you straighten. Planting a hand between your shoulder blades, he adds: Go on now.

Yes, he's younger than you are. His eyes still contain all the things he thinks he has to look forward to.

Today was the day you were hoping to be courageous. To keep away. You already have kept away. You've broken the habit. Save for last night's slip, last night's momentary sighting, you've avoided Henry Plageman for three months and counting.

Today is the last truly hard day, the last date with a hook in it. An anniversary. Not yours. Theirs. But you've lashed your dinghy to their boat.

You move through the darkness to the engine room.

Henry's at the cemetery entrance by now, unshaven, scratching his chin, checking his watch, hoping against hope you'll appear along the path, a pair of gloves extended, even though you said you wouldn't, even though he agreed you couldn't, even though you wrote him: *No more. We cannot continue. Please,* and he wrote back, two words underlined: _I know_.

Three coal-fired steam engines rumble in the rear of the station. A utility door protects the controls, the network of pipes and gauges. You pry it open. Here's a lever. Here's another. Should you pull the one on the left or on the right? Stone said the second. Second meaning left or right? You'll guess right. The lever's stuck. Everything in this pump station has rotted. Salt and sea damp creep inside, seep through all pores.

You hit the lever again, bear down with all your weight, the bar pressed against your sternum. You'll wear a bruise there tomorrow.

Fish her out. Fish her out. J. B. Stone, fish her out of this well.

You hear nothing but engines pounding, feel nothing but your pulse tripping.

—*Almost there,* Stone shouts.—*Almost.* I've nearly . . . hold on. *Shut it off!*

The lever moans as the engine begins draining itself of power. The clanking continues. This pump takes years to stop, takes centuries.

—There! C'mon. That's it. Come on back, lady.

He leans over the rim of the cistern while you fly to him. The way is clear. The pump releases Blue, abandoning its tug of war. She rises, floats upward to the surface, her sailor jacket the first part of her you see. She's facedown.

Stone reaches in and drags her to him, catches her tartan skirt with the pole. One of her arms drapes over the rod as he guides her to safety.

—Hold on. Help me lay her down. Need to put some breath into her.

His eyes flicker up to yours. The engines emit a plaintive final whistle. His eyes briefly say: *I'm here.*

No. You don't want that look. Not today. Today has sufficient worries of its own.

Together, stretching and straining, the two of you lower Blue to the station floor. You can't feel anything from the neck down, can't tell which arms are yours and which are Stone's. Squatting, he brushes the wet hair away from her eyes and mouth.

Pray, Henry would tell you.

Crouching beside her, you check for breath. Stone places a hand on her breastbone.

—She breathing? he asks.—Oh, rot. There's glass stuck to her.

Breathing? Yes. No. Not yet. You pat her back and roll her to her side.
—That's it, he says.—Wake her up good.

Splinters of glass poke through her black stockings. You slap her back. Hard. So hard you see stars. As hard as you did the other day when you were trying to write for the *Banner* about the new macadamized paving and caught her holding her breath; she frightened you into thinking she was choking. Be careful what you punish—this is the mother's comeuppance.

—Let me do it, Stone says.

He takes over and claps her on the back twice. She retches. She coughs water all over his chin and neck. He nods.

—Good girl. Almost there.

She's awake; she's in his arms, sodden, crumpled, resilient. Henry's child. Your child. Her eyes flutter.

—Mother . . .

—I'm here. I'm here. Sweetheart. You're going to be all right.

—I'm very sorry, she whispers, and she passes out again, faints dead away. But she's breathing. That's all you care about; that's all a person can hope for some days.

Stone nods energetically. His ears are a vigorous pink.

—The French Hospital's closest, he says, and his clear eyes lift again to yours, and remain.

What time is it? It's late; that's what time it is. And Henry's still holding out hope you'll meet him today. It's habit. It's tradition. You've done it for nearly a decade.

You two never discuss the oddness of it, the sheer folly of helping your lover tend a graveside garden his wife will visit. It's a tale you'll never submit to the newspaper, a headline you'll never report. Jack's garden isn't yours. It's theirs. But Marilyn is not able to help her husband care for it. Marilyn can endure the city cemetery only so many minutes before her heart gives out.

Henry will have to pull this year's weeds on his own.

Blue

I'M AWAKE. AT LEAST I THINK SO. The redheaded man totes me in his arms. He's jogging along the Great Highway. Leaving the pump station. He calls over his shoulder to Ma, who's running behind:

—We'll bring her to the French Hospital. They'll help. They'll stitch her up.

—What about the Life Saving Service? she calls back.—Those men are trained to deal with emergencies.

I look up at him. My eyes are stinging from salt water. He regards me solemnly.

—I was one. Bunch of drunks. French Hospital's better.

—I can't afford it, Ma says.

—Not to worry.

He winks at me and charges uphill. He's a saddle bum, a cowboy, maybe. But his shoulder makes for easy leaning. I rest my head in the crook of his neck and let him keep carrying me. I can hear the sea slap the rocks beneath the new Cliff House. They built that house too close to the edge. I've been inside only once.

—That place'll slide into the water someday, I'll bet you two bits, the redheaded man says.—Though it's a beautiful sight, I'll say.

He dashes off a smile and hustles up the hill.

Is his smile real? I'm not used to any man but Pa. Neither is Ma.

What kind of *fee-male*—that's how the fellows on the estate say it—spends her days setting glass eyes in the sockets of deer and gluing hair on the bald spots of leopards? They say Ma has a screw loose. If she does, I do too.

A woman is to be a keeper at home, my grandmother wrote to us from Omaha.

Whose home? Ma wrote back. She tore up her reply and didn't mail it. I rescued it from the waste bin.

Grandma likes to accuse Ma of deserting her for no good reason. She likes to write us about her own life, how she crossed the ocean at seventeen, following relatives from Sweden. She wound up in Nebraska. She married her second cousin but lost him to the flu one week after Ma was born.

I prayed to God to grant me a new life, she wrote me and Ma, remembering.

—She should have prayed for something more specific, Ma said when she read that part. Grandma never married again. Eleven months of a fellow was enough.

I'm cold, soaked through from the well. And my ear hurts as bad as a body can imagine. We're closing in on the depot.

—How much longer? I say to the redheaded man.

He says: A few more minutes. Folks at that hospital will put you right in no time.

He looks at me like he fears I'll start crying. He seems shy, like he's not used to talking to girls. He's not as good of a talker as my pa.

The wall is thin between where Ma and I sleep and where we eat, so on the nights Pa visited, I used to be able to hear what they talked about after she put me to bed. One time, she read a letter from Grandma out loud. After she finished, Pa said something about needing to take Ma's mind off things. She said something about what did he have in mind. They whispered for a minute, too low for me to hear. I don't like it when they do that. And then he laughed and said:

—How about a round of chess, then?

—In that case, you're the bishop, Ma said.

—I'm a pawn. At best.

—You underestimate yourself.

—I wish I did, he said.

She should have told him he was the king. That's what I would have said. I can't wait to tell him a well almost swallowed me!

Lucy

— WHAT'S THAT? STONE ASKS. — What's she saying?

— Nothing. She likes to talk to herself.

He raises his eyebrows. You've nearly reached the depot, and you're matching him stride for stride now.

— Let me carry her, you say.

He refuses. — I've got this.

You should be holding Blue, not him. You should take over. But your arms and legs are pistons, pumping without your guidance; they march in time to the word *hospital*, repeated. Rain pelts the brim of your hat, a plain straw sailor with a single pin stuck through it. The pin has worked its way out. Forget the hat. Good riddance. It tumbles off. The sky hangs low, unsettled. A heron passes overhead, so close you can feel the air its beating wings displace. It disappears into fog.

— I see the car, Stone says, and he charges ahead. — There. It's at the depot.

The streetcar depot lies beyond the entrance to Sutro's Baths and Museum. Your employer has aspired to greatness with his baths, has aspired and not quite achieved it. His tourist attraction boasts glass-domed roofs, heated saltwater pools, stadium seating, diving boards, and more than five hundred dressing rooms. His taxidermy workshop — the same workshop where you spend your days — resides upstairs, tucked away on the promenade level. Saturday mornings you're almost always there, aproned and wearing a white skullcap. At your request, Mr. Claude granted you time off today. Without pay, of course.

Stone reaches out to steady your step. The passengers up front turn their eyes to Blue's waterlogged and shivering form as you board. She still rests against Stone's chest.

—You all right? he asks quietly. He's directing the question to you, not your daughter.

You shake your head and remain silent. When you're with any man but Henry, your words fall flat; your vocabulary contracts. What's left to say?

You started the tradition, joining him on May 22. You were the one to intrude. Because you wanted to help him, to see him through it. And then it became part of the ritual:

Show up at nine, before anyone else. Wait for Henry. He arrives; his attempt at a smile collapses. Walk north. When the two of you reach the mariners' section, he stoops, bends over, his hands on his knees; this is God knocking the wind out of him. The sight of that granite angel never fails to flatten him. You hang back; you wait for God to return him. Maybe you're still waiting.

After a few seconds, he reaches for your hand, grips it once, and releases it. Next, the two of you get to work. You don't talk. You labor side by side until the garden is ready. By noon, or half past, your arms and back will ache. You'll rest, sitting on your coat in the sand until he says it's time.

Henry does not like to acknowledge the constraints of his situation, the straitjacket he wears. He prefers to pretend he can breathe.

Your task each year is to dig weeds; clear driftwood; haul trash, the remains of a raptor's kill. Planting new cuttings is Henry's responsibility. You remove the old; he delivers the new.

You vacate the garden no later than one o'clock. Marilyn arrives no earlier than two. What Henry plants never lasts.

—Ten minutes, Stone says, motioning past the passengers toward a bench in the open-air section. —Here's a space. Ten minutes to the hospital. Look, color's coming back into her.

He surrenders Blue to your lap as you take a seat. Her tiny body sags forward. You pull her close, kiss her hair, her eyelids, her nose. You lower your forehead to hers.

Stone remains standing. He doesn't bother with the handrail. Maybe he doesn't need it; maybe his balance is that good. The car lurches forward. Electricity powers the People's Railway, and sparks rain from the trolley pole. Your seat faces outward, offering a view of the passing landscape, roads half paved, half wild. Industry and isolation cohabiting on the same street.

—I can tell you two are related, Stone says, inclining his head toward Blue as the car picks up speed.—I'd have figured that one out a mile away.

—How?

—Stubborn. Both of you.

He laughs, and a half grin escapes him, an expression you haven't seen on anyone in a while: joy arising.

The car hits a rut and shudders. Blue shifts; she's returned to full alertness. You unlace her wet shoes, then pry them off. You'll rub the circulation back into her. Those were good shoes, with stitching around the eyelet tabs. Henry bought them for her.

She stirs again, her lithe little body stretching, seal-like.

—You're stubborn, but at least you can run. Don't know many ladies can run like that, Stone says.—You're fast.

You look down at your feet.—Not as fast as I used to be.

You used to be a fast runner. You used to be a lot of things.

10:00 a.m.

Henry

YOU CAN'T COUNT HOW MANY TIMES people have asked why you and Marilyn didn't bury Jack in Laurel Hill. There are no Chinamen in Laurel Hill, and no paupers. No stink of shallow graves, stale incense, or sour urine where the living indigent have lain. Flowers bloom in Laurel Hill.

— People like us don't bury their loved ones in the city cemetery, one of your parishioners, a manager of a street-improvement company, admonished you, wagging his index finger as if you had blundered on an examination.

— Really? you replied. — It's a cemetery. *People like us* bury their loved ones in a cemetery. What am I misunderstanding?

You spoke with a kind of spastic violence in those days, a rage that pushed people, well-wishers, away.

— They're your parishioners, Marilyn warned.

— Meaning what?

— You're supposed to shepherd them toward goodness.

— We're Lutherans, you replied. — There is no shepherding toward goodness.

That street grader honestly thought you'd made a mistake. He assumed you and Marilyn had buried your son in the city cemetery out of ignorance. Even if that had been the case, which it emphatically was not, what good could his words have accomplished at that point? People are tactless.

According to Martin Luther, a man is simultaneously righteous and a sinner. Man's will is a mule forever ridden by either God or the devil. There is no middle ground. A man is never *not* being ridden.

In the months following Jack's death, you preached your way through the Gospel infancy narratives. The time wasn't right for these passages; it wasn't Advent. Your parishioners studied the floorboards: *This man is talking about the Bible? Whose Bible?*

—Intercalating, you said; you almost begged them—It's the key to understanding Mark's Gospel.

Intercalating is a showy word that means "sandwiching." You have your two pieces of bread, and your meat or a hunk of cheese between. The Gospel writers carry out this sandwiching; they convey meaning by wrapping their stories in series of threes—pericopes, you explained as two elderly women in the front row punctuated your pauses with snores.

—Now, what purpose does this serve? you asked.

Quizzing might be why you lost them, your congregation members, their confidence trickling away year by year, pericope by pericope; you asked questions you didn't need them to answer.

—The purpose intercalating serves, you said, supplying the correct response, is to overlap, intersect, and disrupt the different Gospel stories we have received. It's a form of dismantling. We are pulled to pieces because it turns out that what we took to be the meaning of the infancy narrative, the birth story of the child called Jesus, is *not* the meaning.

—What *is* the meaning, then? one of the elders called out. No one ever calls out in the middle of a Lutheran service unless the situation is desperate.

You glanced up from your notes, bewildered; you had forgotten anyone was listening.

—I have no idea, you said.

Yes, you were frightening them, your parishioners; your grief, your barrage of questions, had begun to alarm them. You weren't behaving the way a clergyman should. Even a clergyman who had lost a son. You were taking too long to recover. Marilyn pushed you to apologize. For causing them to lose heart, she said.

The following Sunday, you stood behind the pulpit, collected your thoughts, and declared:

—My problem isn't you all. My problem is time.

Outside Irving Hall, a stray dog, a roly-poly puppy, no more than a couple of months old, darted across Post Street, and a bicyclist struck it. Its shriek reverberated through the hall. The cyclist cursed and pedaled on. Again your parishioners kept their eyes on the floorboards.

—Excuse me, you said, and ducked around the podium.

—He's getting worse, one of the elders whispered as you strode outside into traffic.

The puppy was on the pavement in the middle of Post Street, rib cage rising and falling, left hind leg broken. Its tail thumped as you knelt. You blocked carriage and foot traffic for a heap of brown fur. Captured heat from sun on the pavement warmed your palms.

—I'm Henry, you said.—And who might you be?

The dog's tail thumped harder.

—Richard it is, then, you said, and you hoisted him into your arms and carried him home. You belonged to that creature from the first moment you laid eyes on him.

Members of your congregation started holding special meetings to confer about your state, meetings to which they didn't invite you. They convened a committee to discuss your condition. Grief run amok, they called it.

You didn't care. You were busy keeping a basset hound puppy with a broken leg from jumping into your bed in the evenings. Distracted, almost ebullient, you tried to teach a neighbor's child to walk Richard on a lead, but the pup's exuberance intimidated him. Marilyn did not like Richard any more than the congregation did at first, and then all of a sudden she did. She co-opted him for her own, began sleeping with him nights.

Your congregation began handing you small assignments, easy tasks, projects no man of reasonably sound mind could muddle. You went ahead and muddled them. You almost enjoyed ruining things; you wanted to watch your parishioners' reactions, their pity metamorphosing into alarm. They began cutting you off, distancing themselves, failing to include you in their usual goings-on. You didn't mind. Being left out quieted your thoughts. It relieved your headache, the dull hammering at the edges of your vision, the knock that took the form of a single syllable repeated: *Jack.*

—Don't abandon them, Marilyn pleaded.—They're your charges. They're the reason you were called out west. The reason *we* were called out west. I moved out here too, remember?

Did she? It struck you, probably unfairly, that she'd never fully shown up. She'd left part of herself back in Gettysburg with her sister.

To your congregation, you were drying up, a madman dying of thirst on the banks of a river. At the end of one Sunday service, a visitor wearing a silk waistcoat approached. He asked, attempting to make conversation:

—So, how many children do you have, Reverend?

—How dare you ask that, you said, and you turned on your heel and walked away.

People should not ask questions about whether or not someone has children. They should not ask if a couple has them now, or had them earlier, or hoped to have them, hoped and failed. If the child is not visibly alive and kicking, gleefully picking its nose or loudly wailing, then people ought to keep their mouths shut. Don't dig in soil whose contents aren't known.

Your elders convened a special prayer meeting. They laid hands on your shoulders, something Lutherans don't normally do, and they prayed, asking God to lift this terrible sorrow from you.

—And from Marilyn, you rasped; you had come down with laryngitis.—Ask Him to lift it from Marilyn. If He can help only one of us, let it be her.

Tears swam in your vision, not from what the elders prayed for or from what the prayer did or did not accomplish but from the sensation of plain hard-working hands placed on your shoulders and head, those rough, uncomplaining, well-meaning hands. When the prayers didn't work, they offered counsel in private. One of them, a coal-shop manager who reminded you of your own father, now long passed, pulled you aside nearly a year after Jack's death and whispered:

—Son, aren't you over it yet?

Another elder, a dentist who the following year would have a dead child of his own to mourn, studied you over his eyeglasses and said, kindly:

—We're worried you've lost your faith, Reverend, your trust in God's goodness.

—I'm worried too, you said.

Everyone's sympathetic the first three days after a funeral. The first three weeks, if you're fortunate. After that, you're pretty much on your own.

Every minute spent in Sergeant Sears's inebriated custody is a minute lost from the day's charge. You're losing time, leaking time everywhere you move. There's no sign he plans to release you and Kerr. He's half asleep at the front desk, head nodding, though every few minutes he rouses himself and feigns an attempt at his paperwork. Softly he belches.

This could be your last year replanting Jack's garden. It's a full day's work, digging holes for plants that don't stand much chance, fashioning an oasis in the middle of nowhere. An oasis encircled by sandbanks. You don't have a whole day at this point. You hardly have half a day. And Lucy will not be joining you.

You shouldn't have assumed permanence. Shouldn't have assumed she would just keep showing up when you needed her. Ten years is not enough time to understand a woman.

Twenty-two years might be pushing it also.

One year after you and Marilyn lost Jack, you told your parishioners:

—People would be surprised if they knew how many clergymen don't believe in an afterlife.

A slate of apprehensive faces stared back.

Two years after you lost him, you declared:

—Everyone must navigate the holes in the fabric of the universe in his or her own way.

Three years in, you began abandoning your own sermons in favor of stringing together quotations from Luther:

Faith must trample underfoot all sense, reason, and understanding.

And: *The fewer the words, the better the prayer.*

And Luther again; Luther said it better than you could. *Bewilderment is the true comprehension. Not to know where you are going is the true knowledge.*

Four years in, you delivered your final sermon, a three-line monstrosity, and walked out before the end of the service. Four years in, you met Lucy Christensen.

Marilyn

ONLY TEN O'CLOCK?

Well, once these plates are done, the saucers will want stacking; that ought to take a quarter-hour. Once the saucers are done, the napkins will need refolding. You'll limp along toward two o'clock; you'll manage An array of housewarming distractions awaits.

The Maria Kip Orphanage marks the third volunteer assignment you've had in as many years, and it's a good one. It offers long hours, unending toil, and numerous opportunities for sacrifice. Not all the children pouring through the doors are true orphans. Maria Kip's annual report, which you helped compile, describes the group's mission as providing for the care and training of "orphan, half-orphan, and abandoned girls." Half orphans have lost one parent, usually the mother, with the remaining parent lacking sufficient means or will to provide for them. Abandoned girls are casualties of poverty, left at the institution's front door.

As the residents of Maria Kip reach their "years of usefulness"—another phrase in the report—some parents come back and claim them. For the rest, upstanding homes will be sought, homes that need workers. An older girl is more likely to find a place if she can scour and scrub and boil and bake and go after misbehaving youngsters with a switch. Call it preparation for wifehood.

A sound from the backroom intrudes. The players have started warming up on their tubas and trombones for the afternoon concert. Their toots and honks combine to form a comforting melody. Henry used to say that people who sang with instrumental accompaniment possessed less talent than people who sang a cappella. He was once part of a men's quartet, though, so he was biased.

In Gettysburg, the early years, the good years, he and three seminarians had formed a singing group. Night after night the friends harmonized, fingers snapping, as they stood in a half circle in the parlor. If you went for a stroll up the lane at sundown, when you returned home you could glimpse their silhouettes, youthful and slim, in your front window, backlit by round glass lamps, their lungs filling, Henry's countenance as clear and earnest as a Yuletide messenger. You would wait for his friends to leave. Then, in the stillness of night, you would climb on top of your new husband in bed; you would find Henry in the dark, hands folded across his chest, lungs tired from all that singing. You'd rest your head on his chest, and though spent, he'd still sing you to sleep most nights. His fingers played with your hair as he serenaded you with old-time hymns, humming more than singing. Your skin absorbed his sound, the baritone reverberations. You both fell asleep before the songs ended.

A grandmother clock stands wedged in the corner of the hall. Has it slowed? Or stopped? Maybe that's your problem. Maybe time hasn't slowed, only this clock. Unfilled minutes are the enemy.

The plates? Taken care of.

The saucers? Someone should arrange and stack the saucers. That ought to use up a few minutes. But you already thought that. You're circling the same terrain.

What would it feel like to be half an orphan? Or half a wife? It strikes you that one of the worst possible things that could happen would be to lose track of one's spouse, to lose one's husband like one loses a ring or bracelet. A woman should keep her valuables on her person at all times.

Wait. You don't believe that. You don't believe your own thoughts.

—You still have Penny, your neighbor Mrs. Chambers recently observed.—Don't forget about Penny.

True. But your little sister has changed. She grew into an adult after you moved away. She developed a mind of her own, without your permission. She married a woodsman and followed him to the northernmost forests of Oregon. She never visits.

The trip is too far, she wrote you and Henry.

There exists such a thing as a train, Henry wrote back when you asked him to reply to her.

Ignoring each other is how you and Penny convey your love, your devotion, your bottomless familial need. Your sister stays busy pretending to be an old-time pioneer woman. She wears an austere bun. You know because she once mailed you a picture, a tintype of herself and her husband. She chops wood, slaughters pigs, sweeps chicken coops, and waits for her husband to saw down enough forest for her to see the sun.

Henry doesn't saw down anything.

He used to beg. He used to plead. In the early days. He bought you bath salts, perfumes, all useless. To this day, they sit in a box in your closet, unopened. He thought you needed to feel better about yourself.

—No, you said.—No, I need to feel better about the world. And that is never going to happen.

He exhorted:

—Marilyn, I understand. I do. But we have to say yes to something. To what's good, to what's left. Let me comfort you. I need you to comfort me too.

—I can't, you said.—I just can't yet. I'm so sorry.

—We can have another child. Let me be with you. Dearest heart. Please let me try.

His urgings felt stilted, forced. His encouragements fell to earth, smashed to shards, to smithereens.

You did try once. Tried twice. Two and a half times, if you count the last fruitless effort. The first time, his hands fumbling at your breasts left you in tears. He stopped and just held you. The second time, Henry cried; Henry could not rise to the challenge. His straining exertion, hands fumbling at his member savagely as he tried to resuscitate it, left you so mortified you took his hand and moved it away from his body.

—Don't, you said.—Just don't. Not this way.

He covered his face and wept.

The last time, he paused just after he'd entered you. He was aroused, breathing slow and deep, hard as a newlywed. He went absolutely still.

—Where are you? he whispered, entreating.—Where did you go? Stay with me. Marilyn, look at me.

You couldn't reply, couldn't meet his eyes. Your innards were chalk. You turned your head.

Without another word he withdrew.

Couldn't reply or *didn't* reply? Henry would frame this question as one of the will's bondage. But you are not a fan of Luther.

You saw a man, a physician. You saw several men, bearded and scientific experts. One diagnosed you with hysteria. A second called you frigid. Both descriptions infuriated Henry, who refused to take you back to either physician. You didn't care for them either.

—She's sad, Henry said. —She's just sad. Someone please help us.

The third physician said: Your wife needs to have another child.

—Tell me something I don't know, Henry practically shouted.

You rose and left the room.

Hypnosis didn't work either. The fourth physician held a brass watch on a chain and swung it until you felt seasick and closed your eyes. He thought he had hypnotized you. He was the suggestible one, not you. He tried to uncover the root of the problem, to retrieve the traumatic event that your conscious mind had chosen to forget.

—I didn't forget anything, you told him, opening your eyes. —I remember the event. My husband and I both do. It's right in front of us.

The physician invited Henry into his study to join them. This doctor was younger than the others, and his eyes held sorrow; he would not last long in this business.

—There is something more here, Mr. and Mrs. Plageman, he said. —This is something more than ordinary grief.

You lifted your head.

—What right do you have to pair those two words together?

Eventually Henry stopped asking. Four years in, he up and stopped. A relief. In a way. He also left his church. He stopped asking and he stopped preaching, both in the same year.

You asked him why. Broaching the subject was not easy.

—What made you stop trying? you said.

He placed his leather marker in whatever he was reading and closed the book.

—I gave up, he said.

—You're not supposed to give up, you replied.

But did you actually say that part? Maybe it came as a thought; maybe the words never issued from your mouth. Back then you had the opposite problem to what you're experiencing now. Back then was a long time ago.

Henry still writes monthly letters to your sister on your behalf. You have refused to correspond with Penny until she agrees to come to San Francisco for a visit. It's a ridiculous standoff. But pride is a demanding mistress.

You sometimes read his letters to her before he drops them off at the grocer's for posting. In one, he assured Penny she didn't need to keep worrying about you.

Your sister manages better and better these days, he wrote. *She stays active; she has become a pillar of the community.*

A pillar! Who wants to be a pillar? They never move.

You left that particular letter on his desk and went and found Henry in the kitchen. He was feeding Richard scraps of smoked pork.

—Stop trying to make it better, you said.—Your trying to make it better only makes it worse.

He straightened, confusion crossing his face, and Richard barked his dissent.

—What do you want me to do? Would you rather I do nothing?

—Yes, you said.

This wasn't true. It was the exact opposite of true. In your defense, it wasn't one of those days when Henry made himself available for conversation.

You can have excellent conversations with your husband, fine discussions indeed; after twenty-two years of married life, you feel confident declaring there is no better listener in the world than Henry Plageman, but everything depends on his mood. One has to strike at the exact right time. The problem is you can never predict when that moment will arrive. Admittedly, your own communicativeness fluctuates too.

You wrote only one letter to Penny after she sent that picture of herself and her husband in the forest.

Sister, you're too late, you told her. *The frontier's been settled.*

She didn't write back.

You shouldn't have phrased it that way. Shouldn't have been such a know-it-all. But you wanted to save her from disappointment, from the realization that life promises more than it can deliver. Maybe she already knew.

Henry

WRITING YOUR FINAL SERMON took eight months. You produced other homilies in the meantime—you were never *completely* paralyzed—but that last sermon, the one you started working on for All Souls' Day, presented a Gordian knot of difficulties that prevented its completion until well over half a year had passed, long after All Souls' and on into the drizzly, damp summer of 1887. You finally tore the sermon up and rewrote it as three lines. Delivering those three lines took everything, depleted every ounce of reserve.

The members of the Women's Memorial Church, named in honor of the Women's Home and Foreign Missionary Society in Cedar Rapids, Iowa, met in a rented downtown storefront crammed between a dry goods store and a dressmaker's. It wasn't fair of you to spring something new on them. Lutherans, even Lutherans in San Francisco, are a wary people. But once the words were ready, they would wait for no man; the sermon had to be delivered. Your voice shook a bit, and you could not pull your gaze away from the fair-haired stranger seated in the front row. Your eyes found hers as she shifted position, orienting herself in your direction.

You cleared your throat and addressed your congregation.

—Here is what I still hold true:

—One: God is fundamentally unknown and unknowable.

—Two: Nonetheless, we seek God's face.

—Three: Grace lies between those two poles.

You closed your Bible and bowed your head; silence washed over the sanctuary.

—Thank you, you said and stepped away from the pulpit. Briefly you thanked your congregation members for their years of kindness, wished them every blessing. A temporary replacement from the bishopric would be in the pulpit the following Sunday.

They would be in good hands. In excellent hands. In better hands than yours, you assured them.

No one made a sound.

Maybe they feared that if they said anything, if they responded with even a single word of sympathy, you might not be able to leave; you might keep drowning right in front of them for four more years.

Down the aisle you trod, making for the exit. You passed the stranger —Lucy—as you left. Her head turned to follow you.

Foreman Kerr feigns a stomach cramp. He doubles over and moans. From his piles of paperwork, the desk sergeant takes notice.

—He's poorly, you offer.—Might be catching. Probably you need to release us both.

Sears scowls as he lumbers to his feet.

When he enters the cell, he ignores you and checks Kerr's pulse, then feels the older man's forehead with the back of one hand. This sergeant doesn't want any fatalities on his watch. He's boozy and sour enough as it is.

Kerr groans.—Somethin' I et, somethin' I et. Fetch me what tonic you possess, Officer, for the love of God.

Sears blinks; he's dubious. Grudgingly, he agrees to help.

—Come on, then, he says.—Hop to. There's a dispensary in back.

Kerr smiles conspiratorially at you and reaches for his cane. What's his plan? You'll go along with anything if it gets you out of here.

It's a quarter past ten. That garden won't plant itself.

You don't see how you could have preached anything else that day. Three lines; that's as much as people want to hear in a sermon anyway. If they're honest.

Besides, you'd been losing their confidence, watching your parishioners drop off one by one like streetlamps blinking out along California

Street on a windy night. *Simplify, simplify, simplify,* you had urged, week after week, your homilies shortening, your silences lengthening.

—Theology is a matter of economy, you had said.—The faster life passes, the fewer words a man needs.

—Even in a sermon? one of the elders asked.

—Especially in a sermon. What's left to say?

They stared at you, expressions sagging.

—Think about it, you went on, a bit desperately.—What can I possibly say that would do you any good?

Hold on. Get ready. There's really very little we can control.

You grasped the hands of two parishioners, both octogenarians with wild white hair.

Hold on to each other, if you can.

And if you can't, be gentle.

Staying away from Lucy is like giving up whiskey for Lent. You take pride in your accomplishment, thrust out your chest and congratulate yourself on your willpower, on how clean you have wiped the slate. Then you fish out your watch on its chain and realize it's eight in the morning, Ash Wednesday, and all your nobility and principle, all your self-congratulations, fly out the window, squawking.

She's vowed to stay away. She's really gone and done it this time; she's broken the chain. She's vowed to leave you alone. Which really means she's asked you to leave *her* alone. You've learned her lexicon. Learned to translate the language of Lucy.

To wit:

Lucy says: I need to let you go.

She means: *I need you to let me go.*

Lucy says: I haven't been my best self of late.

She means: *You haven't been your best self of late.*

Lucy says: I agree with you completely.

She means: *I couldn't disagree with you more.*

How long since you've held her, pulled her into your arms? Blue's birthday. Over three months.

You don't want to be left behind. Too late. You don't want to grow old. Too late. One or the other, you could handle. But both?

Does such a protest matter to any powers that be; does it count in some divine book of fairness? No.

Kerr directs himself to Sears.

—Let Plageman come too, he says, plucking at the sergeant's dark sleeve.

Sears scans you unsteadily, absorbs the fact of your height.

—Name?

—Plageman. Henry.

He consents.—All right. Come along, Plageman Henry. Let's fetch the old man some medicine. But don't cause me problems. I have problems enough on my own. I don't need new ones.

You hold up your hands: you're problem-free. You're old and pitiable too. See? You slump and shrink low so your height doesn't jar him. Your height tends to agitate ordinary men.

The calla lilies had better be in decent shape this year. Marilyn prefers what's grown in a hothouse. She does not trust the outdoors to sustain life on its own. She adores tulips, tuberoses, heliotrope.

She prefers the hothouse version of you too, the supervised version. She wants indoor Henry, the man you were before moving to the Outside Lands. A husband of means, standing, gravitas, a man on his way up, not down, not descending into the catacombs. A man who says the right thing always. Outdoor Henry? Not a chance.

Outdoor Henry is a wreck, a hulking wretch, a Goliath who stoops, roams dunes, flings out the wrong words when the right ones don't suit him. Outdoor Henry fled his pulpit, unable to tolerate the supplicatory countenances of his parishioners, men and women asking him to help them make sense of their lives, to assure them that their brief, brooding lives somehow *mattered*. "The life of man solitary, poor, nasty, brutish, and short"; thank you, Thomas Hobbes. The old philosopher knew nothing about love, though. Or maybe he did.

You've never taken Marilyn to Sutro Heights, even though she's asked, even though she would adore the horticultural extravagances, the groundskeepers who have wrested control away from nature; she'd admire the engineers who had tricked the ocean into pouring itself into a catch basin. Tourists daily peer into that basin, scanning for trapped marine life. She has asked to visit Sutro's, but you can't take her. If she wants to see it, she'll have to make that journey alone.

Marilyn has all of the Richmond district, all of San Francisco, if you're honest. She has your house, your shop, your income, your basset hound, your food, your coffee, your coat when she's cold. She has your history, your youth. She has the top drawer of your bureau for her earrings and brooches.

Sutro's belongs to Lucy.

Next year will be your eleventh in this predicament. How can you be marking anniversaries with two different women? You are and you can. It appears not to be a scientific impossibility. Other men should be warned.

Marilyn

JUST TWO NIGHTS AGO, you almost asked him if something was wrong. You almost said: *Where are you? Where did you go?*

But if you force Henry to talk, to tell you how he's doing, he'll answer by way of the cemetery. He'll tell you how the city cemetery is doing. You cannot abide hearing how the city cemetery is doing. Therefore, you cannot abide hearing how your husband is doing.

Chambers stopped by two nights ago. He wandered across the street at dusk. He and Henry settled themselves into chairs on the front porch, where they gossiped and confabulated like two spinster sisters.

—How are you, neighbor? Chambers asked.

—Holding up, Henry said.

Holding up is your husband's most common reply. *Bearing up* is the alternative.

As Chambers settled in to smoke his cigar, Henry looked around for Richard. He called the old dog outside while he and Chambers swapped tall tales. From the parlor, seated at the writing desk by candlelight, you heard them laughing. You stole a glimpse out the bay window. Henry scratched Richard's velvet ears. He lit a cigar and let the darkness steal over.

Mrs. Wood beckons you into the kitchen through two swinging louvered doors.

—Now, Mrs. Plageman. We certainly do appreciate your help.

She plants her hands on a table filled with platters of finger sandwiches that leave behind the humid odor of eggs past their prime. The first orphans and early arrivals have started to file inside, the guests powdered and primped, the girls anxious to please the adults, to say the right thing always.

— But I must tell you, Mrs. Wood continues, we haven't placed you on any committees yet for the summer. We'll have to wait on that.

— Wait for what? you ask.

— I have to request the rector's input. Since you're not a member of the Episcopal Church.

— Or any church, you can't help but add.

Are you really forty-one years old?

— Well, Mrs. Wood says with an embarrassed laugh. — Well, I don't quite know what to say to that.

— Your rector needs me. This orphanage needs me.

— Of course we appreciate —

— I'm the only one who can balance your accounts. I've been tracking all the income and expenses. I compiled your annual report.

— And, as I said, we are all so grateful for your service. Now, if you'll excuse me a moment, our little inmates need supervising.

The new building being celebrated today cost more than fifty thousand dollars. You should know; you kept the books. It's brick, three stories, with stone ornamentation. When the chapel's ready, it will boast a stained-glass window, a portrait of a sitting Jesus with children clambering into His lap. Under the window, a plaque with the words SUFFER LITTLE CHILDREN TO COME UNTO ME will hang.

You were not involved in the selection of that window.

Two of the orphans, squirming with excitement, race each other to the kitchen. The littler one skids on the newly waxed floor. Mrs. Wood pushes through the louvered doors and snatches the offender by the wrist.

— Mind your manners, she barks.

She looks back at you and smiles, a bit self-conscious.

— I tell my nieces the same thing I tell these little inmates: children should be seen and not heard.

—I disagree, someone calls out.

Your hand goes to your mouth. Dear God, that was *you* talking. What you think keeps turning into words.

—Pardon?

—My mistake, you say.

Another new arrival, an older girl, gangly, with a brace on one leg, walks up to the little one and leads her away without a word.

Time is not a cure. Time is a reminder. Anniversaries slit the envelope wide.

Henry

SERGEANT SEARS LEADS THE WAY down a long, dull corridor with neither vent nor window. He ushers you and Kerr into a storage room crammed with unused chairs. In the corner sit an ancient medicine cabinet and a desk whose drawers no longer close.

Sears heads for the cabinet. From its depths he retrieves every conceivable medicinal option: dyspepsia powders, arsenic complexion wafers, liver pills, peptonic stomach bitters.

—No, no, no. Kerr moans, shaking his head each time something's offered. —Need something stronger.

— Stronger than arsenic? you say.

Kerr frowns at you.

While Sears searches for the right tonic, Kerr asks him questions, befriending him. How long has he served at this police station? Too long. Does he have young ones at home? Yes, and they're wringing the life out of him. What's the weather like outside this morning?

— Foggy, Sears says, and he produces a bottle of Orange Wine Stomach Bitters, which promises to cure gastric ailments, indigestion, want of appetite, malarial diseases, low spirits, nervousness, and "that tired feeling." You're tempted to take some yourself.

— Good, Kerr says and snatches the bottle. — Very good. Now grant me a minute, friends.

Without ceremony, he lowers himself to a chair, settles into a comfortable slouch, and takes a swig.

— It'll pass. Just takes time. I'm old. Bear with me, Sarge.

Now it's you and Sears standing around wondering what in God's name to do while Kerr's having himself a tipple and an impromptu snooze.

You reach for your watch, check the time. Nearly half past ten. Sears finds a chair for himself and pulls it up to the desk. Gloomily, he eyes the scored surface.

—Hard morning? you say.

One kind question is all he needs. It's all most people need. One kind question, and the sluice gates open, and in swims the sea.

Sears counts off a list of troubles. A son with nervous tremors. Debt collectors. A daughter with an abscessed tooth. A wife who won't touch him, not even after he strung up a retractable indoor clothesline for her to use. He had thought she might feel gratitude.

You remain standing before his desk, still garbed in your velveteen robe. You listen, nod, and make sympathetic noises, because what else is there to do when your captor confesses his sorrows? Sears's eyes are watery.

Kerr interrupts.

—Plageman? he says, still slumped in his corner, bottle in hand. —Tell our fine guardian why they locked us up here.

That's easy enough.—They locked us up because of the cemeteries.

—The cemeteries? Sears says, eyeing the stomach bitters.

—Plageman, tell him.

So you introduce the sergeant to the problem of San Francisco's burial grounds.

—In the 1860s, some politicians decided to move Yerba Buena Cemetery out of the way.

Sears observes you distrustfully.—Out of the way of what?

—City Hall.

—It was in City Hall's way?

—It was about to be, Kerr chimes in, straightening in his chair and helping himself to a second swig.—Just as soon as they built it.

You nod.—They dug up the cemetery and moved the bodies to the edge of the city. They thought they'd moved them out far enough.

Sears cocks his head. He listens to your recounting, forgetting himself. People are at their best when they're forgetting themselves for a moment, a month, a year. Ten years, in some cases. That's what Lucy would say.

—The city was on a self-improvement mission, Kerr says.—They dug up the old pioneers. Buried 'em in what's now the city cemetery.

—Did they get all the bodies moved?

—No, you say.

Kerr pats his stomach.—Tonic's doing its job. Thank you most kindly, Sarge.

—Kerr? you say.—Those bitters contain more alcohol than what a man can purchase in a tavern.

Sears eyes the bottle with new interest.—Is that so.

—And thank goodness for it, Kerr says.—Now: The city cemetery lay in peace almost twenty-five years. It lay in peace, doing what cemeteries do.

Sears: What do they do?

—They let the dead sleep. Protected and undisturbed. Everything was fine until some rich folks noticed all those old pioneers, all those Chinamen and seamen and Jews, occupied the best damn property in all of California. *And what do those old bones have that we don't?* they started asking. What do the dead have that the living want?

—Rest, you say.

—Land, Sears supplies, pallid face brightening.

—That's right, son. Kerr nods. He hands the stomach bitters to the sergeant. Sears scrutinizes the bottle. He takes a cautious swig. Then he takes a second.

—That's right, Kerr smoothly repeats.—You're absolutely correct. Go ahead, have another sip, son. You've had a long morning. *Time to move the dead out;* that's what the neighborhood's now saying.

—My landlord's telling me I have to move too, Sears says and drinks again, helping himself to a liberal swallow. He returns the bottle to the desk and puts his head in his hands.—He's going to tear the house down and grade the property so it's level, then build a grand Eastlake. I won't be able to afford the rent.

—That's terrible, Kerr soothes. He tilts his head meaningfully at you, then at the tonic.

So this is what he wants? So this is his great escape plan? A drinking contest? A trial by jury would be faster.

You reach for the bottle and help yourself to a small sip. Good Lord, it's sweet. Good Lord, this whole morning is a nightmare of a headache.

The people of the Richmond want their cemeteries to disappear. They want to shove them south. The Outside Lands are no longer sufficiently outside.

The people of this district can see the day when they'll wake up to find dead paupers across the street from their houses. They do not want the dead to dwell so close. They can't abide the reminder.

And as for you: You can see the day when you'll wake up and across the street will be Lucy's cottage, having crept inland overnight, having picked itself up and tiptoed in from Sutro's estate, unable to deny the truth any longer, unwilling to remain exiled on the continent's edge. The continental ledge. You and Marilyn will stand in the window of your house, and Lucy and Blue will stand in theirs. Lucy will regard your wife, and Marilyn will regard Lucy, through panes of leaded glass. This day is coming too.

You replant Jack's garden annually, show up hours early, tools in tow, so Marilyn doesn't have to admit to herself what's patently obvious, so she doesn't have to admit the truth. Nothing in this terrain survives except what's born here: the natives, spiny growths, abandoned scrubs with their resistance to touch.

Lucy asked for things to stop. But you carried it out. The head you removed turned out to be your own.

You hand the bottle back to Sears, who takes it and drinks again. One more swallow, then two.

— Goes down smooth, he says.

— You're right to feel maltreated, son, Kerr soothes. — You're right to be riled up.

— Am I?

— Yes, indeed.

The more Kerr talks, the more tonic this sergeant drinks.

— Everyone's in such a hurry to improve his state of affairs. Look here. You're a good man, Sarge. A conscientious man. You're one of the good ones.

— Fat lot of help it's been.

And now it's another sip, and then Sears offers the bottle to you, his newest friend. He swipes at his eyes. He's used to spirits. You and Kerr can hold your own right along with him. Among the three of you, there's well over a hundred years' solid drinking experience. All that training is coming in handy. All those nights spent filling and refilling your tumbler—they're paying off at last.

— So they threw us in here, Kerr continues.—They locked us up for no good reason. Have another sip, son. You understand us.

— I sure do, Sears slurs.

— They threw us in jail because we stood up and said, *Enough.* We stood up for the pioneer bones, for the souls born in foreign lands, for all the people that don't have a loved one to bury 'em. Because who has the least voice of all in this country? It's not just the poor man. It's the dead man. Who will speak for him? That's what I want to know.

Sears lifts his eyes.— I thought the city cemetery only held Chinese.

You shake your head.— You'd be surprised.

Blue loves the city cemetery. You've taken her several times, but never to the mariners. Only near the entrance.

Living in the Outside Lands has turned your daughter into a naturalist, a botanist, a collector of feathers, bones, shells. A snail rescuer. And if she can't find any snails to save in the burial grounds, she'll ask you to take her home, where she'll pluck them from puddles and deposit them at the front door of the cottage. She relocates them so they don't drown, she says, so they have a fair chance.

— A fair chance at what? you asked once.

To Lucy, Blue is a marvel, a singularity, a star she discovered and named herself. But your daughter feels no need to explain to her parents the inner lives of snails. They live and breathe and have their separate existence, just as you and Lucy live and breathe and have your separate existence; they wander into the mud along Merrie Way, just as her parents appear to have done; and if God did not opt to pluck her ma and pa out of the muck of their own making, at the very least, He can help ensure the snails have a better chance. Her hands on her hips, planted in the open door in the rain, Lucy used to watch Blue's salvage efforts in action. Mist would dampen her face as she peered down at your daughter, who in turn peered down at the snails. And you would watch Blue as well, on the Wednesdays you visited, hovering, fussing over them both, a series of worries traveling southward, traveling down in size, the larger striving to comprehend the smaller, the known to grasp the unknown. Lucy would look over at you and cover her mouth, try to cover her laugh, her smile, her glee, her spilling over with all that was good and bright and full, for love of you and this child you two had created, this unreasonable sprite. The two of you together could not possibly have made her, Lucy once declared; the two of you together could not possibly have conceived such an absolute original.

Another letter, penned to her last month:

> *I want you to know that you are not, and never were, my mistress. You stormed the bastions of my soul and won me as your lover or, better still, my dearest companion. I sometimes, perhaps too often, pressed to make that impress greater, for which I apologize; I became too eager to advance the idea of how precious this all was. Not a wise plan.*
>
> *As much as I am a student of understatement, I find myself sometimes still in the grip of hyperbole. That might well be excused in other circumstances, but at present, in the face of what words cannot express, and commitments that still run deep, quiet gestures speak more.*
>
> *So the clock, the pictures, the confounded kitchenware I gave you over the years were really no more than gestures. I hope you will keep them even though I am no longer there. They gesture toward that for which there are no words.*

You've received no answer.

—'Twasn't fair they clobbered you two for being good citizens, Sears says, raising one hand in a half-cocked salute and then lowering it heavily to the desk. —'Twasn't fair at all.

Kerr stands. The stiffness in the old foreman's knees isn't an act.

—I believe we've found in you a kindred spirit, Sergeant. You understand what it means to defend one's home against the incursions of greed and grandiosity. I wonder if you might come to our aid.

—Grand-osity, the sergeant repeats.

Move a cemetery; how does anyone move a cemetery?

Will they scissor the turf away, snip and trim as if shearing a bolt of fabric? Will they cut away parcels of land, tie strips of earth to hot-air balloons, float them overhead? Clods of earth will fall from the sky. *Take the bodies to Colma.*

—Son, you look like you need a moment, Kerr says.

—I do, Sears whispers.—I'm so tired. I believe I've never been so tired.

He might be thirty. He's got a lot more tired coming.

You pull off your velveteen getup and drape it over the sergeant's shoulders. He leans his head on the desk, mumbles:

—You two shouldn't be locked up here.

—Good man, Kerr says.—I am in full agreement. Would you be willing to sign something to that effect?

A faint, delicate snore issues forth. Sears rouses himself, snorts.

—'M not allowed.

—But it's justice, you say.—It's a question of justice. And what is the law for if not this?

Too bad this storage room doesn't hold a pulpit.

Sears nods. He's a convert; he's weeping again.

—Do you have a pencil? Kerr asks.

Inside the desk the sergeant finds one. Kerr produces a sheaf of writing paper. He drafts two release notices for the sergeant's signature, your ticket out of this station. Tomorrow Sears will have such a headache, he'll be able to count the blood vessels pounding inside his skull.

—Now, if you'll just sign right here approving our release, Plageman and I will be out of your way. Here, I'll add the date to make it official. What's today again?

—May twenty-second, Sears says.

Like you need a reminder.

10:30 a.m.

Lucy

YOU SHOULD HAVE TAKEN ANOTHER ROUTE. Should have borrowed a bicycle, hired a hack, flown, swum, or floated. You would have reached the hospital faster.

On its eastbound route, the streetcar hit a rut and swayed so erratically that the trolley pole sprang away from the overhead wire. The conductor climbed down and coaxed the pole back into place. He stopped again a block later, yielding to workers pushing wheelbarrows. He stopped a third time to point out two firemen installing a firebox on the side of a telephone pole.

This neighborhood builds itself up from the dunes brick by brick and pipe by pipe. You compose two-sentence updates for the *Richmond Banner* whenever the fire department installs one of those new boxes. Those updates are the only real success you've had with that newspaper.

The French Hospital occupies a full block on Sixth Avenue, between A Street and Point Lobos, close to one of the problem sewers. The Richmond district's sewage plan generally involves letting rainwater pour into these sewers to flush stalled waste along the pipes. Eventually the mess hits the strait and makes its way to the Pacific Ocean.

You wrote about that sewage plan in a longer article. The editor rejected your effort, had no interest in publishing it.

— No one wants to read about a sewer, he said, looking over his reading glasses at your breasts.

— But it's about informing the public, you argued. — People don't know where the sewage winds up. They don't see it. They need to be told.

The editor lit his pipe, puffed, and exhaled a gratified plume.

—To be informed is not why people move to the Richmond, Mrs. Christensen. People move here for the land. For the land and to be left alone.

He waved you out of the editorial room.

You sent him another submission a week later. You'll exhaust the man into accepting your material. You'll wear him down. Let him leer all he wants, as long as he prints what you've written.

The car clangs to a stop near the hospital. Blue lifts her head from your lap. She coughs and coughs until your own lungs burn. She smells of seawater.

Henry has no idea she fell into that well. No idea she came within a hairsbreadth of drowning. And today of all days — the news would send him reeling.

You glance at her. She's curled up, half buried in your skirt, elfin, her brows and lips precisely sculpted, diminutive versions of what they'll look like on the woman she'll become. That pointed chin — it's strident and vulnerable. That mouth — it's your mouth on a smaller scale.

When a man has that mouth, people call him tenacious. Driven. When a woman has that mouth, people call her headstrong.

Your cousin moved here first, and you followed. Your cousin Dean left Omaha, land of unending horizons, to try his hand at the silver mines of Virginia City, Nevada. He discovered no silver, only claustrophobia.

He wrote to you back in Omaha. *I could not abide descending into the earth.* He made his way to the Pacific Coast next; he wanted the sea on three sides. He wound up on land belonging to Adolph Sutro. He told the famous tycoon he'd worked the Comstock Lode, didn't mention he'd worked only twelve hours. Sutro, feeling magnanimous, feeling nostalgic for the mines that had made him his fortune, hired your cousin as a groundskeeper.

When you turned twenty-one, you boarded the Overland west to find him. Your mother walked behind you the mile-long road to the ticket office, her arms folded across her chest as she muttered to herself in her native Swedish. Dried pie filling crusted the bib of her apron.

—Our people will never survive California, she warned as you stepped up to the ticket counter.

—Why not? you threw back.

—The temperateness. Our blood's not suited.

But your toes were tapping, your valise bursting; your train ticket panted to be stamped. For two decades, you and your mother had been a couple, a forlorn twosome. She came close to remarrying one time, a thin-lipped telegraph operator who'd liked your mother all right and you more, but she sent him away after they quarreled over the choice of herbs she used in her meatballs, and he never returned.

When the Overland pulled into the station, the conductor called all westbound passengers to board. You could not look at your mother to say goodbye. If you looked at her, at this woman who'd borne and fed you, if your eyes found hers, observed her loneliness masquerading as severity, her isolation disguised as self sufficiency, then you would lose your resolve; you would not be able to set one foot onto that train, would not be able to take a single step forward into your own life.

—What does that mean, your own life? Henry asked the day you recounted this story; he had drunk one beer too many. You nearly slapped him.

You boarded that train with eight dollars and a piece of paper with your cousin's address on it. Dean was as close to a brother as you'd found. You closed your eyes so you would not have to see your mother, unyielding in her disconsolation, arms still crossed over her apron, judging the vanishing train. Eyes open, eyes shut; you saw her anyway. You still see her.

But you did not see why a woman should not be allowed to try.

Don't use the double negative, Henry would tell you.

Stone helps you down from the car. His grip is firm and warm. The French Hospital lies a long block south. An uneven, rough boardwalk leads there.

—Watch it, there; watch your step. Just a short ways now. Doc'll get your kid fixed right up.

He extracts Blue from your arms. He's old-fashioned in his way. Protective of her. Blue's head nestles right back into the crook of his neck. She opens one eye and comfortably gazes at you from the safety of his arms. She's pleased with this little arrangement.

Henry couldn't take his eyes off Blue last night. He spied the two of you at the back of Simon's Hall.

What? you wanted to ask, wanted to shout over the heads of the neighborhood men. *What are we going to do now?* But you kept quiet.

You should have asked him: *How come?*

That's Blue's favorite question. It's so general, it goes with everything. Every occasion suits. *How come* you're quiet, Mama? *How come* you're still crying? *How come* you're sitting out on the front step surrounded by empty bottles of steam beer? *How come* you cry when I talk about Papa?

Because where he goes, I go too. I am myself with him.

You never actually say those words to her. You're the mother; you're not allowed to have feelings. And any feelings you do hold are your own fault, your own doing.

You nearly lost her to that well, to that cistern. Henry nearly lost her too.

The French Hospital is three stories, new brick construction, with high arched windows. It's the finest facility within blocks of nothing. This Maison de Santé, or house of health, is so grand and opulent that more than one wealthy couple has paid for the privilege of renting a private room, even though neither husband nor wife was ill. There's no way you can afford to step foot in it.

Stone, reading your thoughts: I said I'd handle it.

—That's not necessary.

—Didn't think it was. Doesn't mean a man can't still help a woman.

Henry would have had a field day with his sentences.

Rain's threatening again. It's odd to walk outside with a man without checking to see who might be approaching from the other direction. Without wondering if someone the man knows might see you. People wouldn't think twice if they saw you with J. B. Stone. Or once.

Henry's better off in the dark about her accident. He has enough on his mind today. He can't shoulder his day and yours too.

Or maybe he should shoulder it. Maybe it's time for him to pay attention to the one who's still living.

Your cousin Dean helped you find your first official income, your first official employment. Your arrival in the Outside Lands baffled him. He had no idea you'd taken the train to Oakland, no idea you'd crossed the bay by ferry and made your way to Sutro's, where you searched until you found him.

Near the estate entrance, sculpted ribbon beds of flowers spelled *Welcome All to Sutro Heights.* Plaster statues loomed above the seaside rocks and posed throughout the gardens. The statues were copies of copies. No marble for Mr. Sutro, no, indeed. Why buy the real thing when one could imitate it? Why buy a living lion when one could stuff a dead one?

You found Dean pretending to be at work in a grove of imported eucalyptus. Standing before your cousin, you presented yourself for his approval: twenty-one years old, beaming up at him and clutching your valise; you were practically an urchin, practically a runaway. He blanched, set down his hand pruners.

—Lucy Christensen. What brings you here?

—You invited me, you reminded him.

—I did?

Hadn't he? You fought back panic. As children, the two of you had chased snakes with sticks behind the neighbors' creek. One time you'd struck a diamondback rattler without meaning to, and it hissed into position, its mouth gaping so wide your own jaw ached. Dean danced a jig to distract it. He smashed its head with a rock.

—When did I invite you? he said.

His eyes were red. Liquor-soaked. Your mother was right about one thing: he would not survive California. But this was your first day, your first hour; the train had hardly pulled into the station. Cousin Dean fidgeted, couldn't stand still, shoved his hands into his pockets, sized you up and down with evident pleasure and equally evident distress: his fellow snake chaser, fellow Lutheran from Omaha. He had left all that behind. But so had you. He couldn't fathom why you'd shown up at Sutro's estate. Neither could you.

—But your letters, you pleaded.

That was the day you learned a letter is not the same as a summons. Even a kind letter. Even a wistful one. To be summoned, one must be summoned. One must not show up unless an invitation has been explicitly issued.

A lesson you should have held on to for later.

Cousin Dean steered you across the estate to Mr. Claude's taxidermy shed. He deposited you after conferring with the taxidermist man to man, saying something about a favor, a payment. Then he kissed you goodbye. He hadn't kissed you hello. He returned to his beloved racetracks. He hadn't written you about those.

Dean was kind whenever he saw you after that. But he rarely saw you. One time, a year later, already up to your ears in Henry, you ran across your cousin weaving along the melancholy fairground lane called Merrie Way. He said hello and pulled you into his arms, his breath sickly, a whiff of cherry liquor on him.

—Good Lord, girl, you're a sight for sore eyes, he said.

He released you and returned to his greyhounds and racehorses.

Mr. Claude, however, had all the time in the world for you. Mr. Claude needed a taxidermy assistant; Dean had volunteered you for the role. And he'd promised you'd work for room and board only the first three months. You were payment in kind on a gambling loan, you learned later.

Is this how it is for other women? The men you don't want to see, you see all the time. The men you do want to see are ghosts.

—Where's Ostrich? Blue whispers; she's still curled up against Stone's shoulder.

Stone looks at you.—Ostrich?

—A friend, you crisply say.

Ostrich is her nickname for her father.

The problem with today isn't two-year-old Jack. It's sixteen-year-old Jack who consumes May 22. It's the nearly grown Jack socking his parents in the gut, demanding their attention, felling his father's thoughts as Henry digs and weeds and plants, garlanded by immigrant flowers. The potentiality does them in, the person he might have been.

Stone crosses the walk a few paces ahead of you. Hurrying, you follow him, chasing a man you just met, tramping in his wake as rain drums the top of your head. Haven't you been here before, haven't you stepped in this same crack in the earth before? Yes. Ten years ago, outside the Women's Memorial Church. But now there's a third person along for the ride, a child. Now the consequences are visible.

Rain has slickened the stairs leading to the hospital entrance.

— Watch your step, Stone says again.

Henry's pulling up the thistles by now. He's wiping his brow, the ends of his hair beaded with rain. You'd place money on him forgetting to bring gloves. You always brought them for him.

Blue lifts earnest eyes to yours.

— Mama?

— Yes? you say, leaning in, leaning close.

— It's not my fault the skylight couldn't hold me.

Stone beams. — What'd I tell you? Going to be just fine.

Blue

THIS IS THE FINEST HOSPITAL anyone could imagine. Ma says
fresh air is the medicine here, fresh air and rest and light.

— It's as fine as the Palace Hotel, Mr. Stone says.

Three nurses in their starched white uniforms spring into action
when they see us coming. There's an old one, a pretty one, and one who
looks too serious.

— Sakes alive! the old one says, and she pulls me close when she sees
how drenched I still am. Ma shows her my cut ear.

— She's going to need stitches, the nurse says. — And she's chilled to
the bone.

I could have told her that.

They hightail it with me upstairs to the second floor. The serious
nurse leads me over to the first bed. Ma and Mr. Stone stick close. The
old nurse brings blankets, and the pretty nurse peels off my stockings
while Ma flits about and tries to tell them what to do. This pavilion has
ten beds, and I am the only patient.

The serious nurse removes the largest of the glass shards first. This
hurts a good bit. Then the other two pull out the smaller splinters, rins-
ing and cleaning, bandaging my cuts with cloth.

— You'll be right as rain by the time we're done with you, the pretty
nurse says.

They tell me to lie still and wait for the doctor. Mr. Stone hasn't left.
He's still hanging around. And for no good reason. Ma doesn't need him.

— Want me to fetch anyone? he asks her. — Your husband?

Fine orange hairs sprout above his lip. If that is a mustache, it is a poor one. The lines around his mouth deepen when he smiles. He must smile a good bit.

— No, she says. — No. Thank you.

Then she adds: I'm a widow.

Her hand squeezes my shoulder. Her hand is saying *hush*. It has said this word before. Upside down, her face resembles a puppet's.

— I'm sorry to hear that, Mr. Stone says.

— It's all right.

— Hard to lose someone.

— Yes, she says.

Her hand clamps my shoulder in an iron grip. I won't spill the beans about the whopper she just told. Yes, it's a lie; yes, my mother lies to people. It's not the first time.

— What time is it? she asks and turns to look out the window.

— Sakes alive, Ma, I say. — There's not a clock outside.

She laughs. Mr. Stone pulls a watch on a leather strap from his pocket.

— It's a quarter to eleven. You in a hurry to be somewhere?

She doesn't answer.

This bed is softer than mine. Someone has opened one of the windows, and a breeze sweeps past the white sheets on the beds, blowing out the germs.

Ma stoops close and tucks the sheet around me, too tight. Beneath the sheet, I feel cold. And when I'm cold, I'm contrary.

She needs to stop telling people she's a widow. The first time she said that to someone, I wasn't ready. I burst into tears. I flung myself into her lap. She had to stand up right then and excuse herself from the newspaperman she was asking to read her work. She hadn't wanted to take me to his office in the first place, but I'd talked her into it. She walked me home right then.

— What happened to Pa? I sobbed once we made it home. She sat me on the bed and rubbed my back for a solid half an hour telling me that nothing had happened, nothing at all. Calling herself a widow was just the way she chose to introduce herself to some people, and she hoped I would not contradict her.

— But why would you say that?

— Because it's easier.

— But how come it's easier?

— Because then people don't pry.

— But why would they pry?

She rubbed my back, harder than my back needed.

— People pry when they're concerned. And when they have nothing better to do, Blue, nothing in their own miserable lives to keep them occupied.

She crossed over to the stove to cook flapjacks, which we sometimes shared for supper. She oiled the griddle. She kept her back to me.

— Think of it like playing chess, she said. Pa was teaching us how.

— We have to be careful. We have to think ahead, to plan how and where we take the next step.

— But why? I said.

She wandered outside after she'd finished flipping the cakes. She sat on the front step. Her sleeves were rolled high, past her elbows. Flour was in her hair, but I didn't tell her. She said she wanted to watch the sunset, but by the time she went out, the sun had gone to bed. It grew so dark the bats came out.

She didn't come inside for a long time. I ate all of the flapjacks.

A man wheels a laundry cart past our door. The old nurse watches him pass and explains that in this hospital, the morgue and the laundry dwell side by side.

— Sometimes we forget which one's which, the pretty one adds, and laughs. Ma doesn't laugh with her.

Ma should be the one teaching Pa chess and not the other way around. Ma has true talent. She can lasso her enemy three or four moves ahead, whereas Pa becomes caught in a net of thoughts and can't decide what piece to play next.

He once crossed Post Street in the middle of traffic to rescue a puppy lying in a gutter. This happened before he and Ma had me. When he told me the story, I asked if I could meet the dog he saved.

Ma said, very quickly: It died.

Pa frowned at her.

But Pa lives with his head too high in the clouds. His head is stationed at too high an altitude. I told him so.

—Ostrich, your head is in the sky, I said.

He never comes with us to Ma's workshop. She used to invite him, but she gave up when he kept saying no. He's always working at his hardware store. He's so busy he has to sleep there. So Ma takes me there sometimes instead.

I like Mr. Claude, but the glass eyes in the animals make me feel strange.

The first time she took me, Mr. Claude announced I would be his right-hand girl, his helper. He assigned me to the birds.

—The birds are the simplest, he said.

Ma snorted. —He said the same thing to me the first week I moved here. Fooled me completely. An hour off the train, abandoned by my cousin, and here came Mr. Claude, handing me a foot of wire. Yes. A foot of wire, a scalpel, and three crows. They were hardly cold.

She was talkative that day. Mr. Claude, smiling, asked me to step closer and have a look.

—We will skin them first. We will skin them before we stuff and mount them. It's a science, Miss . . .?

—Blue.

—Miss Blue.

The pouches beneath his eyes quivered.

—Taxidermy is science *and* art. Never forget that.

Ma reached into her box of projects, pulled out what looked like a feather duster.

—A juvenile horned owl, she said. —A fledgling shot out of its nest by a tourist. Are you sure you want to stay for this, Blue?

—Sure as a hog at a trough, I said.

I wanted to see that owl's insides.

—An excellent beast, Mr. Claude said, and he smiled. —He'll be your first.

—It can't be more than a few weeks old, Ma said disapprovingly.

—You'll have to work around the buckshot to cover it up, Miss Blue.

—What for? I said.

He rested his hand on my shoulder.

—It's the first principle of our profession. Your mother learned this lesson long ago: Never allow the cause of death to remain visible.

Mr. Claude showed me how to record the owl's measurements and clean the talons, so tiny. Small enough for a doll. Ma broke the upper wing bone so I didn't have to do it. I think I could have, though. She taught me to feel the bones and sinews. She helped me arrange the owl on its back. Its snowy fuzz made me sneeze.

She separated the down along the breast and cut into the owl with a scalpel. She worked her way around the whole bird. She separated the owl's skin from its muscles. Her face didn't change the whole time. I peeked into the owl. I saw gristle, something that looked like an ear of corn, and stringy blood vessels.

—The first time I did this, Ma said, not glancing up, I cried all the way through.

I looked at Mr. Claude, who nodded again.

—It's already dead; that's what I told her. I said that to your poor mother her first day doing this work. *Don't you worry, Miss Lucy, it's already dead. You can't do anything to hurt it.*

—And what did she say? I asked.

They couldn't remember.

The old nurse has disappeared. She returns to announce that the doctor's on his way.

—Just a few more minutes, she says and pats Ma's hand.—He'll stitch up your daughter's ear in just a few more minutes. And he'll have a look at those other lacerations. He'll examine her behind that curtain.

She points to the far end of the ward.

—There's a bed in the back, the pretty nurse explains.—For privacy during minor operations. Only doctors and nurses allowed.

—Not a chance, Ma says.

The old nurse frowns.—He doesn't want you fainting on him. Your husband can take you to the dining room.

—I won't faint. And that man is not my husband.

—I'll take him off your hands, then, the pretty nurse offers.

Ma rolls her eyes. Mr. Stone blushes.

Lucy

EARLY ON, YOUR MOTHER WROTE from Omaha: *Do you understand what you're doing?*

Of course, you wrote back. Yet another untruth. But a mother does not want to hear that her child is lost, is hanging by the fingernails from the cliff rocks.

Of course you knew how one Sunday at the Women's Memorial Church, your third Sunday apart from your mother, twenty-one years old, new to San Francisco, new to your life, would metamorphose into an afternoon with a once-preacher whose sermons had dwindled to haiku. *Of course* you knew how that one afternoon would divide into two, and then four, and later would transform again, becoming an hour in your room at Sutro's boarding house, gas lantern sputtering, Henry uttering your name, incantatory, as if he had never before laid hands on a woman.

And of course you knew how that one afternoon, that lone blazing hour, would turn into a decade, your whole life, such as it is, yours and Blue's. The requirements of daily concealment have so shaped, so altered your topography, that some days you catch sight of yourself in a mirror and fail to recognize the woman looking back. The editor at the *Banner* thinks the Richmond is busy reinventing itself. He hasn't seen anything yet; he should try being a woman.

You cannot remember what you looked like before Henry. That girl —you cannot recall her face.

You do recall your cousin's face. Rough. Contrite. *Good Lord, girl, you're a sight for sore eyes.* Then back to his gin and greyhounds.

The day you finally lost him—lost Dean, that is—the day your cousin took his life, plunged from the highest available altitude, Blue saw him. Blue bore witness to an act she was too young to comprehend. She was not yet four at the time.

—He was trying to fly, she told you afterward.

For every man who has lost his way, God has assigned a woman, slavering to save him. Has God also assigned a man to every lost woman? No.

You first saw him in church. You went because you were homesick. Because your cousin had mentioned a congregation. Before he abandoned you to Mr. Claude and his creations, Cousin Dean had said, apologetically, as if he bore responsibility:

—There's only one good Lutheran church in this city. The only one where the pastor speaks English. It's downtown.

He made it sound like he attended. He didn't. He didn't attend services at any house of prayer except the one in his letters home to his parents.

You went only the one time. You arrived late. A tall man loomed over the pulpit. An overgrown stalk of a man, weighted with intelligence. Too much intelligence. The front row held the only available seats. He noted your entrance. He observed as you sat down, smoothed your skirt, and folded your hands in your lap. When you looked up, his eyes held a question.

He remained silent. Long enough that you shifted in place, grew uncomfortable. Then he turned to his Bible, not to read but to close it. He had fair hair that hung past his collar. No beard and no mustache, which was rare for a man in those days. He still doesn't have them, which is rare in these days too. His brow made him look angry, locked in a private argument. Never fall for a man whose chief antagonist is himself, whose chief conversational partner is the man in the mirror when he shaves.

You watched him. He wasn't getting anywhere biblical. He gripped both sides of the podium and studied his shut Bible. A muscle in his jaw tensed. In the row behind yours, a woman rustled her skirts, whispered to the man beside her:

—He never got over it.

Got over what? You would help him. By God, any woman would help that man get over anything.

Her companion whispered back:

—That was so long ago.

—Yes. Years. But you know how these things are.

—I forget what happened to it.

—Choked. Choked to death in its crib. And with both parents home.

He began his sermon. He stopped talking after the third sentence. *God is fundamentally unknown and unknowable. Nonetheless, we seek God's face. Grace lies between those two poles.*

You sat in the front row and couldn't move. The austerity of those lines cut through you. Grace is a living thing. Grace means *Stay alive. Keep moving.*

You couldn't stop looking at his hands. You thought: *This man has given up trying to save himself. Someone else will have to do it for him.*

He stepped away from the pulpit, reached for his hat, said his good-byes, and then walked out. He took in the sight of you as he strode down the aisle toward the door.

Here I am; you looked right at him. Your eyes locked with his. Yes, you started it. The opportunity spread itself with feathered wings across the table. All it took was one cut. All it ever takes is one cut, if your hand is steady and you stick to it.

He pulled his eyes away and opened the front door, shoving his hat on his head. He was bidding them farewell, leaving his congregation to face their Sundays alone, to handle their own burials and weddings and baptisms. He was leaving his calling, years of study set aside, abandoned.

Later you asked him why he left.

—I couldn't answer their questions, he said.

His own. He couldn't answer his own questions.

His shoulders straightened as he walked out, and his head lifted; his shoulders and back both straightened. His stride was long and sure. He paused in the door's frame. You reminded yourself to swallow. He stepped out onto the walk. A cable car clanged past in the rain. The door sighed shut.

Five minutes later, you rose and walked out. You followed him. You went after a stranger, a man, in the rain.

Ten years have followed those five minutes.

Stone steps aside for the nurse. He's alert to his surroundings, constantly observing. The world and its inhabitants interest him. His easy movement reminds you of a dance. You must be two centuries older than he is.

He'll never be bored a day. He's hard-working. Resilient. He still thinks a person gets to choose.

Do you believe in free will? That's what Henry asked.

I'll believe whatever you want me to, you thought but did not tell him.

Henry Plageman, the early days, the ravenous days: He was lean and tall and blond and narrow-hipped with an unnatural height and a mouthful of incoherent poetic language about self-knowledge and knowledge of God, and all of it seemed to be life or death for him; all of it served to make him more vitally and essentially male. Listening to him doubled your pulse. He could have read the names of city streets, recited the *begats* in Genesis, and your heart still would have raced. The cadence. The pitch. The meter. The hope in his voice. Newfound. Like he wasn't expecting it.

The decision was easy. Was it even a decision? Henry would say it wasn't. He would say it was given to both of you. Fine. Yes. If one can say that a windstorm is given. If one can say that an earthquake is given.

For a Lutheran, faith is not something one achieves. It is not assent, belief in propositions, or striving. Faith is trust, and trust is a gift, not a feeling. Emotions make an unreliable measuring stick. You don't have to feel anything to be a Lutheran.

Maybe that's why he left his congregation.

You found him four blocks from Irving Hall. He was journeying west on Post Street, a clergyman fleeing his congregation in the rain. He ducked to miss an awning, to dodge the swinging sign of a tailor; he passed a large plaster molar hanging outside a dental parlor. Hands behind his back, he strode, coatless, beardless, craggy as a sheared cliff. You approached, stepped alongside him, matched his pace. He looked over and there you were, walking next to him, like you'd meant to be there, like you belonged. An excellent fake. An outstanding imitation of a confident woman.

Well. Hello.

That's when it begins. When you've trotted up alongside him and there's nothing strange, when your body and his body are already fine, already talking to each other.

Do you believe in free will?

Depends who's asking.

Did you consider propriety, duty, fidelity, society? Yes. Did they stop you? They turned to sounds that day; they lost their meaning. They fell to the ground untouched, a jumble of consonants and vowels. Later you would have to retrieve those words, spell them out. You are spelling them still.

Henry's kindness is the hardest to relinquish. Today, especially, keeping away feels cruel, feels like kicking a dog. He was unfailingly gentle.

And except for the very last time, he never left the cottage without kissing Blue's hands, one first and then the other. And her knuckles.

—You have the most beautiful hands, he would tell her as she glowed up at him. —And I am the luckiest father on the planet to have held them.

He talked better than he wrote. He talked like he touched. Lightly.

Stone's gaze never strays. His eyes are nothing like Henry's. Nothing about this fellow is in the same species. How is this possible? How does the male animal operate?

And how dare you think such things when your daughter lies injured, waiting to be seen by a doctor who is running late, a doctor who is slow in coming?

Dissociation; another word Henry taught you. The splitting off of a group of ideas from the conscious mind. But you're tired of men teaching you things. You'd rather teach them things.

You glance up. Stone's still observing you, his eyes resting steadily. Are you blushing? No. You don't faint, and you don't blush either.

That first Sunday in the rain, Henry asked your name.

—Lucy, you told him.

—Lucy who?

—Christensen, you said, shy all of a sudden.

—Lucy Christensen.

His voice thickened with resignation.

He had no place to store this information, no place to hold a young woman named Lucy from Omaha, a woman who'd ridden the train west alone, searching for a cousin who did not want her, a woman who chased a minister after he delivered a three-line sermon that had taken eight months to compose, she being the only one who had understood it.

Twenty-one. What does anyone know at twenty-one?

Enough. You knew enough. And better.

He repeated your name.

—Lucy. I don't think I've seen you before.

—It was my first time.

—Will you return?

—Will you?

You countered his question with a question. It steamed up from the base of your ribs, flew out before you could retract it.

He shook his head.

—I don't think I can. I think I just left Irving Hall for good.

—Then no, you told him. I don't think I can either.

Blue

— SHE MANAGED TO LAND IN GLASS, the doctor says, talking as if I'm not right here in front of him. — Why wasn't anyone watching her?

— I *was* watching her, Ma says.

Now that the doctor has appeared, a flock of white-uniformed nurses surround my bed.

— Really? he says. — These lacerations would suggest otherwise.

Ma has put on her emergency face again. She's pinched and solemn. The doctor makes a note in his clipboard as he talks.

— She needs sutures along the earlobe. The lacerations on her lower legs will heal, but keep them bandaged. How in the world did you let a child her age roll in a bed of glass?

Ma stiffens. — I didn't *let* her—

— And why is she soaked through? Do you want her to catch pneumonia?

He glares at her. I glare at him. If Pa were here, he would tell that doctor to stop speaking to her that way. May and June would defend her, too. They're her friends, maybe her only friends. I have more friends than my mother does, if you count the snails that live on our front step.

— They're our reinforcements, Ma said to me the other day. — Our backups.

She was talking about May and June. Not the snails.

— Backups for what? I asked.

She didn't explain.

May and June live on the other side of the estate. During the day, they sell tickets to Mr. Sutro's museum. At night, once in a while, they play hopscotch with Ma. They hoot and howl over whatever tale Ma is telling. They toss pebbles where they've scratched lines into the sand. When the game's done, the front step will creak; that's May sitting her big bottom down. Their laughter wanders back into the cottage, where I am supposed to be sleeping.

They both came over the night Ma found out her cousin had died. She didn't hear the news until it was almost my bedtime. She and Mr. Claude had spent the day cleaning up Big Ben for his first public viewing, and she was telling us about it. Big Ben is a sea lion who washed up dead on the shore. Mr. Sutro decided to make him part of his collection of stuffed animals.

—How will they do that? I asked Ma.

—Put him under glass.

—Mr. Sutro?

—No. She laughed.—The sea lion.

She was standing outside, wiping her hands on her skirt, leaning her hip against the door. May and June were sitting on the step.

—It's nature made permanent, she went on.—That's what Mr. Claude said. Nature made permanent.

May chuckled.—Permanent, my hide.

—Meanwhile, there I was, up to my elbows in sea lion guts.

May said: You wear it well.

June sipped her steam beer and snorted.

Ma didn't learn the dead man was her cousin until Mr. Sutro stopped by with the news. By then she was too full of beer to say much one way or the other. May and June stood and helped her inside. All four of us sat together in a row on the bed. To help her, June said.

Ma looked at her hands in her lap. Finally she shook her head like she was trying to ward off a headache.

—I had better write my mother.

That was all she said. May and June asked her if she needed anything. I kept waiting for her to say she wanted Pa to come over. But she turned her face to the wall and asked us to turn down the lamp. I don't remember if she sent the letter.

Lucy

HE TOOK YOU TO LUNCH. He didn't drink and he didn't eat. He ordered two roast beefs on rye. You dislike roast beef, the chewy texture, the spongy pink. But you ate the entire thing. Henry picked up his sandwich but never took a bite.

— What's wrong? you asked when you noticed him not eating. — Is something wrong with your sandwich?

— Not at all, he said, and set it down untouched. — It's delicious. I'm sure it is.

But beginnings are easy; beginnings are the ignition.

— Where's your family? he asked. — Do you have anyone?

— I have a cousin, you said. — And a mother.

After that, you didn't know what to tell him. Your swirling thoughts refused to be coaxed into speech. So you sat there and nibbled at the rye crust, thinking to yourself, *He must believe I'm slow; he thinks I'm dull-witted.* Henry kept quiet. Sipping his sarsaparilla, he never once took his eyes off you. People came and went at the other tables, and he didn't see another person. Not a single woman interested him. Only you.

— You don't have to finish eating if you're not hungry, he said.

— When I was young, you abruptly confessed, leaning in, when I was young, my mother boxed my ears for something I did. I can't remember what anymore. Something minor. When she boxed my ears, my eardrum ruptured. Only instead of losing my hearing, I lost my speech.

— You lost your speech? Henry said, mirroring your posture. He pushed aside his plate.

—Yes. I mean, my ear rang for a few days. But I wouldn't talk at all, not even after my hearing returned. My mother never could figure it out. Not for a month. I didn't say a single word for over a month.

You paused, considering. —I think I was protesting.

He nodded. —Not everything needs to happen all at once, Lucy. You don't have to solve everything all at once. Things have a way of working themselves out over time.

—There will be detours, you said, nodding.

His smile returned. —Yes.

He was thirty-nine, which back then seemed old; the skin at the base of his throat had started to weather. That was weathered? You hadn't seen anything yet. But his eyes were kind. And his hands: you could not stop looking at them.

—You fascinate me, he said.

He needed to lie down with you. That much was obvious.

One hour to lie down with you in his arms. Just one. That was enough. After that, he could return to his regular life.

You could do that for him. In days to come, you'd have an hour to spare.

Or a thousand.

The estate workers shared a dormitory, and your room lay at the end of an unlit hall on the second floor. It boasted a gabled window and an iron lamp that hissed and smoked. A deer head missing its antlers stared from the wall over the bed, a leftover from the taxidermist, a failed attempt from an earlier apprentice. A fox head with a bald patch observed from its station above the bureau.

You had worked for Mr. Claude just a few weeks, and already these creatures seemed to wander after you, to pin you in their sights. The day you brought Henry over, his shoe caught on the edge of a rug made of deer hide and leftover raccoon pelts.

—Deuce, he softly cursed. —What is that?

—Castoffs, you said, and you guided him inside, shut the bedroom door, and locked it. You were getting used to all this. Henry wasn't. All he'd seen of the Outside Lands was the city cemetery. He hadn't moved here yet. Though that was coming. Though you would do that to him also.

Your room smelled of mildew and leather. Henry skittered, nervous, a mariner missing his compass. He thought you two might take a stroll near the water's edge first.

—There is no water's edge, you told him. —It's all rocks.

His hands trembled when you reached for them. Beneath your feet, the carpet of hides was soft.

Later he told you he was afraid. Nervous he would not be able to satisfy you. Satisfaction was never the issue.

—You said you were a widow, Stone says as the doctor steps away to confer with the chief nurse.

—Yes, you reply, not meeting his eyes.

Widow and *widower* refer to people who have lost their spouses. *Orphans* are children who have lost their parents. What's the word for parents who have lost their children? There isn't one.

And Henry has no idea he nearly lost his daughter today. Half of you wants to keep that information from him, to protect him. Today isn't the day. The other half of you wants to shove the news down his windpipe.

Because Blue is still here. Isn't she? Lying on her back in this hospital bed while this doctor stands here haranguing you. She's above the ground and not below. She's eight years old. She needs her father.

You can hear him: *But you sent me away.*

—What happened to him? What happened to your husband? Stone asks.

—Lungs, you say flatly. —He was a lunger. He ran out of air.

Blue

ANOTHER MAN IN A UNIFORM rolls a stretcher down the corridor. The noisy wheels interrupt the doctor, which is good because he has started lecturing Ma again. When the doctor takes a breath, she says:

— You're not giving me a chance to explain.

— Her injuries speak for themselves. You were careless.

— It's not her fault, I say, interrupting them.

I reach out and pull at the doctor's sleeve so he will stop picking on her. She's the only mother I have. I need her to last.

— I fell through a skylight and landed in a well full of the ocean, I say. — Ma didn't see. A monster at the bottom of the well tried to swallow me.

— Blue, she says quietly. — It'll be all right.

But he's absorbed now; my tale has given this doctor something to think about, something to occupy his time. More nurses crowd into the pavilion. They crane in and ask how I'm doing. They pat me and stroke my hair. I can't remember when so many people have paid me so much attention. The nurses marvel over how close to death I came, how brave I must have been. Ma's supposed to be the brave one.

— That's what hospitals do best, Mr. Stone says as he watches the nurses petting me.

— What's that? Ma asks.

He shrugs. — Make a person feel important, feel like the most necessary body in the world.

———

My parents never take me anywhere together. They never take me to Golden Gate Park together. Well, they did once, to the midwinter fair there, but I was only five. Three years have passed since then.

I'd never had so much fun as I did at that fair. Ma and I hid inside the fine arts building. We came out in time to let Pa buy us gum from the Wrigley Gum Girls, who snapped their gum when they chewed. We saw exhibits of the world, genuine native Eskimos, rowboats on Stow Lake. And buffalo in a paddock. The last thing we did was tour the Forty-Niner mining camp. Ma clapped her hands when she saw the men dressed as old-time cowboys. They wore ten-gallon hats and had six-shooters strapped to their hips.

— It's a world within a world, she said.

Pa left before we had a chance to finish the tour. Someone he knew saw him and called his name, a man named Stevens; I heard Pa say it. Ma froze. Pa whipped around and bolted. He sped out of there three ways from Sunday. He disappeared in less time than it took Ma to grab my hand and turn me in a different direction.

Which direction? Away. It's the only direction she pulls.

She moved me so my back faced the man who had waved and my nose was pressed against the window of the camp store.

— Who's Stevens? I asked. — And what are we looking at? Ow.

Her nails dug into my shoulders. — Shh. Blue. Please.

Behind the window was nothing but unfinished wood. The store wasn't real.

A nurse carries a tray of instruments over to my bed. When she sets it down, I raise myself up on my elbows to see. Yikes. There are tweezers, a metal bowl, scissors, a scalpel, and some other sharp things I don't care to look at. I can't help but shrink a little. Ma makes a strange face too.

— I'm staying with her. Let me stay, she says to the doctor.

— You're half fainting already, he says. — Go have something to eat in the dining room. We'll have her stitched up by the time you return.

— I'm not leaving her.

— Seems to me you already did. What a poor excuse for a mother.

He points at Stone. — You, sir. Please take your wife out of the operating area.

— I'm a widow, Ma snaps.

Her hand finds its way through the wall of nurses to my shoulder; she pinches me, reminding me again of my duty.

— Mother, *I know,* I declare from my throne on the cot. — I won't say anything to them.

11:00 a.m.

Marilyn

ONE OF MRS. WOOD'S little inmates trudges in your direction. She could have stepped straight out of Maria Kip's annual report. She's the spindly one you saw earlier, the one with straggly chestnut hair and a metal brace on her right leg that clicks whenever she takes a step.

— Hello, you say.

— Hello. She bobs, her cheeks coloring. — Would you please help me?

She produces a comb that has seen better days, hands it over, turns, and presents the back of her head. She might be twelve.

— We're supposed to wear braids, she says.

— I see.

— I forgot until Mrs. Wood reminded me. She said I have to keep my hair neat or I won't be allowed a deviled egg.

You nod. — That sounds like Mrs. Wood.

— I'm not good at braiding. And I have never had a deviled egg.

You take the comb. — Not to have had a deviled egg is a tragedy.

The girl twists around and follows your movements with warm brown eyes. The flatulent sound of practicing tubas continues from the side room. Mrs. Wood has migrated into the kitchen to dispense wisdom to the cook. And time has slowed to the pace of—what? A snail. A stone. A snail glued to the underside of a stone, buried at the bottom of the ocean.

This is how it is, this is what you have become: a volunteer at whatever sad place will take you. When they send you away—and they will —you'll find another institution that gives women something meaningful to do. When you die someday, people will say: *Marilyn Plageman braided the hair of orphans.*

That's all right. That's fine. You've moved on. Passed through. You've reached the other side of wishing life would make sense. You're fine, perfectly fine, thank you.

Each year on your son's birthday, you think: *Today he would have turned* . . . three. Four. Five. Six. Seven. Eight.

Year nine was especially bad.

Ten was as rough as could be imagined. Eleven you don't remember. Twelve — you came down with the flu, which helped, because you couldn't walk anywhere, were too feverish even to swivel your eyes left to right to take in the gold-patterned wallpaper. Sickness allowed you to stay in bed, which is all you want to do on this date anyway. Stasis is the temptation; it is the enemy.

—It's fine if you stay home, Henry said.

But it's not. You mustn't. He should know this. You must fight each year, each time this day descends. You must not let the day vanquish you.

You explained this resolution to Henry, and he seemed to understand, but then the next year he said the same exact thing, as if he hadn't heard anything you'd said, as if he had completely forgotten your conversation from the year before. He sat on the edge of the chair, the skin beneath his chin starting to sag, the vulnerability of his flesh taking you by surprise, affecting you so much you had to turn your head.

—I can't stay in bed all day, you said. — Don't you see?

—But you're not well.

—I'm as well as I will be.

Henry has gotten better on his own but doesn't say how. You asked him about it a while back, a couple of years ago, it must have been.

—How did you do it? you said.

—Do what?

It was late; he sat hunched at the kitchen table, knees bumping against the underside because they do not make tables for people with legs as long as his. He was eating salted peanuts and riffling through committee reports from the Richmond Property Owners Protective Association.

—Get better, you said.

—I'm not sure that I did.

You pressed him. —No, you *are* better. You used to have no hope and now you have it.

—I'm not sure it's that simple.

—I didn't say it was simple, you said.

—What, then, Marilyn?

Your eyes felt drier than usual. Dry and gritty. —How do you do it? How do you get through? you asked.

—Get through what?

—Through the day. Make it through each day. How do you do it? He peered at you over his reading glasses.

—I wasn't aware we had a choice.

Normally you two are not so direct. And yes, this is direct, at least for you. Normally you and Henry sail in and out of each other's day, in and out of each other's peripheral vision, peripheral marriage, gently and without jousting.

A few hours later he resumed the conversation. In the parlor, he pulled your chair close, pulled it with you still sitting in it. He slid you away from the bay window, so that you lost your view of the curtains. He grasped your hands and raised them to his lips, kissed your fingertips, and urged:

—We have to give thanks.

—For what?

—For the gifts of each day.

—What are those? you shot back, wounding him.

You felt guilty, but Henry has this effect.

—I don't always know what they are, he admitted. —The point is to keep searching. The point is we have to remain open.

—Be more specific, you commanded.

—More specific?

—Yes.

—All right, he said. —I'll give you specific. I give thanks for *you.* Every day. Despite everything. For you. My wife. Marilyn the Impossible. Marilyn the Irascible.

—Despite everything?

—I give thanks for the way you clomp your boots in the rain. For the slenderness of your fingers. See?

He held your hands up for you to take stock of yourself. The touch was kind. Not romantic.

—My fingers aren't slender, you said.

—And for the way you rest your chin on your knees when you're reading curled up in a chair and no one's watching.

—No, you replied, suddenly unaccountably lonesome, suddenly feeling yourself the object of pity.—I need you to be thankful for something that isn't about me. Or you. I need a gift that's outside us, that's away from here, as far as a person can see. Find me one of those, Henry.

And you rose, tripping over the hem of your dress, and swept out of the room.

—What do you want? you ask, rotating the girl so she's facing you. She might be older than you thought. A wiry thirteen.

—What kind of braid, I mean. One or two?

—Two, please, she whispers.

—French?

—Is that all right?

—Of course. What's your name, child?

—Ida.

The girl studies the floor, eyes huge. She's not used to having her preferences consulted.

—Ida. Tell me what kind of hairstyle you *really* want.

—Like yours, she whispers.—Yours is swell.

—I can't remember what I did to my hair this morning.

You reach up to pat your head. Your hair's in a heavy twist at the nape of your neck, beneath your hat. Henry hates this hat. It's sage green, velvet, and topped with a genuine Mexican merle. They sew the birds on everything these days, whole specimens, or at least the quills. A woman can't buy a decent hat anywhere without a dozen feathers attached to it. Henry says San Francisco is becoming a city full of hats but without any egrets or herons.

—Are you sure you want your hair styled like mine?

—Yes, Ida says.—Yes, please.

So she wants to wear her hair up; she wants to be a woman. Mrs. Wood won't stand for it. That's all the incentive you need. Gently you turn her again and begin combing out her tresses.

—I used to braid my little sister's hair every morning, you say.

—You have a sister?

—Yes. Her name's Penny. She lives in Oregon now.

You wait for it, for the inevitable question: *How many children do you have?*

—I used to live in Sacramento, Ida says.

A relief. She's not going to ask.

Year thirteen was mild, almost peaceful. You walked through the cemetery at the appointed time and, without thinking, reached for Henry's hand. He searched your eyes and regarded you with such troubled perplexity that you dropped his hand.

—It's still me, you said. —Sorry to disappoint you.

—Don't talk that way, he urged.

He walked you down an overgrown path, until a stench near the paupers' graves overtook the clearing. He gave you a handkerchief to cover your nose and mouth. He wrapped you in his arms and hugged you, pressed you to him. You removed his arms and stepped away.

If you are not able to be with your husband, to make love to him, if your desire has died, then surely his desire has died too. You expired together. You both went down with the ship. Correct? If your sex shrivels, his must shrivel too. You cannot permit yourself the thought that he might still be alive down there.

The two of you wound up before a lookout point not far from where the strait connects the Pacific Ocean and the San Francisco Bay. The water resembled a pane of green glass. Shoreline to horizon awaited. You rested your head, fleetingly, against Henry's arm and looked out at the strait. You could feel his intake and exhalation of breath; his lips brushed your hair. For a week afterward, you slept poorly.

Year fourteen was worse than anything that had come before. You were headed nowhere, growing worse instead of better. But you couldn't *not* go; you couldn't *not* visit. If you don't remember your son, who will? The only two people on this planet who can keep Jack Plageman's memory alive are the same two people who can no longer keep each other alive.

Year fifteen: You tripped on the lane leading to Jack's grave; you twisted and nearly sprained an ankle. The pain helped. It distracted you from the blank unyielding sky. You stood, balancing on one foot, and clung to Henry for balance, the two of you alone together once again, alone as you always are on this day. The grave lay feet away. Coyote brush had tried to invade the garden just beyond Henry's ridiculous granite angel. You could see the places where your husband had failed to vanquish the brush fully. Patches of wild thistle poked up. When you pointed out these areas to him, he said:

—I guess your old mule is wearing out, Marilyn.

You stayed longer than usual. When you returned home, Henry drank more than usual. He did not ask to lie down beside you. You lay in bed with your ankle elevated. Richard would keep you company; Richard was not allowed to leave the room.

May 22 is hard on the dog too. Richard's fourteen now. Sometimes he urinates inside. He cannot decide if he should stay in the front room or in the back, if he should ally himself with you or with Henry. He becomes immobilized on the porch steps, where you'll find him halfway up or halfway down, eyes wet with panic. He will whine, unable to move. When he sees Henry, he'll moan louder and fling himself up or down the remaining steps, nails scrabbling, until he reaches the landing: safe, ebullient, *whew.* Until the next time, whereupon the cycle begins again.

You and Richard are pretty steady most of the time, pretty ordinary for 364 days out of 365. Does that help? Yes on most days. No on May 22.

Lucy

STONE STOPS IN THE CORRIDOR as the door to the pavilion closes. He turns to regard you. He's out of place here, with his overalls and uncombed red hair. He's rough-hewn.

—What that doctor said? About you being a poor excuse for a mother? That wasn't right. He shouldn't of said that.

He takes your elbow. —C'mon, let's feed you something.

Together you make your way downstairs to a second hallway streaming with natural light. This floor reeks of antiseptic solution and lemon. At the end of the hallway, the kitchen pavilion is airy and almost empty, with windows overlooking a courtyard, a green lawn precisely manicured, its shrubbery tasteful and trim: a private oasis for those who can afford it. A decorative fountain plumes at the end of the quadrangle. It's the kind of place for a woman who walks around with a parasol.

You can't remember the last time you carried a parasol. Certainly not in the Outside Lands. The wind would take it.

In the dining area, servers are setting tables for the noontime meal. Stone pulls one of them aside and prepares to order.

—What do you want? he asks you. What'll it be?

Henry would have ordered two roast beef sandwiches.

—A cheese and cucumber sandwich? you say; the words feel stilted.

—Sounds good. Sounds like a very good plan to me. Waiter, two cheese and cucumber sandwiches, please.

He points to a small table in the corner.

—Here's a spot. Ladies first.

White linens drape the table, and a single yellow rose in a glass vase stands alone as a centerpiece. You seat yourself without allowing Stone to pull out a chair for you, without giving him an opportunity for chivalry. A poor excuse for a mother? Try a poor excuse for a woman.

—Do you think about your wife when you're with me?

You posed this question to Henry once. Early on, in the first months. His hand lowered to the table, relinquished his fork.

—I hadn't until you brought her up.

—How can you not think of her?

—Because I'm with you. When I'm with you, Lucy, I think of you.

You leaned forward, pushed aside the remnants of the meal you'd hastily cooked, stewed tomatoes and beans. With your thumb, you rubbed a speck of tomato off his chin.

—And do you think of me when you're with her? you asked.

His eyes stayed calm, desolate, his contemplation steady.

—Yes.

—You sound unsure.

—I try not to.

—You try not to sound unsure, or you try not to think of me when you're with her?

Henry lowered his head, toed the tightrope.

—Yes.

Stone tears into his sandwich. It's fancier than the ham rolls he packed in his lunch basket, the same basket he abandoned back at the pump station. The gulls must have devoured those rolls by this point.

Behind him, kitchen workers push in and out of swinging doors, getting ready to serve lunch. Hospital workers in their crisply starched uniforms will gather soon for their repast.

—See here, you say to him. —You've been extremely helpful—

He cocks one eyebrow. —Never good when a woman starts with *See here*.

—But I don't want to inconvenience you more than we've already done.

—There's no inconveniencing. Not from where I sit.

—No one's watching the pump station.

—Pump station'll be fine for another hour. It's not going anywhere. It'll survive for you to beat it to death with questions another day.

He's smiling at you.

You don't have the concentration to look at this man. Let alone talk to him. You can't string two sentences together. So much for working on being a reporter. What time is it? Your clock is still set to Henry. You memorized his routine ages ago. You wanted to be able to imagine what he was doing during all the hours and days you couldn't see him.

When it's six in the morning, Henry's rising. When it's seven, he's shaving and putting on coffee. By eight, on a normal day, he's walking to his store. By half past, he's behind the counter, waiting for customers, who ask advice. Everyone wants a piece of Henry Plageman. They walk into Plageman's Hardware and General Merchandise, with its scuffed wood floors and crowded glass display cases, lean against the counters, and unburden themselves to him. A wife who won't stop crying. A diagnosis: tumors mushrooming along the spine. Henry listens. He absorbs every word. He's still a pastor. He's just changed venues. He sells tambourines, castanets, veterinary medicines, tonics for digestive difficulties. Poultry netting, rat traps, electric rings for rheumatism, birdcages. What else? Box cameras. Lamp wicks. Almanacs. About the only thing Henry's store doesn't carry is buttons. If you can't find what you want at Plageman's Hardware and General Merchandise, Henry will order it for you.

Right about now, he's knee-deep in weeds, clearing refuse. The city cemetery is one of the few places where you can hold Henry's hand in the open and not worry about being seen.

But you've called a halt to all that. You have given May 22 back to him.

Stone reaches for a tumbler and fills it with water from a pitcher. He sets it before you. In the glass, your reflection is visible. You're washed out. Pale and peaked, your mother would say.

—You look like you'd rather be someplace else, Stone observes.

—I need to be with Blue.

—Course you do. But you're wandering. You have a wandering look.

If you give up Henry for good, then Blue forfeits him too. She grows up fatherless.

—I was thinking about a place I used to visit, you say.

—Good place?

—I used to visit there every year. On this date.

—Gravesite? Husband's grave?

You look at him, and he shrugs, a little embarrassed.

—My ma used to do that, he offers.—My pa passed fifteen years ago, rest him, and she still shows up once a year at his grave. Doesn't bring him flowers. Bakes him an apple tart. Ma's losing her reason, demented as they come, but she still remembers once a year that Jimmy Senior needs his tart. She sets it out on the headstone, and the crows eat it.

—I visit the city cemetery every May twenty-second, you say.—Or I used to.

—The city cemetery? God Almighty. That dump?

He helps himself to a swallow of water.

—You interest me. You're interesting, Lucy Christensen.

He points at the sandwich you haven't eaten.—Something wrong with your food?

—Nothing's wrong, you say.—It's delicious. I'm sure of it.

You slide the plate in his direction.

—Lucy, Henry said that very first time.—I have a family. I have a wife.

—I know, you said, and you stood on your tiptoes to reach him, on the carpet of mismatched hides.

He stopped talking. His hands were hard and soft both.

He kissed the top of your head, a fatherly gesture, and rested his chin there. For a minute you thought that would be all; that would be enough. Then he tipped up your chin and kissed you on the mouth. That was the moment you understood Henry Plageman would not be any one thing in your life. He would have to be everything. You would require of him both too much and not enough. There was no one else you could ask.

The gas lamp snapped and smoked. The deer head thrust itself forward from the wall. That reminder of an untamed life cut short hung in your line of vision, behind Henry's shoulder.

He should have turned you around.

Did you think he would leave his wife and marry you? No. Never. Not in a million years. And yet.

Henry

—TOLD YOU I'D WRANGLE US OUT.

—That you did.

—Help me track down those potatoes, Plageman. Famishment is my middle name.

Escaping that police station took time. More time than you wanted it to. As you and Kerr headed toward the exit, release papers in hand, with Sears in the storage room snoring off his stomach bitters, the station head banged through the front door and demanded to know what you were doing. Showing him your papers, you explained that Sears had signed them and your release was therefore legal. You didn't mention the Orange Wine Stomach Bitters. Beside you, Kerr suppressed a gaseous belch.

The supervisor called for Sears, who slouched from the storage room, swiping at his eyes and stinking of rancid citrus.

—Saphead, the supervisor said and cuffed him twice. —Half-cut sot.

You had to summon all your powers of persuasion, all those rusty homiletic skills, to keep Sears from losing his position. You succeeded, but the process took time, chewed through half an hour you didn't have, half an hour the garden didn't have. Marilyn will show up at two o'clock and find your efforts wanting.

Kerr tugs at his broad-brimmed hat as the two of you step along Stanyan toward the station stables. His belly droops between his suspenders. Shuffling forward, he makes good use of his cane.

—Let's stop at that diner on Point Lobos.

—There's no time for breakfast, you remind him.

He looks at you as if you've lost your mind and not just your appetite.

—There's always time for breakfast, Plageman.

—I need you to drive me to the city cemetery first. Please. I'm asking for your kindness.

Kerr, shrugging, acquiesces. —My chariot awaits, he says.

He doesn't have anyone expecting him at home. His home is the Odd Fellows' Cemetery. And by *chariot*, he means an old gray mare. An old gray swaybacked mare hitched to a hearse.

Kerr drove you and your arresting officer to the police station last night. Always a gentleman, Kerr is. His hearse is a plain black coupe, modern, lightweight, with room in the back for a coffin. The letters *IOOF*, for International Order of Odd Fellows, are printed on the side. The vehicle can seat two, three if you count the deceased. There's an empty coffin in the back right now. A spare, Kerr calls it.

He's your ride, your one chance to reach the cemetery on time. His mare will haul your plants and tools to the mariners. But he and his Bess had better be long gone by the time Marilyn arrives. You don't want her seeing the hearse. Not on this anniversary.

You glance up. A rare easterly wind is blowing this way, delivering the acrid stench of foundries and slaughterhouses south of Market Street. The good winds in San Francisco are westerly. At the far edges of your vision, the densely populated neighborhoods rise up, jagged and formidable in their newness, shops and flats jammed so close against each other even the fog can't find its way in. Looming behind the flats are the silhouettes of factories, and the warehouses with their blacksmiths, and the sausage makers crowded in with the paint shops, the hay-and-grass sellers. The Richmond is nothing like those streets. Not yet, anyway.

You'd do a year's hard time in that park station for one full night alone with Lucy. You'd give your right eye. Or your left eye.

You told her so. Early on, in the first year. She'd moved out of the workers' dormitory and into a tin-roofed cottage hidden on the far side of Sutro's estate. It was remote. More secluded than the dormitory. No one would come by.

She moved there for your sake. You were aware of this fact and not entirely comfortable with it. She was trying to protect your good name, to safeguard your privacy for the times you visited. But she seemed genuinely pleased with the new arrangement. She liked the quiet and the austerity of her surroundings. She had detested the dorm, workers coming and going at all hours outside her door.—I couldn't hear myself think, she told you.

—My right eye, you confessed to her several days after she'd moved into the cottage.—I'd give my right eye to spend the whole night here with you.

—Then I have just the thing.

—What?

—Glass eyes. A tray of them. Back in Mr. Claude's workshop. Pick your color.

She dissolved into mirth. Before you departed, she kissed you. Lucy kisses best when you're on your way out the door. This particular demonstration was not one of her mediocre kisses, not one of her wondering-what-life-could-have-been kisses. It was one of her original kisses, the kind that inflames the loins. Lucy's kiss could resurrect a dead man. Maybe it did.

Maybe that's why you're still clinging to her tether months after she sent you packing. Jailbird; that's you. Or *half-cut sot*, the phrase Sears's supervisor used. You still write her letters. You, at forty-nine, old enough to be the father of a father, still pine in your nightly dreams like a schoolboy while Marilyn, your wife, your noble, disenchanted wife, lies in the next room waiting. For what? For you to come to her? No. Marilyn doesn't want you to come to her. She expressly told you not to. You spent four years asking; she spent four years refusing. She pushed you out of the room. And when she could no longer push you out, she vacated the room herself. She took over the nursery, added a bureau and a bed. Jack's room became hers.

That's another reason you wound up in this predicament.

See how easy that was? See how convenient it is to lay the fault at the spouse's shut door? For shame. You should be ashamed. *Chastened* might be the better word.

―――――

Inside the stables, Kerr calls a boy to fetch his horse and gig. The youth returns with Kerr's beloved Bess. The mare picks her way forward glumly, loath to abandon her dry room and board. Chewing the remains of a crab apple, she refuses to acknowledge you; she has eyes only for Kerr; right out of the gate, she does not wish to be associated with this business.

—How long have we been at this, Plageman? the foreman asks as he adjusts her gear and bit. Bess nickers.

—Two years.

—Feels longer.

—That it does.

—Think we made any headway last night?

—No, you say. No, I don't.

—Maybe we slowed 'em down, anyway.

Marilyn thinks you moved her from the Western Addition to the Outside Lands to be closer to Jack's resting place. That's partly true. You also followed Lucy.

Kerr climbs up and situates himself at the driver's box. He extends his hand to you; you step up, take a seat beside him. Bess sets off, the hearse wheels rattling behind her. She wends her way beneath a pewter sky. She'll head north along Stanyan to the carriage road that leads through the Panhandle. Then she'll jog left along Masonic before heading west at Point Lobos Avenue. Always, you are heading west. Albeit with detours.

Two almost-fugitives, one middle-aged, one in his seventies. Free now; out in the open. Your destination: the Outside Lands. The outermost edge of the Outside Lands. The end of the road.

—I need to stop at my store, you tell Kerr.

—Thought you were in a rush.

—I am. It's on the way. It'll take ten minutes. It's close.

—What do you need?

You tick through your mental list. —Pruners. A trowel. And lilies. I ordered calla lilies, two crates' worth.

The foreman pulls on the reins, shifting to appraise you.

—Lilies?

—Yes. I order flowers every year.

—Why?

Two years, you've worked side by side together on the cemetery problem, and you've never once mentioned your real reason to him. Never explained why you're in this fight. In your defense, he hasn't asked. Until now.

— Plageman?

— I had a son, you say.

And then you can't say another word.

The old foreman stays fixed, studying you, until recognition arrives. Something in his countenance gives way. He bows his head, clicks at Bess, and resumes driving.

— Never really gets better, does it, he says under his breath.

No, it doesn't. Not on birthdays and not on death-days. And when both anniversaries fall on the same date, a parent is done for.

Marilyn

IDA WINCES AS YOU RAKE OUT the last of her tangles.

—Ma'am? I think I should have two braids after all. I'm sorry. But that's what Mrs. Wood told us.

—Are you sure? Because I'll do yours up if you want it up. I will. Let me worry about Mrs. Wood.

Ida bites her lip. —I should take the braids. But thank you.

—All right. Braids it is, then.

—With green ribbons to tie the ends? she whispers.

—Do you have a green ribbon?

—No, ma'am. But . . .

Shyly she tilts her head toward the bunting you earlier strung along the staircase: pine-green ribbons in abundance. She smiles hopefully at you. No one could deny that face.

You nod. —Fetch me a pair of scissors, Ida, and you'll have your green hair ribbons.

Beaming, she limps away. Mrs. Wood will not be pleased to find the ends of the bunting snipped for a child's hair decoration. You halfway hope she finds out. You halfway hope she tries to forbid it.

The task for today is to get through, to endure, to cross over to the other side of the calendar. How you do it doesn't matter. It doesn't have to be pretty.

Returning with the scissors, Ida tries and fails to hide her excitement; her cheeks are flushed; she's breathless. She's had too much stimulation. These Maria Kip residents rarely escape their fixed routines. They don't know what to do with a morning of comparative freedom.

—All right, Ida. Here I go. Shield me.

She moves to stand between you and the arriving guests so no one can see what you're doing. You reach out, snip one of the fancy satin bows tied along the stair railing. Ida covers her mouth with her hand.

—Keep watch, you tell her.

She nods energetically.

Finished snipping, you come away with two sleek green ribbons. You pull her into the corner, away from the staircase.

—Come here, then. Let's see what we can make of these.

Threading the ribbons through her hair will allow you to create two lovely braids, special and festive, against the rules. None of Mrs. Wood's other charges will be wearing such finery. Ida hugs herself with delight.

Will this be your most important accomplishment of the day? Quite possibly. Of the year? That too.

Henry's putting in the plants by now. He won't want you to witness his struggle with the roots. He wants you to think things come easily for him.

But you've learned a few lessons over the past few years. It's time to catch your husband in the act of improving nature.

Henry

YOU'VE LEARNED A FEW LESSONS YOURSELF:

1. When with Marilyn, don't think about Lucy.
2. When with Lucy, don't think about Marilyn.
3. When in the black-and-white-tiled kitchen, stay in the black-and-white-tiled kitchen. When on the ferned front porch, stay on the ferned front porch. Don't mix and match locations.
4. Remain immutable. Stay the same in both places. You can't have your worlds changing and you changing too. Something has to remain the same. The only one who can achieve inalterability in this situation is you; the inconstant one must become constant. Achieving this equilibrium will take effort; it will take some doing. It's one reason you will be tired all the time.
5. There won't be enough of you to go around. Get used to it. This is what you've chosen. Or what chose you. The solution to this deficiency does not lie in enlarging yourself. Nor does it lie in bisecting yourself, splitting your heart down the middle. The solution requires presenting your whole person, whatever in God's name that means, to each woman at each location and then withdrawing entirely, leaving everything behind when you depart one or the other so that you can offer your whole person all over again the next time.

In theory, this plan works. In practice, it fails. It assumes you can just pick up and leave. Which you can't. It's not possible.

You've left vital organs behind, you're sure of it, when you depart Lucy's, when you try to leave and Blue has not yet fallen asleep, when she patters out of the bedroom after you, spies you tiptoeing toward the front door, attempting to slip out without disturbing her.

—Ostrich, she'll say.—Ostrich. Why are you leaving? I still have things to tell you.

You leave your heart in one place, your stomach in the next. You return to Marilyn, then sneak off to Lucy and Blue, and then back to Marilyn again, disemboweled, hollow as a carved pumpkin. You shake it off. Shake off the disequilibrium and become steady Henry again. Whereupon the cycle recommences.

An hour with Lucy, and you want to be a better man. An hour with Marilyn, and you know you're the worst man in the universe.

The other problem with that last lesson, with lesson five, to be precise, is it assumes your wife and your lover each have nothing better to do than sit around and wait for you. It assumes that they both desire your company. And it paints that yearning as a well that never runs dry, as a continuous impetus for reliving thirst. *Relieving* thirst, that is.

This depiction isn't true. It's so far from true, so much more mercurial, that thinking about it makes you splutter, makes you cough until you double over.

—Where's this store of yours again?

—Tenth and California.

—Let's swing by the Big Four on the way. See how Odd Fellows' fared last night.

Kerr saws at the reins. The mare veers right, turning from Stanyan onto the tree-lined carriage lane of the Panhandle.

—We don't have time.

—Won't take but a few minutes. Right, Bessie?

The mare slows to a halt in the middle of the thoroughfare. A black horse and racing buggy speed past. You glimpse the driver standing in his seat, cracking an impatient whip. Bess, standing still, flicks her ears. She thought it was time to stop. She'll land on any excuse. She's stopped three times now, and you've traveled only a few blocks.

—Is this her top speed? you ask.

—It's close. Kerr clucks her back into motion. The world's slowest outlaws crawl on.

Last year, the mayor signed into law an order prohibiting any further sales of burial lots within the city and county of San Francisco. The city cemetery doesn't sell individual plots, so it wasn't affected directly. But it's next. Marilyn didn't take the news well when you told her.

—Some meeting, Kerr says; he's obviously thinking about what's next for his Odd Fellows'. —Mark my words, Plageman, they'll shut us down. They'll shut us down and then they'll move us. In five years no one will remember any of us existed.

—But people need cemeteries.

—They need 'em, but they don't want to *see* 'em. People don't want to be reminded every day where they're going to wind up.

You called your wife cold-blooded that day you told her about the mayoral order. The two of you were quarreling. You wanted her to be informed. She wanted you to solve the problem.

Was it fair to call her cold-blooded? No. Did you apologize? Yes. Did she accept your apology? She never responded.

Kerr clicks twice. Bess will trudge north on Masonic, traveling past the cemetery of the same name. She'll pass Calvary Cemetery on the right, the burial ground for Roman Catholics. There's no cemetery dedicated to Lutherans. There aren't enough of them out here.

The foreman straightens his shoulders and hums an old-time hymn. He's entering familiar territory.

Lucy's first year joining you: Nine in the morning, May 22, her nose running as she shivered in the mist. You found her at the entrance waiting.

Bewildered, you halted in the middle of the path. You had told her about May 22; you had relayed to her the day's course. You'd hoped she might think of you that day, might remember what you were doing. You didn't dream she'd want to involve herself in the actual work. The two of you had known each other less than a year. This anniversary wasn't hers.

—You're here, you said to her.

—I thought we might need these, she replied, and from the folds of her skirt she produced two pairs of gardening gloves.

—Thank you, you said and, confounded, fell silent.

She walked with you north to the mariners' graveyard. As you reached Jack's grave, she tied the strings of her straw hat tighter beneath her chin. Resolve took over her features. Then she dropped to her hands and knees and began pulling up thistles and weeds. She knew exactly what needed to be uprooted and what needed to stay. She was a natural at it. The two of you worked three hours side by side. Under your gloves, blisters bloomed.

Midway through, you paused and studied her. She was still on her knees in the sand.

—You're spent, you said.—You're exhausted.

—I'm all right, she said, wiping her face with her sleeve, streaking her cheek with grit.—I'm fine, Henry.

You told her you could handle the rest of the work; you'd been tending this plot of land on your own for four years now. She didn't have to stay. You'd be all right.

—I don't want you to be compromised, you said.

She met your eyes. The wind whipped a stray lock of hair free of her hat.

—That word makes sense only in hindsight, she said.

You had no idea what she meant. You tried again a few minutes later. She was still attacking the weeds, although they had surrendered some time before.

—Lucy, you said.—It'll be all right. You can return home.

—No, she said, and in that moment she looked younger than you'd seen her. Younger and more damaged.—No, don't send me away yet, Henry. Please.

You were living on borrowed time. Stealing fire from the gods. All the clichés you hate, pathetic, overwrought phrases. You needed them anyway.

She spoke once more after the garden was ready. Standing, she brushed off her gloved hands and regarded the scrubbed granite of Jack's marker. The blue of her scarf reflected the clement sky.

—My life isn't large, Henry, she said.—It's not large. But it's mine. It's not anyone else's.

Then she turned and went from you.

An hour later, Marilyn arrived.

Bess clops past the Masonic Cemetery. The reservoir for the Olympic Salt Water Company lies ahead, off Josephine; it's the companion to the ocean-side pumping station below Sutro's estate.

Lucy will be spending her Saturday morning inside that museum's workshop, buried in sealskins and fox hides, draped with cotton batting. She'll be efficient, composed, focused. The task of preparing a 4,800-pound sea lion for mounting and stuffing doesn't give her a moment's pause. She's clearheaded at the taxidermist's. She doesn't complain, doesn't question the hand life has dealt her. She saves everything else up for you.

You should have left last night's meeting before things deteriorated. You should have chased after her, should have flagged her down in the rain. She did the same for you once. Last night should've been your turn.

What would you have said? *Don't leave. Don't let go.*
Forgive me.

Her second year joining you: Two Chinese men tending a burial ground to the south lit bonfires. Smoke blanketed the cemetery. As the haze drifted into Jack's garden, Lucy asked what the Chinese ceremonial fire symbolized.

—*Adiaphora,* you said. —Though that's my word. Not theirs.

She frowned. —Speak plainly.

—They're letting go. Burning what's not needed.

—Letting go?

—Of the nonessentials. Of everything that's not necessary to salvation.

She was with child then, mere weeks along; she had just found out, and you were overcome with terror and calm. Your secret was about to spin out of control. You were gearing up to tell Marilyn.

—How does a person decide? she asked as the smoke filtered skyward. —How do we know what's essential and what's not? How are we supposed to figure that out ahead of time?

———

And then came months of sweating it out in secret, of tracing the veins in her swelling breasts, a violet web under thickening flesh. She forbade you to tell Marilyn. She didn't want to cause more harm. *To whom?* you wanted to ask. Her ankles thickened. Her dresses developed permanent stains in the armpits. Her body was raining. She didn't understand what was normal, what wasn't.

— It's all normal, you tried to tell her, tried to say. — It's life arriving.

And every day searing and unbelievable, and every day wrestling dread, worrying Lucy would leave, worrying she would stay, expecting her to flee, fly away, board the train back to Omaha, where she could return to her previous life, her previous incarnation, the girl she was before she collided with you. In Omaha she could write you off as an error in judgment, a yearlong mistake.

When you asked if she planned to leave, she shook her head.

— Where would I go? I can't travel backward.

It was a second chance. But for you, not for Marilyn. Therefore, not really a second chance. And Lucy couldn't have a second chance yet, because she was still in the middle of her first one.

She concocted an unlikely tale for Mr. Claude about a husband killed in war, a husband she'd neglected to mention, some faceless chap in uniform who'd paid her a conjugal visit before his untimely end.

— Which war? you asked her.

She had to think a minute.

Bess steps into the late-morning light, head resignedly bobbing. The day has stayed quiet, has retained the curtain of dawn.

You hunch forward on the driver's box. Mist spits in your face. What did Luther say? Man is a mule forever being ridden.

And then, February 1889: Anna Christensen slid with a robust howl into Dr. Emma Sutro's capable arms. You didn't witness Blue on her first day. You remained locked all afternoon in disputations with Marilyn over some trifle and could not travel, could not leave your front porch.

You didn't learn you had a daughter for three days, not until your usual Wednesday afternoon. You showed up late for your own second chance.

This was no longer a dalliance. It never was. The horizon split wide.

Marilyn

DECKED IN PEARLS AND PEACOCK FEATHERS, the plump women of the Episcopal church surge into the reception hall. The women parade their cinched waists and ballooned sleeves; the men sport four-in-hand ties and top hats. One woman wears a hat modeled after a windmill. Another has donned a headpiece topped with a stuffed bluebird.

Mrs. Wood wanders the tables, her eyes as glassy as the bluebird's. Waiting orphans line the staircase.

Ida stiffens. She won't join the welcoming committee. You won't either. This isn't your day. You worked for it, sacrificed many an evening for it. But it's not yours.

Henry used to pull you to the bay window practically every hour on Sunday afternoons. He'd push aside the Nottingham lace curtains you had hung to shield yourself from the vacant lots across the street. He wanted to show you dark-eyed juncos and black phoebes pecking at seeds along the walk.

You tried to support his hobby, his birdwatching. You presented him with a notebook so he could catalog nature, record its comings and goings. My ornithologist, you called him.

He never wrote a thing down. You asked him why not.

—I didn't want to write the birds' names down, he said. —I just wanted you to see them. I wanted you to watch them living their lives.

—Whatever for? you asked.

Henry's face fell. Later, you apologized.

Yes, he'll be there at two today; he'll replant the garden, such as it is, and then he'll stand back and wait for you to admire it. He'll build an oasis of green against the backdrop of the strait and the Marin coast.

Maybe a woman dwells on that rocky outgrowth across the water, someone living a parallel life to yours, a mirror to your own marriage. Maybe across that expanse of sea, another wife watches another husband plant the same hopeless lilies year after year while trying to think of things to say to him.

Henry never wants to talk about how the two of you lost Jack.

—What is there to say? he'll declare. What's left to say? We loved him.

The two of you have reached an impasse. Your husband has friends, or if not friends, customers; or if not customers, people, basic everyday people. He surrounds himself with persons with whom he never has to speak. And you, well, no one surrounds you, and you have all these words that need to come out. Henry has the audience, and you have the speeches. You, Marilyn with words galore, have no one to listen to you, no one except a basset hound losing his hearing.

Ida has stayed by your side. Ida will hear you out. This girl's already a better friend than most.

The guests have devoured the salmon croquettes and moved on to ham and mustard on biscuits. Two red-cheeked elderly women suck on lemon drops and ogle candied cherries displayed in a china bowl. In the background, the band plays a lively tune. Today's program includes Sarasate's "Spanish Dances" and Schumann's "The Gypsies."

Ida fingers her new braids. Her leg brace protests as she steps aside to make room for the benefactors.

—Poor little thing, one of them says, staring at Ida's leg brace.

—Such a sad sight, the other agrees, and dips her hand into the cherry bowl.

Ida looks up at you.

—Ignore them, you say.

The last time you and your husband made love, *really* made love: a lifetime ago, a Sunday afternoon, the middle of a middling Sunday, a mild late-spring day, breeze teasing the curtains, sunlight cascading through the bedroom. A galaxy of dust particles floated between the closet and the bureau.

You remember white linens, white curtains, white pillows, Henry wearing a white shirt. He removed his collar, unbuttoned the shirt. His eyes filled with the afternoon light. You closed your eyes, not because you wanted to avoid him, but because the sun hurt. It was the first time it had shown up in days; you'd fallen out of practice with it.

You remember thinking: *Maybe this will work; maybe our lives here will work. Maybe we can build a home here. All this vastness, this raw earth, means breathing room.*

Two-year-old Jack lay sleeping next door in the nursery. Your skin warmed when Henry touched your face.

—I'm going to kiss every inch of you, he murmured. —Every blessed inch.

You had a son; you were a mother now; months had passed since you and Henry had shut the door on a Sunday afternoon. Why? Why had you waited so long? You loved this. You reclined on the pillows, laced your hands behind your head, and waited again for his touch, which came.

Things were easier then. His words carried you. Do they still? No. Do you carry him? No. He's too heavy.

But the brilliance of that day split him into two Henrys, like stereo images that together produce a three-dimensional view. A stereopticon. That was Henry, two versions of one man, the man of God and the lover, the paramour, his hair falling into his eyes, the way he kissed your mouth, his tie slung over the sitting chair, the tie he would not wear again. It was a new beginning. But you didn't say that to him because it sounded trite and because it raised the question of what was ending. Also, he was entering you. He had preached that morning on Abraham's sacrifice of Isaac and the ram that God sent.

Afterward, he pulled you to his chest and hummed a soft tune. You fell asleep. The sun crossed over the top of the house, and the light withdrew.

Women want a man who wants something other than themselves. Does that make sense? You're not sure. What was it Henry wanted? You can't recall. But his capacity to attend, to pay attention, impressed you. The rest of the world ceased to exist for him. You had full breasts, full hips, full thoughts, a full life. You still have the breasts and the hips.

You have not put a halt to loving Henry. Loving Henry has put a halt to you. To the both of you. You're in this separation together. It is not a clean break. It is not a break. You're more married than ever. The farther apart you grow, the more tied to each other you become. You're twin boats caught among ice floes, dinghies lashed together with cord. The farther apart you drift, the more your shared line tenses; the more you feel the rope.

Is that the clock gonging? Thank God. So it's not broken.

You really should leave this place early. Yes, head to the cemetery ahead of schedule. Show up while he's resurrecting the garden.

You could join him, surprise him, lend a hand. What's there to lose?

11:30 a.m.

Lucy

WHEN BLUE WAS BORN, Henry said:

—I'll tell her. I have to. I'll tell her everything.

Your newborn lay swaddled on your stomach. Emma Sutro Merritt, physician daughter of Adolph Sutro, had assisted with Blue's birth three days before. She had asked no questions. A wise woman. And efficient, with no tolerance for the nonessentials, no interest in anything less than shepherding new life into this world.

—A girl, breathing, sizable, with all limbs and all appendages, she said before pausing to brush the hair from your forehead. She clicked her black bag shut and departed, leaving May and June to keep watch.

—I have to tell her, Henry said again; this was during his first visit. —I have to try.

He paced in front of your bed, overcome by fatherhood, secret fatherhood, overwhelmed by the sight of his newborn daughter. And by the sight of you as a mother.

—She's an infant, you replied. —She won't understand.

Henry pressed his fingers against his eyelids.

—I'm talking about Marilyn, he said as Blue wailed her three-day-old thoughts on the matter. —I need to tell her. She needs to be told.

—No, you said. —No. Absolutely not. What good could that possibly do?

Yes. That was you. Blissful, distracted, useless. You refused to allow him to tell his wife, to end the world right then. If the world is going to end, better to do it in year two than year ten.

But you didn't need Henry to make some scene, to abandon one family and lay claim to another. You would be his secret life, his secret wife; you would parent in the shadow of his existing family. That was enough.

Also: You were ashamed. You did not want Marilyn finding out. You could not bear the thought of her finding out.

If people ever learned the truth about you and Henry, they would want to know why. Before they condemned you—and rest assured, they would condemn you—they would want your reasons. *Plageman?* they would say. *Him? Whatever for?*

You would tell them about the time Henry lugged a bucket of water from the groundskeeper's shed and wrenched his back in the process, about how he wound up on his hands and knees in agony on your black-and-white-tiled floor while Blue pirouetted in circles, declaring her father's injury a game of ride-the-pony. You plied him with whiskey to blunt the muscle spasms and did your best to keep Blue from bouncing on him. He nearly missed the last streetcar of the night. He peered up at you, long-suffering in his gaze.

—Mother of God, I'm never picking up a bucket again. I'm too old for this.

—I am too, you told him.

You are seventeen years his junior.

Yes, you will tell them, you will inform your interrogators that the longest length of time Henry stayed at the cottage was the day he truly couldn't move. There's a lesson in there somewhere. There's a lesson everywhere if one chooses to live that way, darting from example to example, moral of the story to moral of the story. It's one way to navigate. It's not your way, but it's *a* way.

People will want to understand. *People* meaning neighbors, imagined or not; estate workers, friendly or not; family members, estranged or not. Your mother. They will want your life presentable, or if not presentable, fathomable, or if not fathomable, doomed. They will want to hear that you could not resist him, that his passion seduced you, that his desire devoured you, that he was swarthy, dark, pent-up, worn, brooding. That his attention never strayed, that his eyes burned into you. Certainly. Of course. Trade the dark hair for fair hair, but of course. They'll want to hear you had no choice but that you still hold yourself responsible. They'll want you to plead the vagaries of womanhood: *Truly, I am only a woman.*

And any *fee-male* with a heartbeat would have thrown herself at him, at the wolf Henry Plageman was back then; any woman living would have begged him to rip her apart, saving and sacrificing both, reducing everything, every motivation, to a single caress, a single unitary moment. Is that how it happened? How will you explain that he was less and he was more —that he was both? Is both? Husband without husbanding, father without fathering, priest without preaching, brother, lover, teacher, friend, everything, all at once, together; too much —that's not his fault, that's yours. You asked for too much and not enough. You climbed up the tree of his life in order to see past your own.

Keeping away might not be working.

Stone eyes your plate, his fingers drumming the table. You're still waiting for the doctor to finish Blue's sutures. And Stone's waiting for you to ask for his help. You can discern that much. This man would like the opportunity to serve as your champion. He'd accompany you; he'd safeguard Blue; he'd escort you someplace safe, whatever your next destination.

—Where's home? he asks. His eyes hold some single-mindedness, some depth you didn't notice before. —Where are you headed? What's next for you and your girl?

Stop being who you're not. Start being who you are.

—We'll be fine, you tell him. —We'll be just fine. Don't worry.

—You're the one with worry on her forehead, he says.

He began giving you money. A dollar here, two bits there, whatever he could siphon off, whatever he could afford. He wanted to provide for you. He wanted to be a good father.

The sad state of Henry's accounting books —that's partly your and Blue's doing. Did he expect sexual relations for his generosity? No. Did he hope? Yes. Men will. They hope. They pine. Were his hopes realized? Rarely. You are possibly the most withholding, the stingiest mistress in the history of the world. You are with him only when you want to be with him, and that, it has turned out, is once in a great while, once in a blue moon. But when you *do* want him, you implode. Nothing will stand in the way; there's no middle ground when it comes to wanting Henry. You're either on or off, ablaze or frozen.

And when the moment announces itself, you hear no sound but his breath deepening, feel no sensation but his hands gripping, the question he forms, half caught, in the base of his throat. His hardness, his softness, the ride of it. He used to look down at the two of you, bodies joined, and say, *Christ.* Sometimes he'd say it twice.

As newborn Blue slept, impossibly small, in your arms that first day he visited her, he sat on the side of your bed and kissed her forehead.

—I can't believe I found you, he said, searching your gaze.—I'd given up believing you existed.

—What about Marilyn? you asked; really, you blurted.—Did you give up believing she existed?

The questions landed on the ground at his feet, as rude and intimate as hawked spit. Henry stood up from the bed, said your name once, quietly. *Lucy.* Then he stepped out.

Blue

THE PRETTY NURSE WHEELS my stretcher into the hall outside the pavilion. I'm successfully stitched up. Ready to make tracks.

—Can we go home? I ask Ma.

—We're leaving, she says, reaching across the stretcher to take over steering. —How do you feel?

—How do *you* feel? I say.

She glances at Mr. Stone. —I'm supposed to be asking her that.

—Believe you've met your match, he says.

—Ma, I say, pointing at the window. —Look. It's starting to pour.

She peers out. —I guess it is.

—The snails will drown. We'd better rescue them.

—We're leaving as soon as we can.

She smoothes my hair away from my ear, which the doctor has stitched. I don't want to think about the needle and thread he used to do that. And it's hard for me to hear from that side of my head now. He bandaged my ear in cloth.

—Leaving for home? I ask again, just to be sure.

She nods. —I just said we're leaving.

—But for home?

My voice sounds tinny and small. Mr. Stone pats my hand.

—You've been a brave little girl, he says.

—I'm not little, I say, and start to cry.

Ma looks tired. Mr. Stone offers me a sleeve on which to blow my nose. He smells like the outdoors. Like the seashore. Pa smells like old books and cigar smoke. I could smell Pa all day long and not grow tired of it.

— How old are you? I ask Mr. Stone. Snuffling, I wipe my nose on his sleeve.

He looks over at Ma. — I'm twenty-nine. That ancient enough for you?

Downstairs, I stick close to Mr. Stone while Ma crosses to the desk and asks a clerk about the charge for my stitches. Apparently I am very expensive.

— The total will be two dollars, the clerk says.

She makes her way back to us. Her brow is wrinkly and upset.

— I told you not to worry about it, Mr. Stone says. — Told you I'd take care of it.

She scowls even more. — It's my responsibility.

— Your kid fell in the pump station. That's my territory. I'll handle it. Least I can do.

I drop his hand, which, yes, I have been holding, and I look back and forth from him to Ma, who surprises me by staying pretty quiet. The electroliers above me are so bright they hurt my head. My bandages itch. Rain slides down the windowpanes.

— Ma? I say, plucking at her sleeve as Mr. Stone goes to take his turn at the clerk's desk. — It's really raining.

— I see, she says, though she doesn't. She's not paying attention. She's listening to whatever Mr. Stone's saying to the clerk.

— We have to hurry, I say and yank harder. — The snails! And I want to see Ostrich. Can we see him? I want to tell him about what happened to me today.

She looks sharply at me.

The clerk says something in a whispery voice to Mr. Stone, who looks back over his shoulder at Ma.

— I'm taking care of this, he calls out to her again. — Wait for me, will you? You shouldn't travel alone. Not with a hurt kid. You're not heading to the city cemetery, are you? That place you told me?

— We'll be all right, Ma snaps. Her voice is tilting too high. She

puts her hand on my back and leads me, pushes me, toward the doors.
—Thank you again. We'll be absolutely fine.

He frowns.—You've said that three times now.

—Ma, when can we see—

She taps me.—Wait till we're outside.

—I mean it, Mr. Stone calls out.—Cemetery's no place for you to be wandering on your own, if that's your plan. Wait for me. Last time I checked, you two pieces of calico were on your own.

—I'm not a piece of calico, I shout.

As the clerk bends over the paperwork, Mr. Stone softens his voice.

—God Almighty, Lucy Christensen. Let a fellow lend a hand, won't you?

Lucy

YOU DON'T NEED A FELLOW to lend a hand. You have two hands
of your own.

And you've grown used to your life, such as it is, to its quietness, to
the coverings you throw over it, like the sheets and blankets you draped
over the furniture the time you left to spend a week with Henry in Sausalito. You used to cut off sections of your life to see if they'd grow back.
When you cut Henry off, he regenerates like the arm of a starfish. When
you cut yourself off, you swim.

—We're leaving, you say again, bidding Stone farewell; he's still ne-
gotiating the hospital bill.

He twists around to take in the sight of you and Blue.

—Thank you, you add, feeling clumsy.—I'm sorry we stole your
morning.

—Don't you worry about my morning. Don't you waste one second
of your time worrying about how I'm doing. Worry about how *you're*
doing.

Before you can sort out what's happening, he strides over, abandoning the clerk. He stands before you. Without hesitation, without pausing a second to consider the matter, he leans in and kisses you. On the
cheek. But still. You don't have to stand on tiptoe to reach this man.
Here are his lips, soft as yours, right at your cheekbone. Here are his
hips, narrow and tight, right up against yours, his hips grazing your
skirt, his hips suddenly all you can think about. You don't have to strain,
not an inch, to meet this man. He is ready everywhere.

He pulls away, and your lips brush the stubble on his neck. The skin under his jaw stings with heat. Accidents do happen. He colors.

—Hey, he whispers.—Hey.

For a second, you wish you were a different woman.

Henry will be through with the weeding. He probably forgot to bring gloves. Of course he forgot. You always brought them for him.

He loves your humble cottage by the sea. He used to call it home. Even though he never spent a full night inside. He adored its cleanliness, its unpretentiousness. Its separation from the everyday.

His everyday. Not yours. He never saw you scrub a floorboard. But you did scrub them.

—It's more barn than cottage, you reminded him once.

He nodded.—The simpler the better.

—More shed than barn.

A better woman would have refused to live in such a place. You'd settle for being an interesting woman. But being interesting is how you wound up living in a glorified lean-to in the first place, hiding on a hill-side in the back of a rich man's estate, a man who collects the grotesque-ries of taxidermy and builds catch basins in the belief that he can control the ocean.

Free will? The tides don't ask that question.

Stone steps aside, still flushed, as Blue moves in to take possession of your skirts, grabbing them with one fist, her lower lip protruding. She doesn't like him standing so close to her mother. She didn't like that kiss. Maybe she wanted one for herself. The bandage covering her ear gives her a rakish look.

You lead your little pirate toward the doors. Stone calls out a final time, bestows a final caution.

—It's dangerous, you know. A woman traipsing around the Outside Lands alone.

You look out at the raining heavens and laugh aloud. If only danger were that straightforward. If only it were visible.

—What's so funny? he demands.

—Nothing. It's very kind of you to offer. Thank you. It is.

But it's your life, not J. B. Stone's. It's your life to savage. To salvage.

Blue

MA TRIPS ON THE SIDEWALK outside the French Hospital. The rain has made puddles on the boards. She catches herself, but she still winds up with her hands and knees on the planks. A small *oof* escapes her. Rain pelts the top of her head. I can see the part in her scalp, the helpless pink.

— *Mother,* I bellow, more sad now than anything.

She stands and brushes off her skirt, which doesn't help. So she turns to me instead. She tries to yank my sailor jacket tighter around my shoulders, tries to improve me. As if that's her problem. My jacket's damp as anything. I push her away.

— Why can't you just accept help? she asks. — Who taught you to be so stubborn?

For reply, I just look at her.

— Pumpkin, she says, trying again. — What is it? Walk with me. Please. We have to reach the streetcar stop.

— I *am* walking. I'm not the one who fell.

She should not have let Mr. Stone kiss her on the cheek.

— I know you're tired, she says. — We need to get you fed and into dry clothes before we do anything else.

— Are we headed to the snails? And can Pa come over? I want to see Pa.

Ma takes a long breath before she replies.

— I don't know if he can see us today, she says. — I don't know if we should interrupt him today.

— Why not?

She shakes her head. I've stepped in it now. She must be collecting her thoughts—that's what Pa used to say. Like her thoughts run outside the house without her permission.

I let her be and trudge forward. What did that doctor call her?

Up ahead lie hills of sand and patches of scrub brush. A few houses too. More and more people and houses are coming to our neighborhood, but not in an orderly way. Not following the rules.

A burst of energy comes over me. I don't know where it came from. I sprint ahead. Ma hitches up her skirt with one hand as she follows me. Usually she's faster than I am. Not today.

—Mother, I wheel around and say.—Be careful. You look like you don't feel good.

Lucy

RAIN SLIDES DOWN THE BACK of your neck. To your east lies the Odd Fellows' Cemetery, its pale gravestones barely visible. A lone nag pulls a hearse up a solitary lane. Two men hulk atop the driver's box. Their heads are bowed, almost supplicatory. But that's not the direction you're traveling.

— Sweetheart, you say to Blue. — I know you're tired. We have to make it to the streetcar stop. We're almost there.

— I'm not tired, she says. — *You* are.

Her eyes are filling. She wants to see her father.

This isn't a contest. It's not a match between the living and the dead, not a competition for Henry's attention. That would be sick. And you would lose.

You started writing about the buildup of the Richmond last year. It began as a game with a purpose. Blue was dragging her feet on a grammar lesson that required her to distinguish subjects from objects. She prefers to play outdoors. To make the lesson palatable, you supplied her with sentences *about* the outdoors, sentences describing the half-finished roads, the paths she'd rather be exploring. You wrote about the newly paved and graded thoroughfares of the Inner Richmond, closer to San Francisco proper. Descriptions of the houses hastily hammered into place along sloping hillsides sprang to your pen with little effort. Blue gnawed the end of her pencil, studying what you'd written. You realized you had a knack for the subject.

You read your first report aloud to Henry before submitting it to the *Richmond Banner*.

—Charles Hawthorne has completed a fine Queen Anne house at the corner of Fourth Avenue and Clement Street, with marble steps. Stewart Menzies has just let the contract for six two-story cottages on Second Avenue, just south of California Street. The timbers of the houses will be exposed and stained. The style is to be old English, patterned somewhat after Shakespeare's house in Stratford-on-Avon. The houses will be very novel, and (in total) will cost nearly eighteen thousand dollars.

Henry applauded.
—It's dull, you said.
—Never, he responded loyally.—Not in a hundred years.
For your labors, the *Banner* paid ten cents—enough to take the streetcar twice. Other than those two-sentence firebox updates, it's the only article of yours the editor has published. Before he accepted your work, he wanted to make sure your husband had approved of you submitting it.
—Yes, you said.—My husband approves.
You were too tired to drum up your usual lie. The ride to Sixth and Clement had taken over an hour. Sand caked the tracks so thickly the conductor had had to recruit two passengers to help him sweep it off. Mr. Claude was back at the workshop alone, stuffing a fox and two pups.
The editor removed his monocle and appraised you from toe to head.
—Writing is a fine hobby for a woman to cultivate once her children are grown. Are your children grown, Mrs. Christensen?
—Yes, you lied again.
You clipped that lone publication and mailed a copy to your mother. She wrote back: *And you left Omaha for this?*
Yes. Yes, you did leave Omaha for this. What of it?
The late heavy rain has played sad havoc with the condition of Point Lobos Avenue. Its surface is a mass of red mud, with an adhesive tenacity equal to a layer of putty.

Henry helped with that last sentence; he contributed *sad havoc*. He sat at your table, reading glasses sliding down his nose as he read and reread your words. He'd challenged your original phrase, which was *fast and loose*.

—That makes no sense, he said, glancing at you over the rim of his glasses. —*Fast and loose?* Rain can't play fast and loose.

—I say it can, you said, and you reached across the table, kissed him on one ear, then the other, removed his eyeglasses, and kissed his nose.

—You're exhausted, he said.

—Not as much as you.

—Never. I'm never tired when I'm with you.

You felt him stirring, sensed the heat rising beneath his shirt. When he swallowed, you watched his Adam's apple. You went and stood over him and massaged his neck, kneaded his neck muscles, the tops of his shoulders as he sat. He looked beleaguered. And peaceful. He looked both.

From the bedroom, Blue whimpered in her sleep.

You removed your hands. You crossed the room to check on her, and then when you returned to the kitchen, you proceeded to boil water for coffee. You extinguished the moment.

Henry tracked your shift. He tracked it, and he kept his mouth shut.

If you two see each other only once a week, twice if you're very lucky, you don't have the luxury of moodiness, of aloofness, of playing cat-and-mouse. You should have been grateful. You were. You should have seized the moment. You did.

But to seize the moment ten years running is impossible.

Blue squirms to free herself from your arms. You're standing in the middle of the rain, in the center of this empty street. The day has started to spiral; the day has started to take over.

And here comes the streetcar. Finally. You'll board it and return to the cottage. Let Blue save a snail from the rain. Be patient with her. Be a mother, for God's sake. Get something right. If not for yourself, then for her.

And after? What happens after the snails?

One second at a time. One self-admonition at a time.

You're holding her tight again; without thinking, you've folded her into a bear hug. She writhes in discomfort.

—Let me go, she bleats.—I want my Ostrich.

—When you're thirty, you'll understand, you say, wrestling her quiet, unable to step away.—When you're thirty, Blue, you'll look back and understand why things didn't work out for us the way they do for other people. I know this is hard. I'm sorry.

—I'm *eight*, she howls.

Henry

KERR PULLS OUT A PIPE, a beat-up T.D. clay. He tamps the tobacco, offers you first dibs.

Declining, you raise your hand. —No, thanks.

—A man can puff and ride at the same time.

—I'll pass. Really need to keep moving.

—We are. Just a quick drive by my place is all.

The foreman guides the hearse west onto Point Lobos. This is his detour, not yours. He can't bear to be separated from his beloved Odd Fellows' more than a night at a time.

The entrance to his cemetery lies just ahead. The French Hospital sprawls in the distance, its brick edifice slick and proud in the rain.

Jack never made it to any hospital. There wasn't time.

It will take all your strength, all your reserves and then some, to rebuild his garden. The task takes longer each year. You're battling entropy. And age.

Past Parker Avenue, Bess picks her way toward the main gate to Odd Fellows'. Kerr draws on the last of his pipe. He doesn't turn into his cemetery; he just wants to eyeball it, give the place a good once-over. This is his kingdom, plain and neat, with a low stone wall bordering the property. Not a cross is skewed. The dead lie immaculate in rows a compass could have drawn. The administration building near the property's edge is a turreted and gabled construction within which he daily neglects his paperwork.

—Call me an officer of the peace, he says jollily. —But the population I serve lives underground!

He whistles a jaunty tune. Bess resumes her labored movement. Surrounded by fallen clouds, the distant hospital resembles a sanctuary from a medieval tale. The walk outside it lies quiet.

The beginning of the end: Thirteen months ago, April of last year, a dour month, the same month Point Lobos Avenue flooded and your route to Sutro's estate deteriorated into a slushy creek, so that for two weeks you could not reach Lucy, could not travel to her on your usual Wednesday afternoons, the same Wednesday afternoons Marilyn understood you to be engaged in bookkeeping and inventory. Regularity of pattern is key when attempting to live two lives, when trying to navigate two streets. Adhere to the pattern, follow the traffic, and no one will question your comings and goings.

But you failed this time. Failed to keep to the plan. Your horse wouldn't cooperate. Your life wouldn't cooperate.

Bailey, your middle-aged roan, abhors the saddle and bit. Rarely do you ride him. You should have left him in the stables. He went down in the mud that day on the way to Lucy's, and you went down with him, landing on a rusted railroad tie the rains had swept into the lane. Bailey screamed and rolled.

Your horse recovered. You contracted an infection. Your neighbor Chambers is a compounding pharmacist; he treated your knee with carbolic arnica salve. Fever grounded you for seven days. Marilyn skipped her volunteer duties to help Stevens cover the store, leaving you to recuperate in the company of Richard. She pounced on the books as soon as she arrived. She proved better with the ledgers than you and Stevens had ever been. This didn't surprise you; she used to keep the books for the Women's Memorial Church. The ledgers surprised Marilyn, though. She couldn't believe in what shape you'd left them.

— I thought you went through the accounts weekly, she said with a puzzled frown as you sat, leg elevated, and sipped broth that needed salting. — Every Wednesday evening.

— I do, you said. — And look what a mere week in your care has done for them.

Your knee improved; Point Lobos Avenue didn't. Lucy lives so far out, in such isolation, that city workers never bothered to seal one of the cesspools on the route to Sutro's estate. They forgot civilization extended that far. As a result, whenever it pours, sewage overflows a portion of the avenue, compounding the difficulty of traveling.

So Lucy went to you instead. If you couldn't come to her, she would head in your direction. You'd written her a letter, a hurried update, informing her of your accident, your knee, the sewers. She knew more about those sewers than you did. She'd warned you about them.

—Watch out, Henry, she had said.—They didn't lay the pipes with care.

I'm worn thin, you wrote her. *The circumstances here are delicate. I need a couple of weeks.*

She mistook this letter for an invitation. Either that or she became tired of waiting. She does this sometimes; she ties your thoughts in sailor's knots and leaves you to unravel the cording.

When you saw her entering the cool of the hardware store, heard her shoes tapping the wood floors, her skirt brushing the stock barrels, your heart sped up; your heart banged out a march. It was only your second day back after your fever had broken. Marilyn was in the bookkeeping office upstairs. Stevens was late arriving. Lucy lifted her head high, almost too high, as she made her way inside. She was trying too hard to be brave. She wore the determined expression of someone who has vowed never to be caught. And by *caught,* Lucy meant *trapped.* Whereas you meant *found out.*

—Is anyone here? she called. She spotted you and her expression softened.—Thank God. You're all right.

Not now, not here. Fast as you could hobble, you left the horseshoe of counters to meet her, to cut her off at the pass. You did not want her to run into Marilyn; you did not want the two of them to discover each other. What if Marilyn should come downstairs?

When she heard you say *not now* under your breath, Lucy's eyes narrowed. You absorbed the sight of her, the dishevelment from her pedestrian trek, mud clinging to the hem of her skirt, and you decided there had to be a better way; the two of you had to find some time together alone, and soon, or you'd both go to pieces. If you weren't in pieces already.

You steered her away from the staircase, as far away from those stairs as you could take her without leaving the store, without leaving the neighborhood, the Richmond, entirely.

— Two weeks, you whispered. — We'll find two weeks together. Or one week, at least. Just the two of us. But you shouldn't be here right now. It's not safe.

— Not safe for whom? Lucy replied.

You paused, then said: We'll travel somewhere, go away together. We'll sort out what comes next. I'll find a way. I promise you. I just need more time.

— Time! She laughed, but her laugh snagged on something. — I walk over an hour to see if you're living or dying, haven't heard a word in days, and all you can say is you need time? You've had time. You've had years, Henry.

— Shh. I did write you.

— Don't shush me. I'm not your wife. Or did you forget that?

You took a deep breath, filled with desperate resolution. Or was it resolute desperation? Whatever it was, the feeling has stayed.

— Hear me out, you said. — Please. I know we've both been hanging by a thread.

— There's no way you could travel with me. Someone would find out. Something would go wrong.

— Lucy —

She twisted away to regard one of the glass display cases. It held brooches and necklaces, skin creams and brushes, items a man might buy to placate a living woman. A livid woman.

— Don't do this, you went on. — Lucy. I'm begging you. I'm trying to help.

She shook her head. — You're trying to help yourself.

You grasped her wrists. — Don't do this. Don't spin around.

— Let go of me, Henry, or I swear I'll make a scene.

— You already are.

— No, she said, and her eyes held yours. — If I wanted to make a scene, trust me, you wouldn't be the only one to witness it.

But she had chosen this arrangement. Hadn't she? She chased you out of the Women's Memorial Church in the rain. She wanted to live her life on her terms and not anyone else's.

— I thought surely you had died, Lucy went on, lowering her voice as Stevens entered through the front door. — Because if you hadn't died, you would have found a way to let me know you were all right. You would have at least done that.

— I did. Lucy, I wrote. I was laid up with fever. Seven days.

— You have a hand, don't you? You have a pen? You could have written a second time. Or can you write only when your blood cools?

The stairs in back groaned. Marilyn was beginning her long descent from the upstairs office.

— Nine years, Lucy breathed. — Nine *years,* Henry!

She tiptoed close, pulled you to her, pressed her body against yours, and exhaled, lips against your ear:

— I miss you. I just miss you. Fool.

She passed by Stevens on the way out. She passed within two feet of your wife. Stevens wished her good day; he assumed she was a customer. Marilyn didn't see her at all, didn't notice the small tornado in your store. Your wife had her own reasons for being vexed with you that morning.

— Henry, she said. — What are all these petty-cash withdrawals for? They date back forever.

Her hand on the doorknob, Lucy heard your wife's question. She turned and stabbed you with another look. She threw open the door and stalked out.

You have not worn Marilyn out. You have not worn Lucy out. The two of them have worn you out. The two of them, working separately, working in ignorance of each other's methods, together have worn you down, cleaned your plow.

On your headstone, the epitaph ought to read: HENRY PLAGEMAN, HUSBAND OF ONE WOMAN, LOVER TO ANOTHER, SLEEPING WITH NEITHER.

Maybe last night's argument with the Richmond associations signals the beginning of the end of this fight.

Maybe you and Kerr made such a commotion, caused such an embarrassment to the neighborhood groups, that Hubbs and his men will back off their plan. It would be a relief if they'd leave the cemetery alone for another year, so you can leave Jack where he lies, so Marilyn can leave her heart where it lies. So you can sort things out, repair what's been broken. Maybe everyone's learned a lesson.

A man can hope, can't he? Yes. And a man can be ridiculous.

Marilyn

IDA JIGS IN PLACE, jittery from the coffee you just supplied her with. The band plays an ebullient march. Housewarming guests stream through the front doors as Mrs. Wood glides through the crowd in your direction.

—There you are, she says, slightly short of breath.—I've been looking for you all over, Mrs. Plageman. Where'd you go?

—I haven't gone anywhere, you tell her.

That's not what you want to say. What you want to say is: *Today would have been Jack Plageman's sixteenth birthday.*

—We're shorthanded in the kitchen, she says.

What would your son have looked like at sixteen? Would he be growing a mustache? Would he have inherited his father's looming frame?

Mrs. Wood is waiting for a reply. You swallow, nauseated, unable to speak.

—Mrs. Plageman?

Today is the day to say it. To remember his name aloud. *Jack.* You have permission; you can be as deranged, as hysterical as you want, this one day of the year.

That's not true. You're not allowed to shipwreck at this stage. The statute of limitations has expired. Visible grief is no longer permitted.

Ida stays by your side. She's so close you can smell her freshly laundered dress, her lye-scrubbed skin, the bitter aroma of the coffee she sampled. Mrs. Wood hasn't said anything about her hair ribbons. She's too focused on you.

—You're quite pale, you know. Are you unwell? I don't think you should help in the kitchen.

—I'm fine.

—Are you certain?

—Yes, you say.—Yes, absolutely.

A lie as sure as any man ever gave.

—Give thanks for what's been given, Henry would say.—Look around. Look at the day, Marilyn.

—What about the day? you replied. You're embarrassed to admit how recently this conversation took place; possibly it might have been yesterday morning.

—Remember what blessings we've received. The store. This house. Our years together. Richard. Come here, Richard; that's a good boy.

Henry bent to scratch the dog's stomach. Your husband had spent the hour before dawn holed up in his study, writing. He makes you feel slothful when he rises that early. Papers fanned across his desk.

—What are you working on? you asked him.

He continued scratching Richard, who twitched an arthritic leg in response.

—I'm just puttering. Just jotting some notes to myself.

—That's probably for the best.

He looked up at you.—What do you mean?

—That you're writing to yourself. Because you're the only one who understands your thinking.

He laughed then, his eyes turning up at the corners, those patient eyes that bear the light.

You began to feel defensive. Henry's laugh made you want to shove something.

—It's true, you said.—Every time I listen to you, I lose track of what you're trying to say. All I can think about are the things that have been taken away from us.

—Marilyn, nothing was ours to begin with.

—That's not true, you returned hotly.—That's not the case at all. And when did you become such an optimist?

He laughed again, but bleakly.—I wouldn't call it optimism.

—What, then?

—I don't know. Surviving?

The two of you never discuss your marriage. Why would you? What possible good could it do?

The band has started playing Brahms's "Kinderland." Ida claps her hands. She's perfect, or almost, leg brace, reedy frame, and all. A good attitude, also; a hard worker. She would never accept grace on its own terms. She would understand a person has to earn it.

—I'm fine, you say again to Mrs. Wood, louder now, possibly bordering on shrill.

—I'm glad to hear it, dear, the younger woman replies. But her eyes now hold concern.

Henry

LUCY CHANGED HER MIND about that week away. She reintroduced the subject after your knee mended.

Yes, she said. Yes. She'd like to try a week away. Just the two of you, if you really thought it was possible. Were you still offering? She'd hoped to see Yellowstone. Or the Grand Canyon. Or just Sausalito. She'd never been to any of those places.

— I've wanted to run away for forever, she confessed.

With you? Or from you? you wondered.

But you needed to appreciate a few things first, she continued. You needed to understand that while you remained free — relatively speaking, she added when she saw your look of incredulity — to contact her, write her at your leisure, and stop by the cottage when you pleased as long as you practiced discretion, she enjoyed none of these freedoms. She could not mail letters to you at your home, could not stop by your store to see you when she pleased lest she disrupt your regular life, the life people thought of when they thought *The Plagemans*. She could not call you on the telephone.

You felt the muscles in your shoulders tightening.

— I don't have a telephone.

— But if you did.

— I wouldn't. Monstrous invention. Besides, it's not true you can't contact me. You stopped by the store last week. Remember?

— Yes, and look how well that turned out.

— I had a fever, Lucy. I had an infected knee.

—Is that all?

—And I'm sorry.

You are not accustomed to apologizing for having a fever, but with Lucy, this is how things work.

—But a vacation, she said.—I would rather hear you talk about that. Where are you going to take me?

She was trying to lighten the exchange. But her eyes were asking a question. When you stepped forward to gather her in your arms, she moved aside so that the table came between the two of you. She sat down and went quiet.

You weren't sure how to respond to that.

But a vacation, planning a trip; that much you could manage. And it was past time. Two people with a secret will need a vacation from the secret.

Thinking about the trip interrupted your sleep for three nights straight. You were too excited to shut your eyes. Sausalito wasn't far. It cost less than other locations. And no one you knew bothered to travel there. It would be the first time you and Lucy had gone anywhere together, had spent a full night together.

You planned the time out in your head. You'd walk beside her at sundown along the boardwalk. Sign the register at the Shoobert House as a couple, using Lucy's last name, to be safe. Take her to breakfast the next morning, observe her slight dishevelment, her rumpled luxuriance as the two of you dined on toast and eggs with perfectly done yolks.

You felt adolescent, alert, and randy as hell. You could not wait to fall asleep with her in your arms. You could die in peace if you could do that. Just once. Lie with her head nestled against your chest, fall asleep feeling her warm breath escaping her nostrils. Your little sleeping dragon. Let the world pass; let someone else keep watch for a night. Let someone else be the bearer of the stricken conscience.

—I can help plan it, Lucy offered. She was suddenly animated, livelier than you'd seen in days.—When should we depart? The end of the month? I'll have your daughter stay with May and June.

Her wording, her reference to Blue as *your daughter*, not *our daughter*, was confusing. Also, you were still exhausted, on edge; your mind scampered back to Marilyn.

—I can't travel this month, you said.—It's May, remember.

You'd said nothing she hadn't known already. But she blanched.

—We can go in June, you offered.—June or July would be fine. That gives us more time to plan anyway.

—I can't compete with your family, Henry.

—I'm not asking you to compete. I would never ask that.

—I'm well aware.

She stood up from the table and crossed over to the front door. She opened it and disappeared into the night.

You should have thought before you spoke. You should have said: *You are my family.*

You searched a quarter of an hour for her in the darkness before giving up. She would reappear when she wanted to reappear and no sooner. You returned to the cottage, kissed sleeping Blue good night, tucked the blankets around her, and departed into the blackness again to catch the streetcar. You could hear but not see the ocean.

—Why didn't you come after me? Lucy asked you the following Wednesday.—I waited out in the cold for an hour. And why did you leave Blue by herself?

You had to work not to raise your voice.—Blue was fine. She was fast asleep. And you wanted to be alone. Clearly, you wanted to be alone.

—Why in the world would you think that?

—You have to tell me what you want, then. I'm not a clairvoyant.

Her hands were on her hips.—Then stop pretending to be.

When you returned home, Marilyn was on the front porch, waiting. A dime novel lay unopened in her lap. She had commandeered the wicker chair, an unusual move. And she was itching to quarrel. Over what? Didn't matter. She and Lucy were taking turns.

Her eyes raked you.—You look like you've seen a ghost.

A ghost, you could manage. The living are what haunt you.

Behind Odd Fellows' stands a single line of newly planted trees. Naked land sprawls beyond that line, undeveloped plots divided by almost-streets, depressions in the earth waiting for builders, carpenters, home-dwellers, crowds yearning to escape downtown. Mail-order cowboys with no West left to conquer.

You wrote Lucy two letters and mailed both. She wanted more letters? She'd rue the day she asked. She'd swim in letters.

You laid out the plan for the getaway. Seven days, mid-July, a ferry ride to your destination, a journey to be taken separately for precautionary reasons. A reunion at the inn overlooking the Sausalito wharf.

Lucy wrote you back, something she had never dared before and has only done one time since.

She mailed her reply to you at the store. You had to seize it from Stevens's curious hands.

— Henry? asked your clerk, wide-eyed. — Everything all right?

— Never better.

You shoved the letter, unopened, in your coat pocket. Later you stole upstairs to read it in the office.

She didn't actually *write* you anything. Her letter contained no sentences. She mailed you two drawings from Blue. Lucy could be wickedly accurate with the blade when she chose.

Contemplating your daughter's drawings, bold compositions filled with horses and racing snails, you experienced something in your spine compressing, wearing down, grinding, bone against bone. You still feel it.

Someday, Blue will realize what her father was. De facto bigamist. Man with two families. She will despise you for it.

Lucy

IN SAUSALITO, A WHITE-GABLED INN called the Shoobert House perches vertiginously atop a ridgeline overlooking the railroad and the ferry wharf. In return for the uphill journey, it offers a staggering view of schooners, steamers, catamarans, and salmon barks dotting the harbor.

Henry suggested the Shoobert House for your escape, your one-week rendezvous, vacation, getaway. Which word is appropriate? None of them.

—Seven days, he vowed.—Just the two of us. I'll find a way.

—Are you sure? you pressed, checking once, twice. You prodded and poked. You wanted to be positive his plans would hold.

He nodded.—Yes. Yes, I'm sure. It's past time. Lucy, let's do it.

—Do you promise?

You'd rather hear him say no right away than learn later that he'd run into problems. You couldn't stomach the thought of being let down, abandoned at a clandestine altar. Also: You didn't want him doing anything out of obligation. Or pity. You'd prefer anything to becoming the object of pity.

—I promise, Henry said.—Wild horses couldn't keep me away, et cetera.

—Bailey kept you away, you reminded him.

But you agreed to meet him at the inn in Sausalito.

You asked May and June if they would watch Blue. They were willing. More than willing; they were delighted. Openly looking forward to the opportunity. Blue wasn't. Your daughter said:

—I want to ride the ferryboat with you.

You shouldn't have mentioned the ferry to her when you introduced the plan for the two of you to have separate adventures.

— You can't, you told her. — Not this time. You'll stay with May and June this time. Next time. This time is just for your father and me.

She wept.

You resorted to bribery. Suborned her with the prospect of a grandmother. You couldn't believe the words coming out of your mouth.

— Or would you prefer to spend a week with your Grandma Christensen? She's always wanted to meet you.

Blue stopped mid-outburst. A wriggle of interest escaped her. A visit with a grandmother? Yes. She approved.

You humbled yourself, wrote to your mother, lured her with the prospect of time alone with her grandchild.

Please come meet Anna. She'll be yours for a week. I will be away.

Your mother wrote back saying one week wasn't worth the time it would take her to travel west. A longer visit was in order. *I will take her for one month,* she wrote. *Arrival date 14 July. Bring her to the station.*

It would be her first time traveling to see you in California.

You took Blue to the Oakland Mole to meet her. The screaming whistle of trains arriving and departing the wharf made your daughter cover her ears. Freight engines wheezed, their sound interrupted by the ticking of steam pumps. The floorboards hummed with commuters. Everywhere you looked, you saw men rushing to be somewhere, filled with self-importance.

When the train pulled into the station, belching and steaming, you peered up into the passenger windows, and the first person you saw was your mother, her face tilted downward at an inspectorial angle. She had the same thin chapped lips you remembered from your childhood. Her eyes held a gloomy certitude that somewhere the sky must be falling.

She did not set foot on the platform until the train had emptied. She observed you in silence through the window. When she stepped down from the train, refusing the arm of the porter, you steered Blue over to her. Your daughter, suddenly shy, clung to your skirts.

— Mother. You smiled. — You look exactly the same.

— And you do not, she said. — You need to take care of yourself. The circles under your eyes are worse.

She turned to Blue and cupped your daughter's chin in her hand, compelling Blue to meet her eyes.

—She's too thin. What are you feeding her? Child, when is the last time you had a solid meal?

Blue's eyes widened.

—Mother, you said.

You didn't want to turn your daughter over to her, but you went ahead and did it. You needed those seven days. You have not asked for much from these last ten years, only seven days.

A poor excuse for a woman? A poor excuse for a person.

Your mother never forgave you for leaving Omaha. She never forgave you for "preventing" her from remarrying when she was young— even though she never wanted a second husband anyway, even though your company was already one more person than her natural disposition could endure.

And she has not forgiven you for producing a daughter with no husband in sight.

He died, you wrote when Blue was an infant.

In childbirth? she wrote back, then scribbled something, likely unrepeatable, in Swedish.

While the porter retrieved her luggage, you flagged down a hackney cab. Blue bounded inside first, face upturned, nervousness forgotten. She glowed with anticipation. Your mother boarded beside her. Blue forgot to wave goodbye to you; that's how excited she was to be a granddaughter. You had to wave for her. The two of them would spend the following month sightseeing up and down the coasts of California and Oregon, a journey you've never taken.

You stood on the platform and watched them disappear from view. As the train pulled away, the wind kicked up stray papers and ticket stubs left behind by commuters. You went around and picked up this trash and deposited it in a waste bin. Your mother has this effect.

You felt thoroughly daughterless. You felt like the woman on the operating-room table who, awakening after surgery, after being carved down the middle, hears the doctor calling out a joke: *Which half goes back to the ward?*

Marilyn

SOMEONE ON THE BOARD OF SUPERVISORS needs to approve a motion. The motion should state that Marilyn McLarty Plageman is not permitted to address a single soul on May 22, not a single blessed soul, save Henry Plageman. And probably not him either.

—Mrs. Plageman?

Mrs. Wood does not want to call you by your Christian name; she does not wish to lower herself to the level of friendship with you.

—We need to put these girls to work. If you're feeling well enough —are you feeling well enough?—could you please help me extract some industry out of them? We're still shorthanded in the kitchen.

—But they're the guests of honor, you remind her.

—So they are. She briskly nods.—And they'll continue to be. They'll be *helpful* guests of honor. They'll earn their keep.

She folds her arms and regards you with trained politeness.

—But we hired help, you argue. Henry's combativeness with the neighborhood groups might be contagious.—We specifically hired help so the girls could stay in their good uniforms.

—The help never arrived.

—Did you actually send for anyone?

Mrs. Wood stiffens.—That was uncalled for.

Sorry. She doesn't frighten you. And she can't make you feel inadequate. If you're going to feel inadequate, you can generate that feeling all on your own, thank you.

Ida squeezes your hand. She wants to leave this place.

—These girls aren't the help, you say again.—You promised them. *I* promised them. You can't ask me to go back on my word. We need another plan.

Says the younger woman, with youthful serenity:

—This *is* the other plan.

Ida squints up at her as if the devil has just come through.

Lucy

ON THAT FERRY RIDE TO SAUSALITO, you leaned over the deck rail to smell the sea, which blew foam in your nose and mouth. You watched the moving water. The fin of a shark or some other mighty fish slapped the ocean's surface. When you looked again, whatever you'd glimpsed was gone.

Mid-July, a cool day, clear and windy, and everyone in that seaside town seemed in a fine mood, festive for no reason. After disembarking from the ferry, you pushed past a throng of passengers to make your way by foot along a winding path leading uphill to the Shoobert House. You carried a valise. It was not light. It contained two shirtwaists; two skirts; one pair of shoes; slippers; two sets of undergarments, including stockings; one nightdress, which you'd bought especially for the occasion; a hat; and three dollars from Henry hidden inside the lining, in case of emergency. You were sweating by the time you arrived.

Inside, a young clerk standing behind the front desk greeted you and asked how he could be of service.

—Christensen, you said, suddenly uncomfortable. —Mr. and Mrs. Christensen. Checking in.

The clerk checked his notes.

—Your husband made reservations for one o'clock. The room's not quite ready. Is Mr. Christensen with you? We can serve you in the dining room while you wait.

—He'll be here soon, you said, and rattled off the explanation you'd concocted days before. —He's coming here on his way home from a long trip. For his business. For his store. He asked me to meet him here—

You blushed. The clerk reddened right alongside you. A finely dressed woman in navy and lace strode past you into the dining room. Perspiration slid down your spine, dampening the back of your dress.

—I understand, the clerk said.—Perhaps you might enjoy yourself in our dining room on your own, then? Until your . . . husband is able to join you?

—Thank you. You nodded and moved out of the way to avoid bumping into another guest, this one old enough to be your mother and wearing a look of judgment.

In the dining room, you ordered a Hood's sarsaparilla, the cheapest thing on the menu, and drank it too fast, because you were nervous. You were the only unaccompanied woman in the room. The only perspiring woman in the room. Sparkling glass and crystal caught the light from the open windows; drinking glasses, shot glasses, rum bottles, flower vases on the tables—amber, topaz, peacock blue. As the noontime sun filled the dining room, the shelves behind the barkeep in the corner burst into color, winking and translucent, like wind chimes that come alive with a single gust, only these instruments produced no sound, only light.

An hour passed. The clerk found you and showed you upstairs.

—My husband must have been delayed at the station. He'll be here soon, you floundered, not sure what to say, as the two of you walked toward the lift.

—Of course, the clerk said and colored again. Yours was not the first such arrangement he'd witnessed.—I'll show him right up when he arrives.

Two hours passed. You reclined, fully dressed, on the bed and stared up at the scrollwork and wainscoting. Gradually your burning cheeks cooled.

Three hours. People do not appreciate that waiting is a skill. It must be practiced. One must run up and down its octaves regularly.

Four hours. The sun retreated.

By half past five the room had darkened to whorls of lavender and charcoal. By half past six, you had rolled onto your side and faced the window with the partially drawn shade, a window that overlooked the wharf and the bay. From this corner of the four-poster bed you could see no water. You lay in the darkening room on the top floor of the Shoobert House. You rubbed your eyes. Rubbed them clockwise, then counterclockwise; you tried to rub your eyes back in time. You opened your eyes. The same story appeared, the same chapter and verse.

Take therefore no thought for the morrow: for the morrow shall take thought for the things of itself. Sufficient unto the day is the evil thereof.

—They should have translated it as simply *Stay in the day,* Henry said one Wednesday evening after you'd mentioned this verse was one of your favorites. — They should have written, *Just don't get ahead of yourself.* That's all Matthew was trying to say.

—How do you know what he was trying to say? you replied. — I thought you quit the pulpit.

He'd returned home soon after.

By seven o'clock, you had curled into a fetal position. You'd unpinned your hair and let it fall loose onto the pillow. You wanted to seize a pair of scissors and cut off your hair, shear off some piece of yourself, something necessary and substantial.

You would not cry. You would bite the inside of your cheek off before you would cry. Any pain incurred was your own doing.

But he had promised.

Lying there in the blue-black twilight, you watched stray beams from the wharf as they bounced and glanced across the face of the inn. Light filtered through the curtain, igniting first one corner of the room, then another. You lay there in the blinking lights from the ships, under a canopy of old crown molding. You lay there a long time. Henry never came.

The following morning you made your way to the front desk and requested the bill for a one-night stay; you would not be able to use the remaining six days of your husband's reservation. The clerk's eyes met yours before dropping to the guest book. His lashes were as long as a girl's.

—I can mail the bill to him, he said and pulled out his reservations book. He made his way to *Christensen,* glanced up, and whispered: Is this the right address?

You remembered the dollar bills tucked inside the lining of your valise. For emergencies, Henry had said. The word covers a wide swath of territory.

—I'll pay, you said.

You returned to the Outside Lands alone.

Blue lifts her head from your shoulder. The streetcar has pulled into view, rumbling your way at a leisurely pace.

—The snails, she says. —Mama, there's too much rain. It will drown all the snails.

You shift her weight from one hip to the other. —The snails will still be there in an hour.

—But they'll be dead!

—Then we'll take them to the cemetery with us, you can't help but say.

Blue pulls her head away and stares at you, perplexed, blue eyes to blue eyes.

—We're going to the cemetery?

What's that flying past? It looked vaguely familiar. Ah, yes. Your self-admonitions.

Today was a habit you were supposed to break. You did. You are. You will. But breaks don't have to occur in a single location. The bone can go in several places.

It was for the best.

You wouldn't have tolerated each other for that amount of time. Seven days is some duration.

Maybe he passes gas in his sleep. Possibly you snore. Probably you would have waded into an argument.

It's good you never found out. It's to your benefit. Because if it was easy, if sleeping with him was like water, like swimming with the day's first current, if when sunlight filtered through the curtain you did not want to leave his arms, could not bear to breathe apart from his limbs twined around yours, well, what then? Where would that leave things?

The day after you returned from Sausalito, you went and visited Jack. You hiked on your own to the northernmost part of the cemetery. You wouldn't see Henry or learn what had happened to him for two days. When you did see him, he would insist on paying you back for the hotel. But it was his money in the first place.

—I know that, he would say.—I need to do it. Please let me do it, Lucy.

You went alone. Blue was sightseeing with her grandmother. Blue was having the vacation you and Henry had failed to have.

You stood in front of Jack's marker, just you and Henry's son, and listened to crows cawing.

—It's you and me, little one, you said out loud.—It's you and me. When everyone else is gone, you and I will still be here.

On the way out, you passed one of the Chinese burial grounds, its path strewn with garments so soaked from earlier rains that the clothing refused to burn. Two elderly men were trying to set them on fire.

You went over and offered to help. They searched your face, skeptical. You must have appeared to be a lunatic. A woman on the edge of acceptable society. A woman trying to pull herself back from that edge, unsuccessfully.

There was a reason he couldn't come. Of course there was. There's always a reason. And it's always a good one.

Something about the store and a problem, or about Marilyn and a problem, or about the store and Marilyn, or about Marilyn and Penny; maybe a distressing letter had arrived from Marilyn's sister, Penny. Or maybe it had to do with Jack; sometimes the reason is simply Jack. How can a child who died fourteen years ago interfere so much with the here and now? He just can.

It's not like Henry tricked you; it's not like he set out to humiliate you. He doesn't mean to disappoint you. He just disappoints you. Besides, you brought it on yourself. You chose this. You consented to it.

Count your blessings, Lucy Christensen; you've escaped relatively unscathed compared to other women in similar states. Compared to the women in books.

Two hours until Marilyn arrives at the garden.

You can get there sooner. You can get there in one. If you hurry. If you board this streetcar right now. Right this second.

People say it always ends. People say the wife always finds out. It ends in the cases people hear about.

12:00 p.m.

Marilyn

—YOU MUST DETEST CHILDREN. Do you have any children of your own, Mrs. Wood?

Two maroon spots of color blaze on the younger woman's cheeks. Childless women retain a sourness about the mouth, you have decided, a faded bewilderment, a whiff of something missing, an amputation. A limb that wasn't.

—I will not take instructions about the care and well-being of children from a woman who never had any, you continue.

Mrs. Wood blinks. —I was a girl once myself.

—Being a child is a far different thing than having a child.

—I know that. That's not what I meant—

—And not having children is far different than having a child and losing him. That should be obvious to anyone. Do I have to spell it out?

—No one suggested it was the same. No one said anything at all about losing children. Are you all right, Mrs. Plageman? Are you feeling ill again?

Ida, chewing the end of her braid, glances back and forth between the two of you.

—What I'm feeling is none of your concern, you say.

—I apologize, Mrs. Wood replies, visibly stung, the blotches of color in her cheeks spreading to her ears and neck.

Oh God. Why won't your mouth stop flapping? She doesn't deserve your vitriol. She's naive, she's a bit officious, but that's not a crime; if it were, the prisons would be spilling over.

—I need some air, you say. —Excuse me.

—Mrs. Plageman? Ida says.

—Yes. Mrs. Wood nods, jumping in.—Yes, that's a good idea. Why don't you both take the air?

Ida, now, she's a human Richard, waiting by your side without needing to be called. Is it strange to love a child because she reminds you of a basset hound?

You make your way toward a side door. The guests mingle and throng, corpulence in motion, the women as round and pasty as confections. The men block your path with their bulky, meaty bodies, signaling to one another, their cronies from high society, calling out across the streamers and bunting.

Mrs. Wood speaks again: Goodness. Are you quite all right?

Her voice has lost its hardness. The room has begun whirling. And this reception hall smells of wallpaper glue. Does anyone else notice that smell?

—Here, child, she says to Ida.—Quick. Help me find a chair. She needs to sit. She's gone white. Be quick now.

Mrs. Wood and Ida grasp you around the middle, one on either side, and guide you away from the reception. They find a high-backed chair in the corner.

—Let's get you off your feet, Mrs. Wood says.

The room revolves. Recalcitrant room.

—My son, you start to say.

Dear God. Here it comes.

They want you to sit in the chair. No. You'll stand and face it instead, clutching the arms, head lowered. A wave of nausea engulfs you. The upholstery stares up. The paisley fabric glows copper.

—My son—

—Pardon? asks Mrs. Wood.—What did you say?

—My son would be turning sixteen today.

—Well, happy birthday to him! she exclaims, and as you turn your head to regard her, the younger woman's eyes light up, briefly warming with admiration, envy, respect.

Don't correct her misunderstanding. Don't say a word. Do not cast one's pearls before swine. And you're not casting; you're vomiting. Or you're about to. Sometimes it happens. This is a live year. Yes, indeed, folks. You've got a live one on the hook.

—Excuse me, you say. Tearing away, you make haste for the lavatory in the back hall. Ida hurries to follow. You shut the lavatory door on her. Sorry, Ida. She'll have to remain outside; she'll stand guard.

The porcelain stares up. Gripping the rim of the basin with one hand, you use the other to remove your hat and rest it on a folded towel. The merle on the hat stares up at you, accusatory. You reach back to pull up your hair. Wait, your hair's already up. You forgot. You forgot your own hair. Perspiration wets your neck, the soft fold beneath your chin. Your heart sledgehammers.

Mrs. Wood has no idea you lost someone.

People are forgetting. No, they're not forgetting; they're too young to forget. Jack's grown older than the neighbors. If you and Henry don't remember him, if you don't make this yearly pilgrimage, no one will. Time will erase your son, will expunge his name from its annals. It will be as if he never existed, as if his birth and his death meant nothing.

This basin is so shiny, you can see your reflection in it. You need to be sick, but nothing's coming up. Wait for it.

Waiting to be sick is worse than being sick; waiting for the end is worse than the end; waiting to find out if your husband no longer loves you is worse than your husband no longer loving you. These things aren't true; you're just experimenting. Of course Henry loves you. He loves you as much as you love him.

Your head lowers again. Ida knocks.

—In a minute, child.

Why do you call her child? The word is pejorative in this case; it suggests no will, no direction, no choice. The whole concept of charity, of helping the less fortunate, functions, you suddenly see, as a ruse, a ploy, a way for the powerful to preen and pat themselves on the back for their own munificent acts. Mrs. Wood will swaddle Ida in an apron and propel her into the kitchen, where she'll clean china caked with half-masticated roast beef, scrape fish blubber from licked plates, get rid of all the messes Maria Kip doesn't want its benefactors to notice. And Ida won't complain. Though she should. She needs to speak up, to say: *Enough.* That's all a person can say some days. Some decades. You have said it to Henry; yes, you have. All those Wednesdays working late.

You can't risk him being happy, for God's sake.

And there.

Your stomach releases its contents into the basin. You pat around for the towel, something to blot your face. Don't look at yourself in the mirror. Don't look into your eyes, glimpse them shiny and wet.

Yet you miss him. You miss your husband: young Henry, from the Sunday of the white sheets, the white shirt, the blowing curtains, the antediluvian quiet, the day he lay beside you, propped on an elbow, and confessed he adored you. He said it twice when your own words wouldn't come.

That man no longer exists. Or if he exists, he no longer desires you. Or maybe you no longer exist; maybe you no longer desire him.

Which one of you gave up first? You did. But Henry's was permanent.

Henry

—WHAT WAS IT Hubbs called the cemeteries?

A menace.—"We must fight this menace," you say, reminding Kerr of the attorney's words.

The hearse is pulling away from Odd Fellows'. Bess shakes her coat, spraying the air with droplets. Reluctantly she plods forward.

—What else? Kerr asks.—I forget. Near the end. It was horseshit.

For reply, you give him your best imitation of the Richmond Property Owners Protective Association chairman:

—"Mr. Plageman. The city cemetery could be made into a beautiful spot, fronting the bay, the Golden Gate, and the Pacific."

—Right. And then you said, "It already is a beautiful spot. It already does what you say."

—Yes, and he ignored me. "These things will all come when the graveyards are gone and the quick, not the dead, inhabit San Francisco."

—That's the line. Kerr nods.—That's the one. "The quick, not the dead." Pure horseshit, I say.

—Then things started to deteriorate.

—I never thought I'd see the day Henry Plageman took to using brute force.

—Not brute force, Kerr. I merely addressed him with my shoulder.

The foreman chuckles. Bess pauses to nuzzle tall grasses sprouting along the edge of the street.

—If she doesn't move any faster, I can walk, you say.

—We're moving, we're moving. Just have to check my chickens.

— Chickens?

— Yep. Won't take but another second. Right on our way.

He grins as you quietly curse. Clucking, he coaxes the mare forward.

The beginning of the end, continued: Nine months ago, September of last year, you took Blue and Lucy to the Cliff House in a rare public outing. You were trying to compensate for your spectacular failure with the Shoobert House. Your invitation followed Blue's return from a month of travels with her grandmother.

You had tried to explain, had tried to tell Lucy what happened that night you didn't show up.

Marilyn had happened.

An hour before your scheduled departure for the Sausalito ferry, your wife received a letter relieving her of her volunteer duties at the San Francisco Nursery for Homeless Children. She had balanced their account books too well. She'd discovered oddities in their ledgers, discrepancies they didn't want exposed. Be careful what you ask Marilyn Plageman to tackle, what problems you ask her to solve.

The letter eviscerated her. She wasn't expecting it. She retreated to her bedroom and locked the door, would not let you inside. You checked the time; you were nearly due at the ferry. You had told Marilyn you were heading off on one of your business trips to Portland to purchase hard-to-come-by goods for the store. You pounded on her door; she ignored you. So you picked the lock with one of her hairpins. It took several minutes. Inside was no better than outside. She had given herself over to the bedcovers. Facing the wall, she lay curled on her side in her old yellow nightgown. The covers half buried her. She would not allow you near her; at the same time, she needed you not to leave.

You didn't make the ferry. You could not just walk out on her, on a wife falling apart in a yellow nightgown. You had failed Marilyn on many occasions. But not this time.

You spent the day at her side. Didn't step out of the house. Didn't even reach the front porch except to let Richard out to heed the call of nature. The ferry to Sausalito departed. The ferry after that departed also. You paced, parlor to kitchen and back again. You considered trying to send word. Could someone deliver a message? Who? Stevens?

You could tell no one. And Lucy was waiting for you. Lucy was wondering what had happened. How long would she wait? Too long. Not long enough. Both.

The following morning, you went and begged a favor from one of your customers, an old Episcopalian priest. Within two hours that retired priest had finagled a new position, complete with letter of invitation, for Marilyn at the Maria Kip Orphanage, whose director needed volunteers.

Marilyn doesn't know you orchestrated the assignment. To this day, she thinks Maria Kip wanted her for her skills.

When you delivered the letter with the news about the appointment, your wife lifted her eyes from the newspaper she was halfheartedly reading. You sat next to her on the edge of the bed, extracted the paper from her hands, laid it aside. You stroked her hair.

—Tomorrow will be better, you said. —You'll start at the orphanage.

—How can you say tomorrow will be better, she replied. —How can you possibly know for sure?

In the morning she drank a glass of milk and ate a boiled egg. As you walked with her to the streetcar stop, her gait looked unsteady, almost somnambulant. But it strengthened during the walk. Maria Kip had opened its doors to her.

That's all a person needs sometimes. An open door.

Lucy said very little when you told her what had happened. She listened. She heard you out. When you finished, she said:

—You did the right thing, Henry.

She buried her face in her hands and wept.

An hour at the Cliff House is a poor substitute for a week in Sausalito. During lunch, Blue called you Pa, and without thinking, you shushed her, right there at the table, surrounded by crab cakes and clams with lemon. Blue flushed, irritated. Being shushed is not something she tolerates. Your attempt to quiet her made no sense anyway; you were already sitting with her and Lucy in public, already risking exposure.

—You're my pa, and I will call you Pa if I want to, she said, glowering, resembling a miniature version of her mother. She reached across the table and, for punishment, honked your nose.

—What if I let you call me by my Christian name? you offered.

—What's a Christian name?

—The same thing as a regular name.

She rubbed her eyes.—Why do people make things so complicated?

—Good question, Lucy said. Under the table she rested a hand on your knee and squeezed, harder than your knee wanted.

As the waiter took away the remains of your meal, the new Welte Orchestrion in the main dining room started playing music by itself, without human assistance. Blue asked if a ghost was in the keys.

—There's no such thing as ghosts, Lucy said.

The three of you left before the end of the concert. Outside, Lucy folded her arms across her chest and scanned the churning sea.

—Next week? you asked her over the pounding of waves against rocks. You were asking when the three of you could next be together.

—Our usual time?

The wind whipped Blue's hair. Your daughter had squatted down to dig in the sand for shells. Lucy took your arm and steered you out of Blue's hearing.

—Don't say you're coming if you're not able to come, Henry. Don't do to her what you did to me. I won't stand for it.

—I'll be there, you declared.

You returned home. An hour later you started to seethe.

Lucy has no idea how much effort you expend daily protecting her, keeping her safe, building a wall between her and your other life. She has no idea what it's like to live with a double conscience. A double consciousness. Every day you must carry her and Blue, and every day you must carry Marilyn. They are all three yours. And every day you must not let them collide, must not allow their spheres to touch. They can't even jostle each other by accident.

Lucy has no idea the amount of energy this requires. Even Atlas shouldered only one world at a time.

Lucy

— *HOW COME* WE'RE GOING to the cemetery?

You'd better think before answering her. Choose every word with care. She's eight. She's too young to understand.

Or maybe it's the opposite problem; you've already waited too long to tell her. Not just about today. About everything.

— We're going to see your father, you say.

— But why?

— That's what you wanted, isn't it? To see him. To tell him what happened to you today. You've been asking for the last hour.

— I think it's what *you* want.

She stares distrustfully up at you. Your voice sounds snappish, high-pitched, even though you don't want it to come across that way, even though a churlish tone is the last thing your daughter needs.

You try again: We'll get you home and into dry clothes first, and you can see your snails. But quickly. Just for a minute, okay? Then we'll walk to the gravesite.

— Pa's in a grave?

Now she's crying. — What happened to him? she sobs.

You exhale. — Oh, sweetheart, he's fine. No, it's not what you think. He's just there visiting someone. And we'll visit him. We're visiting your father while he's visiting someone. Does that make sense?

She shakes her head vigorously as, once again, you fold her into your arms.

—Just for a few minutes, you say.—That's all. That's what you wanted, right? Please, Blue. I'll explain everything on the way.

—Who is he visiting? Put me down!

Stop trying to carry her. Let her be. She *is* eight. She's starting to awaken to her life.

Marilyn

IDA HAS NOT LEFT HER STATION guarding the lavatory. She's still at her post when you reappear in the hallway. You've splashed water on your face, blotted your nose and mouth with a handkerchief, but the damage remains; you're officially in disarray.

—It's all right, you tell her. — Come with me.

She complies. Her cheeks are delicate, the skin across the bones nearly translucent. She's thinner than she ought to be. You elbow through the guests and return with her to Mrs. Wood, who stands outside the kitchen, surveying her domain.

—I'm afraid I can't stay, you tell her.

—You're ill. I understand, she says, nodding.

—I'm sorry. I'm all right; I just have to leave. I'm expected elsewhere.

Brow furrowing, Mrs. Wood retrieves a piece of paper from the pocket of her skirt and unfolds it: the volunteer schedule.

—According to what I have here, you aren't supposed to depart for nearly an hour. You're leaving us terribly shorthanded, you know.

Childless women have no sense of what constitutes an emergency. That Mrs. Wood is about to be left shorthanded—that is not an emergency. That you are about to go stark raving mad—that is not an emergency either. It's uncomfortable and it's unpleasant; an emergency, it is not. Yes, you can feel the madness creeping in through the corners of your eyes. Yes, you see redly. What of it?

Ida holds tight to your fingers. *Yes, Ida, keep the faith. We are on the same team here.*

—Mrs. Plageman . . .

Mrs. Wood has recovered the poise she lost following your earlier exchange about childlessness. She has smoothed herself into position, calmed everything down, save those maroon spots of color on her cheeks. But she will not forget the child she never had. Years from now, after age has dried up her womb, she will still think of it.

—Mrs. Plageman, she says again, quietly.—If you need to leave, of course I can't stop you. But I must let you know I'm not sure we'll have a place for you on the summer volunteer schedule. You've been with us only ten months. I'm afraid I cannot guarantee your future.

Your laugh surprises you.

—Only God is in the future-guaranteeing business, you say.—And He doesn't do a very good job.

Ida begins to babble something about taking responsibility, about wanting to help with the reception. She's nearly hyperventilating. She dreads arguments; she'll do almost anything to placate an angry person. She fears confrontation.

Mrs. Wood darkens.

—Hush. No one gave you permission to speak, girl. Mrs. Plageman and I are talking.

—Her name is Ida, you say.

—Pardon?

Your throat stings with leftover stomach acid.

—Her name. If you're going to reprimand her, please use her name. It's Ida. And she and I are both leaving.

Ida, astonished, looks up at you.

—You can't remove a child from the orphanage. That's tantamount to abduction.

—I'll return her before day's end.

—Don't be absurd! Mrs. Wood exclaims.—I cannot give you permission.

—That's all right, you say.—I'm not asking for it.

You do not believe children should be seen and not heard. They should be seen and heard both. They should not be quiet. They should not hush. They should not pray, go to bed early, say please and thank you, or finish their mathematics schoolwork. They should not obey their parents at all times. Children should stay alive. That's all. You have set the bar exceedingly low where these things are concerned.

Ida seizes your hand once more. Holding hers tightly, you weave through the crowd to the door, past wallpaper decorated with hummingbirds, a gauntlet of pearl-bedecked women.

Outside, a cocoon of quiet replaces the pumping of trombones and trumpets. Light rain dampens Ida's countenance. Never before has someone rescued her, never has someone plucked her up from the muck and set her on dry ground.

—Mrs. Plageman, where are we going? she asks.

In the course of a single morning, you have lied about your husband not being locked up in the park station; you have *left* said husband locked in the park station; you've thrown up, quit your volunteer position, seen redly; and now you've stolen a half orphan. The only thing left is the cemetery.

12:30 p.m.

Blue

MA'S EYES ARE CLOSED, but she's not sleeping. It's the face she wears when she'd rather be alone but can't get away from me.

This car we're riding in smells of new paint. It's electric. We boarded at Sixth and Clement. Ma hasn't said a word since we sat down. She's not watching where we're going.

I know the way home.

We'll ride west to Thirty-Third. Then we'll jog left. The trolley pole will strain hard, and sparks will skid skyward. We'll rumble along Point Lobos Avenue until Sutro Heights rises up. Behind lies the ocean. We'll smell sugar and beer and mildew. We'll pass the penny gaming Ma never lets me play. We'll smell the salt from the sea.

I sneak a glance Ma's way. A fat man smoking a pipe across the aisle is watching her too. She looks unpresentable. She's hatless, for one. Her hair isn't pinned. And she has those lines at the corners of her eyes that show up when she's tired.

She wouldn't look so poorly if she hadn't spent the morning fishing me out of that well. That makes this partly my doing. At least Mr. Stone helped take care of things. But he's gone now too. She left him behind to pay our bill. And there are no men left in the Outside Lands except those whose names spell trouble.

That last line is what Ma told Pa the night of my birthday after they'd given me two sticks of licorice and one book and put me to bed. She was talking loud enough I could hear her.

Usually I don't bother listening when they talk at night. They sit around the table and yammer on about the same things, paddle around the same subjects: Pa's store, Ma's taxidermy, Ma's sense that something has gone wrong with her life. Whenever she talks about that last one, my stomach hurts. Pa doesn't talk about what's gone wrong with his life. He just listens.

This time I paid attention. I sat up in bed. Pa's voice when he answered her dropped so low, it was hard to hear. I had to press my ear against the wall to catch what he was saying.

—I'm well aware, he said. —I'm well aware of the problems here.

And Ma replied: You've said that before, Henry.

—I meant it before, he said. —And I mean it now.

Ma coughed. —We have to make a change.

—And how do you propose to do that?

—Carefully.

—What would it look like?

—It would look like we talked about, she said. —We'd stop. We'd just stop, Henry.

—Let's talk this through, he said.

—We have. We've talked it through a thousand times, and each time we wind up talking about parting instead of actually parting.

—I'm glad we haven't been able to do it, he said. —I'm proud we haven't been able to tear ourselves away from each other. I can't imagine no longer seeing you. Or Blue. I can't fathom the prospect.

My ears pricked up when he mentioned my name. No longer see me? He must not have been right in his upper story. Ma wouldn't want that.

Ma stood up to pour a drink, which she does sometimes to help herself think, because next thing I knew, I heard a slip and a thud, followed by breaking glass and a groan—and Pa saying: Are you all right? And the joints in his knees cracked, which happens when he squats, and I heard Ma say: Blue's Raggedy Ann doll. I didn't see it. And she started giggling. Relief swelled in my chest. Whenever Ma laughs, I laugh. If she bangs her elbow, mine throbs. If she trips on Raggedy Ann, I hit the floor too.

—You're my sympathetic nervous system, she once told me, with a half-proud, half-worried look.

This particular time, her chortling lasted so long I poked my head around the bedroom door and asked them to please keep it down, I was trying to rest.

—I can't sleep, I said. —I need help falling asleep!

Why my voice sounded so cross, I could not have said. Crossness just sprang out of me. My throat and eyes felt angry.

Pa was crouched with his arms cradling Ma. She was pretty well settled on the tile where she'd slipped. Pretty well not moving. She looked happy to have his arms around her. She had leaned her head against his chest. She was in her stockings with no shoes on her feet.

—Now *that* I can do, Pa said, talking to me. —I might bear the mark of Cain for everything else these days, but I can still help my child fall asleep on her birthday. That much even I can't bungle. Right, Blue?

He stood and left Ma's side, pausing to collect pieces of glass near her feet. He set them on the table. Ma swiped at her eyes, suddenly quiet. She watched as he went and found the *Little Soldier Boys ABC,* the book he had brought for my birthday. I was glad for that book. I'd grown tired of hearing only Bible stories. Too many Abrahams finding rams in bushes. Too many Solomons waving their swords over babies, deciding which half of love goes where.

—Let's read, Pa said to me. —I'll read you to sleep from your new book.

And then, over his shoulder, to Ma, his voice cracking:

—Don't you give up.

The streetcar clangs to a stop. I look out the window as the conductor climbs down and crosses over to a toolshed along the roadside. He'll relieve himself behind that shed. We'll have to wait for him. The rain comes steadier here. And harder.

Pa's store lies a block south, down the street and past a vegetable garden. We won't pass it directly. A turkey vulture waddles through the weeds near the toolshed. It stops to shrug rain off its feathers.

I've never been inside Pa's store. The few times I've asked, Ma always says:

—We can't go in there.

—Why not?

—He stays very busy, and he can't be interrupted.

He's so hard-working, she explained, he has to live in the office over the store.

—I don't like that, I told her.

She gave me an odd look. I think the look said: *I don't either.* But she didn't say it in words.

I'm still staring out the window when I see, far away, an old mare trundling up to the front of his store. She's a gray mare with white blotches on her nose and forehead. Blotches I'd like to pet. She pulls a black coach with the letters IOOF printed on the side.

A white-haired man sits on the driver's box. He wears a hat wide as a sombrero. He lifts his eyes to the sky. He's stewing over something. I look up also. Has he spied a hawk? A pelican? What am I missing?

Someone had rattled the cottage door partway through the *Soldier Boys ABC.* It might have been the wind. It might have been a grounds-keeper. It might have been May or June, bringing a tin of coffee.

Pa shot to his feet at the sound. He whirled around like he expected a peck of trouble. The rattle came right after he read me the letter *J* for *Judiciary,* which he mispronounced as *judicious* and did not take the time to correct. I had to say the right word for him. He closed the book and pressed it into my hands, leaned down, kissed the top of my head, and whispered, *I'm sorry.* Then he threw open the bedroom door and left, pausing to touch Ma on one cheek before he went out the back.

Vamoosed. That word isn't in the *ABC* book.

Ma watched him leaving. She didn't say a word.

Afterward, she walked outside and sat on the front step and eyeballed the moon awhile. Whoever or whatever had banged on the door was gone.

I came out, and she patted the outside step, meaning for me to sit beside her. The moon turned her hair silver.

—Are you mad at me? I asked her.

She studied me. She looked at me for so long, I felt like someone else's daughter.

—No, she finally said. —No, child. I'm not angry with you.

And then she added, softly: No more.

She stood up, picked me up, and carried me inside. I don't need to be carried, but I didn't remind her. For almost the whole night she stayed up trying to write a letter. I could hear her trying on words as she sat at the table and crumpled papers. I fell asleep before she finished. Either it was a very long letter or my mother is a very slow writer. Or both.

In the morning I walked with her to the main estate so we could post the letter together. She said it was important that I join her. Pa's name was on the envelope, *Henry*, along with his last name, *Plageman*, which I had never heard before.

—I thought his last name was ours, I said.

Ma stopped in the middle of the path. She placed her hands on my shoulders and said:

—I'll explain everything to you. I promise. I will. Soon.

Since that night, since my birthday, Pa has called on us only twice in almost four months, and both times Ma has not been at home to receive him.

—It's just you and me, half-pint, he said during his most recent visit.

He walked me around the estate three times without asking me if I wanted to walk that long. Then he bought us tickets to the baths and took me to the upstairs exhibits Ma had helped create.

—*Curate*, he said, correcting my word when I said the wrong one.

He was sad that day, or nervous. As worried as a cat in a roomful of rockers. To calm him down, I led him around and showed him the Bengal tigers under glass. I know the museum better than he does. We didn't see Ma once.

Pa studied her creations. He watched those tigers for a long time, until my stomach started hurting again.

He hunched his shoulders into his coat, and we moved on.

The conductor boards after he finishes with his business. Our car lurches back into motion. I can still see that old gray mare over on California Street, so I wave goodbye to her.

Someone's hotfooting it toward that mare. Someone tall, in a hurry, half hidden by leaves. He's carrying trays of plants with petals shaped like pig ears. Calla lilies. Pa taught me those.

I can't see any part of the moving figure except his legs. But I would know those legs anywhere. Even from this far.

—Ostrich! I call out.

Ma rouses herself from her nap.

—What is it? What's wrong?

Across the aisle, the fat man stands up. He holds his pipe in one hand, and with the other, he reaches for the handgrip above Ma's head. He's standing too close. His legs part wide for balance. He moons down at her, waiting for the car's next stop. He's almost brushing her legs. He *is* brushing her legs.

I don't have time for this smelly old goat. Not in the middle of a father sighting.

I reach out and kick the man in the kneecap, kick him with my shoe, so hard his leg buckles. The cuts on my own leg are stinging.

—Little cur, he snarls.

Ma instantly trains her eyes on him, instantly begins tracking his movements.

—What did you say? she says.

He's roused the hawk. Or is she a falcon? Whichever's meaner.

The man mumbles a foul reply, but he steps away. By the time I can get Ma's full attention to show her what I saw, the car has traveled a good ways, and the store is out of sight. The store and my father.

Henry

—GET WHAT YOU NEED, Plageman. I'll wait.

Kerr lights his pipe. He's losing steam, and in this weather his lungs must be raw. The two of you have stopped outside the hardware store.

—I can take it from here, you say —If you need a rest. I can borrow Bess and finish up on my own.

—Nonsense. We've come this far. We're nearly there. Right, Bessie? He pats the mare's rump as his speech dissolves into a hacking cough.

—You all right?

He gestures you away. —Will be, he says, gasping. —Get on now.

The ramshackle structure on the northeast corner of Tenth and California houses your store. Stevens lives on the second floor, in a room next to the bookkeeping office. A vegetable garden, your own untended vegetable garden, occupies the vacant lot next door.

—I'll tend it in my spare time, you told Marilyn a couple of months ago when introducing the idea of vegetables to her.

—What spare time? she said.

But you do indeed have time, now that you've stopped trekking every week to Sutro's. You're drowning in time, buried in it, second by second filled with these ticking nerves, this clock that won't stop chiming.

The front door wears a sign you painted by hand: *Plageman's. All Orders Filled.* Lucy used to tease you about that sign.

—Which orders are those? she would say. —Because I can think of a few you haven't filled for me.

A sleigh bell jangles as you step inside and pass the potbellied stove and the wooden bench for customers. Floor-to-ceiling shelves line the walls behind the counters. Stevens uses a step stool to reach the higher shelves. You use your arms.

Your clerk is stationed at his post behind the counter, wire glasses perched on his nose, perusing the morning *Call.* He's taken to calling your wife the Mathematician because of her deft handling of the ledgers. The two of them, Marilyn and Stevens, have grown fond of each other. In another life they would have been friends, or more.

He rests the paper on the counter. His glasses reflect the gleam of his small tabletop lamp. Beside him squats a new Smith Premier typewriter with a toothy metal carriage.

—You're late, he announces.

He knows about May 22. He's been around this block with you before.

You nod.—Wound up taking a little detour.

—I just read the news article. I can't believe they sent you to the police station, Henry!

—That they did.

He straightens his string tie.—How can I help?

—I just need to gather the usual supplies.

—Most of it's ready. I started to pull things together when I realized you were running behind.

—My thanks, you say as he trots off to help retrieve your gear.

And here are the bait-and-tackle shelves, the same corner where you and Lucy quarreled over your infected knee, where Lucy breathed: *I just miss you. Fool.*

—Pruning shears, right? Stevens calls.—I have them. And a jug of water?

—Yes. That's right.

—And I dug up a shovel. Ha! I didn't even think about that before I said it.

—Maybe not a shovel, you tell him.—Maybe just a trowel. A shovel could be excessive.

—Is it?

—Depends on the hardness of the soil.

—Take it just in case, he cheerfully advises, as if you're packing for a lengthy expedition, an exploration of unknown territory.

Tomorrow things will return to normal, at least where Marilyn is concerned. You'll travel past May 22; you'll round the corner on the calendar. The rain will pass. Kerr's cough will pretend to dry.

Tomorrow will not return to normal where you and Lucy are concerned.

Lilies are the last item on the list. And the most important. Calla lilies, as many as a man can carry. You order each year from a nursery south of Golden Gate Park and have them delivered in advance. You should have gone with some type of hellebore instead. Hellebores are mean plants in disguise. They sicken anything that tries to eat them; absolutely nothing fazes them. Perfect for a cemetery. But Marilyn distrusts native plants.

—Stevens, where'd you put the lilies?

Around back. I was letting the sky water them. I'll fetch them.

—I appreciate it.

He hands you the shovel before heading out the front door. You stand, restless, your arms and legs suddenly heavy. The *Call* lies on the counter. Its pages will contain a report on last night's neighborhood meeting. This shovel is a lead weight. It takes more effort to accomplish the same task each year. Good thing you have Kerr and his hearse. You never thought you'd see the day when your closest friend was a seventy-year-old who drove coffins for a living.

But this is your life. Don't knock it. Don't trade it. You'd trade today, trade May 22, but not the rest of it.

Then again, today can't be divorced from the rest of it. The good and the bad dwell together in the same house. Christ, you miss Luther.

—Why don't you read him, then? Marilyn asked recently.—No one's made you stop.

—I don't have a reason to read him. I don't write sermons anymore.

—And whose fault is *that?* she said, shaking her head.

Stevens reappears bearing a wooden crate. Lilies peek through the slats.

—Goodness, he raves.—They're lovely this year. And there are some more out back. Where do you want them all?

—In the hearse. Out front.

—A hearse! I hardly noticed, I was so focused on these blooming beauties.

Your clerk is an honorable man. Unmarried, a lifelong bachelor. You hope he's having a good life. You hope his losses have followed the natural order.

What would Jack have been like at sixteen?

—Extraordinary color, Stevens says.—And in full bloom!

They'll last a week.

Lucy could change her mind about showing up at the cemetery. Couldn't she? It's not likely. It's bound to be too late. But anything's possible.

And is it true that she saved you? Yes, though that's an incomplete portrait. There's Blue, for one. And Marilyn. All three are implicated in this business of Henry Plageman's resuscitation.

Are you that much of a problem? Yes.

Stevens retrieves the remaining lilies while you walk outside to see how Kerr's faring in the rain. The foreman reaches down to help you settle the first crate of plants at his feet in the driver's box.

—Let's get moving, Plageman, he says, shivering in the damp.

A long block to the south, the Sutro streetcar clangs and starts moving. You glance up at the sound. That car could take you straight to Sutro Heights, straight to Lucy and Blue. In theory, you could drop these lilies, make a run for it, board. In theory. You could chase after her. Do it once and for all.

Say it: *Don't leave me.*

But if she's the one who left, why hasn't she gone anywhere?

Stevens returns bearing the second crate and lifts it into the driver's box. The plants burst with heart-shaped leaves, each protecting a long white spathe.

—I'm grateful, you tell him.

—My pleasure. He beams.—Give my best to the Mathematician . . . to Mrs. Plageman.

—I will.

—You'll be glad when today is over, won't you?

You nod.

Kerr reaches over to steady the crate. As Stevens watches his effort, his countenance clouds.

—Henry? Did anyone at the police station tell you how things turned out last night after you left?

All these plants have turned the driver's box into a moving terrarium, leaves and stems and petals all crammed together. The white spathes bob as the returning rain strikes them.

—No one told us anything, you say.

Kerr looks up from the plants. —What's the word? What idiocy have they tried now?

—Wait here, Stevens says.

He disappears inside and returns with the morning *Call*. His wire glasses are flecked with rain.

—See for yourself. I'm sorry to tell you. They took a vote last night. They called a vote without you, Henry!

—That's illegal. Kerr frowns. —We weren't there for it.

—It's not illegal, you say.

—Blackguards, the foreman sputters.

The *Call*'s pages are damp. Water has blurred the ink. Either that or your eyes are deteriorating. Kerr shifts in his seat, his newly petaled quarters. For the remainder of the journey, you two will sit knee-deep in calla lilies.

Stevens helps you find the relevant page.

—There. The news is right . . . there.

Page fourteen contains the offending column. Huddling in the rain, you and Kerr digest the words in silence.

The Richmond Property Owners Protective Association unanimously passed a resolution last night. They did it right after you left, after they'd hauled you and Kerr off to the park station. They held a stealth vote.

Therefore be it resolved that we, the citizens and property-owners of the Richmond district, in mass-meeting assembled, do petition the honorable Board of Supervisors of this City and County to take immediate steps to exchange the City Cemetery property for other property outside the County and prepare the acquired lands for burial purposes and have all bodies removed thereto from the present site.

Have all bodies removed from the present site. Have the bodies removed.

Kerr straightens, tries to relight his pipe, curses when the flame sputters out.

— God for us all and the devil take the hindmost.

They're going to dig up Jack.

Marilyn

HENRY WON'T BE READY. His lilies won't all be planted. He'll have to live with that fact. He'll have to accept imperfection.

Little survives this far west but wind and whatever can survive wind: beach sagewort, sticky monkey flower, Franciscan wallflower, its golden petals shaped like a cross. Scrub jays and great blue herons dwell here too, as do wild turkeys. And mourning doves. Their calls, their distinct clarion messages, fill your ears. Two egrets perched on a utility pipe watch Ida limp past.

She's doing her best with her brace, but she shouldn't be walking this far on it. Taking her with you wasn't prudent. But she wanted to come, and so she's yours, at least for now.

— Are you feeling any better, Mrs. Plageman? she asks.

The bitingly cool air has relieved your nausea.

— Yes. Yes. Thank you, Ida.

— I think she was an awful woman, that Mrs. Wood.

— She has good intentions. She tries.

Ida makes a face. — She's mean.

— How so?

— She orders us around twice as much as the assistant headmistress. She makes the littlest girls run her personal errands. She told one of them to wash her stockings while she was sick with mumps.

— While Mrs. Wood was sick with mumps?

— No. The girl.

— Then maybe Mrs. Wood will catch them. The mumps.

Ida tries to cover a smile with her hand.

—It's all right to laugh once in a while, you tell her.

It's advice you'd do well to take yourself.

Women endure the anniversaries of lost children all the time. Some more than one. Maybe you make this pilgrimage every May 22 less from sorrow than from anger, voyaging year after year in pure celestial rage. You are not the victim, the martyr everyone assumes. Because you didn't lose just Jack that day. You lost Henry. You gave them both up, Jack and Henry, young Henry of the white sheets and the curtains billowing as you sank against the eiderdown, the day you slipped into sleep afterward.

Ida's stomach rumbles. If you're going to abduct her, the least you can do is feed her something.

—You're hungry.

—Not too much, she says loyally.—Not very.

—And you're tired.

—No, ma'am.

—We'll catch the streetcar. Can you walk a few more blocks? If we head south, the Clement Street car will take us straight to the cemetery. I should have thought of it sooner.

You'll board the car at Eighteenth. This girl has earned it. It'll be easy to catch the line headed west, the one that comes from the French Hospital. You can ride together for the remaining distance. Save her some wear and tear on that leg.

—Where are we going again? she asks.

—Potter's field. The city cemetery. To meet my husband.

She looks at you trustingly. You haven't earned that look.

Are you unmoored? No. You are, however, dry-docked. You can pretend you're floating, but you're not. You've struck earth. Rather: you struck water once and it turned to earth, just as Moses struck his staff once and it turned to serpents, all because he wanted to prove his rivals wrong, all because he wanted to show them his God was powerful.

Henry doesn't believe in miracles. Lutherans as a whole remain skeptical of the concept. Ages ago, in Gettysburg, back before life horsewhipped him, you asked his opinion about events of a supernatural nature, and Henry quoted Luther for his answer, some arcane reference to the unchanging nature of divine revelation.

—Don't tell me what Luther said, you returned.—Tell me what *you* say.

He smiled.—It's not that miracles never happen. I suspect once in a great while they do. It's just that they make unreliable forms of communication compared to what God has already revealed to us through His Word.

—Meaning what? you pressed.

—We don't need them.

You should have married a Roman Catholic.

A low bank of clouds slides into view at the crest of the next hill. A few more blocks until you start falling apart in earnest, Cinderella at the tail end of the ball, only where today is concerned, there is no ball, and no gown, and no solicitous prince, only a headstone and a husband shabby as a lean-to, a husband with a spade and a scowl who will not be ready. Henry needs time to himself. He needs more time to himself than anyone living. He will never be ready for you.

—Why is Mr. Plageman in the cemetery? Ida asks.

—He's gardening. Planting lilies.

—I see, she says, though she doesn't.

You soften your voice.—I've really stolen you away from your special day, haven't I?

—I don't mind, ma'am. I prefer it. It's quieter here.

Maria Kip's new facility will test this young woman's reserves. More square footage means more orphans. And more orphans means more chaos, the lovely and unavoidable noises of childhood. Even unhappy childhood.

—I'll stay out of your and Mr. Plageman's way, she vows.—I will. Anything's better than Mrs. Wood.

She bends and adjusts one of the buckles on her brace. When she straightens, her cheeks are rosy.

—Mrs. Plageman? Do I have to return to Maria Kip?

Oh no. She thinks you want to adopt her. You have no intention of adopting her. You don't have room. You're stealing her, kidnapping her for a single afternoon; someone to keep you company, to distract you momentarily—a cruel reason, a cruel use of a person always.

She scuffs her shoes against the grimed street and waits.

— Oh, child, you say.

And then you can't think what else.

You still harbor hopes your sister will visit someday. One day Penny will bound through your door, husband or no, children or no; in your mind's eye, these details don't matter. You'll fall to your knees, wrap yourself around her solid pioneer waist, and beg her solid pioneer heart to come back or, better, to take you with her, to whisk you away to the Oregonian forests, another place where the trees are older than nations.

Ida smoothes a stray lock of hair off her forehead. Her green ribbons have begun fraying. The streetcar stop is within sight.

— Ida, you say. — You'll have to return to Maria Kip. I'm very sorry. But not just yet. Not for a little while yet.

— Yes, ma'am, she says. — Though I do prefer it with you.

Henry

—I CAN TELL HER WHAT IT'S BEEN LIKE, Kerr says.—Battling these buffoons. You did everything a man could.

The city will move Jack's remains south of San Francisco. Strangers will dig up his coffin and rebury it half a day away, three rail transfers away. And Marilyn will hold this latest disaster against you. She'll prop it up, lean it up against the others. She's built a shelf of your shortcomings. She'll clap this newest one on as a bookend.

—I'll tell your wife you did everything a man could, the foreman goes on.—Up to and including criminal behavior. Think where we spent the night.

No, Marilyn won't survive the news. She'll endure, but that's not the same as surviving.

None of this helps Lucy either. Lucy, whose name still ruins you; Lucy, the thought of whom has not ceased to upend you; Lucy, who's busy cutting the tether to release herself from you. And you watch her progress, admire it. It's like swallowing a razor, but you admire it. She saws and saws at her bonds each night, severing the cord, but in the morning when she rises, the rope that binds her to you reappears, fibrous and new. You feel frantic when you contemplate her efforts, her Sisyphean labors. Lucy Christensen absolutely needs to be free of you. And you are the only one who can help her do it.

When Marilyn shows up at the cemetery, she'll take one look at you and instantly comprehend the truth. She'll wonder what you spent the past two years fighting for, if only to lose.

—Plageman? Penny for your thoughts.

—They're not worth that much.

You try to fold Stevens's newspaper, but the pages are tearing. So you ball it up and pitch the whole thing into the sand. It lands in a wet clump in front of Bess, who lowers her head and sniffs at it. Silver grit streaks her coat.

Everyone praises the man obsessed with a long-shot cause who winds up on top. But what about the man obsessed with a long-shot cause who winds up on the bottom?

Stevens rails, decrying the vote; he paces the length of the hearse as Kerr from his driver's box begins to fulminate. They suggest next steps, concoct potential reprisals. You remain apart from them, head lowered against the rain, and wonder how to persuade feeling to return to your extremities.

—I don't see how they'll ever relocate a cemetery, Stevens says. —They don't know how to plan a mass disinterment. Those fellows are so disorganized!

Kerr says: They'll figure it out.

—What'll they do with the Chinese? Do they have any idea how many bodies are in that ground?

—Thousands, Kerr replies.—And no.

For the love of God, your son is in that ground.

—The Chinese won't let their kin be touched, Kerr continues. —The Chinese will dig up their own, at midnight if they have to. They'll ship the bones back to their homeland. Bury them next to their ancestors.

Stevens tugs distractedly at his hair.—How will the city know who's who? How will anyone keep the names straight? Most of them don't have names.

Your head lifts.—They had names.

Kerr nods.—Just not on the headboards. By Jove. What rotten idiots.

He sighs and continues.—I saw the disinterments back at Yerba Buena. Years ago. Leg bones in one corner, skulls in another. It was hell. And I'm a cemetery man.

———

You have started to imagine a time when not seeing Lucy will feel routine, will be commonplace. The requirements of life are stepping in to fill the gap, to crack the whip. You slog on, defiant. You resist. You obey and resist both.

You'll keep visiting Blue. You'll see her whenever Lucy allows. What else can you do? You cannot keep her.

Kerr clears his throat. — Plageman . . .

You look over at him, still enthroned on his driver's box.

— It's nearly one o'clock. Do you want to keep on or swing back? You're in charge here.

Adds Stevens: This time next year, there might not be any city cemetery left to visit. I'm afraid it's over, Henry.

You shake your head. Just because someone says it's over . . .

That's lesson six, if anyone's counting.

— So here are our options, you say. — We can forge ahead.

— Or we can stop, Kerr offers.

— Stop and howl in place, Stevens says.

— No one's doing any howling, Kerr replies.

You meet the foreman's eye. — Day's not over.

— Henry? Stevens says.

You raise both hands, signaling *enough*. — I have to put these plants in the ground. All of them. And in the next hour. That's as far as I can plan today. That's as far as I can travel.

Stevens briskly nods. — Let's get you two on your way, then, he says, and bids the foreman goodbye. Next he embraces you, not something he ordinarily does. He pats your back with such filial steadfastness your eyes involuntarily water.

Sometimes you think Stevens grasps the truth about your life, about you and Marilyn. Sometimes you think he sees and understands a great deal, and says nothing.

Bess pulls into the widening lane. Stevens stands outside the shop door and raises one hand in a farewell salute. The calla lilies shudder in their crates as Bess pulls her burden forward.

Blue's birthday, that last night, before things fell apart: Lucy stood and bent over the infinitesimally small bald spot that recently has appeared on the top of your head. She kissed it and called you her ostrich, borrowing Blue's word. She resumed her seat on the bench, sliding in beside you, her hip touching yours. She was in her stocking feet, and she slid her toes up your calf as you two shared a steam beer from the same glass and waited for Blue to come inside from playing outdoors.

She looked over the rim of the glass.—I need to tell you something, Henry.

—What's that?

You were weary. The two of you had not been right for months. Not for a year, if you were honest. You'd tried to hold things together, but more and more you were holding things together *for* her, not with her. You were losing her piece by piece.

This only works if we both believe in it, you had said to her.

—What do you need to tell me? you repeated.—What is it, Lucy? I'm here.

—If I say it, don't let it travel to your head.

—Not much does at this stage.

She reached out and took your hands in hers.

—You're still the only one I want to talk with, Henry. Your hand is still the only hand I want to hold.

The lamp glowed at her side. Her eyes reflected an oceanic light.

Just then Blue burst through the door, spackled with mud and seawater, your daughter on her eighth birthday, a miracle, yes, a miracle, dripping with sea and sand, wielding some wonder of nature, a starfish, a fossilized fern, a living mole.

An hour later, your conscience battered the door.

Kerr pats Bess's rump. He prefers being on the move. A tortoise's pace, but a pace. Half an hour to the cemetery.

—Good to be back on the road, he says expansively.—Good to be wandering the great wide open.

Bess's eyes are filmy and milky, with almost no lashes. She must suffer constant conjunctivitis from the sand that flies her way, ground-up minerals spewed by the sea, traces of gold dust lingering over Lands End and Point Lobos.

A couple of weeks ago you caught Marilyn plucking out her own eyelashes, pulling the offenders out one by one, leaving bare patches. They've started to grow back, though slowly.

When you discovered her pulling them out, you gripped her shoulders and propelled her away from her mirror, which sits in the corner, where the crib used to be. She paled, and her chin trembled above the high collar of her nightgown.

—How dare you walk in on me, she said.

—Stop, sweetheart, for God's sake, stop, you pleaded.—Is this about Jack?

In that moment you thought: *She knows.*

The rain has given way to the fog. The fog unfurls like a scroll. The mare groans west.

Lucy

AT EIGHTEENTH AND CLEMENT the streetcar clangs to a stop. Three passengers disembark, pulling their coats tight against a rising wind. The rain is letting up.

You passed Henry's store some blocks back but couldn't bring yourself to look out the window for it. You can't afford what's inside.

In a few minutes you'll arrive at Sutro's. From the depot, you'll hurry home, change Blue's clothes, let her inspect her snails. Then: to the cemetery. It's close. Within walking distance. Practically a hop-skip, if the walk's brisk. Very brisk.

You'll be in and out of the mariners' burial ground before Marilyn shows up, before you have time to regret it. Blue will be able to see her father. And time will come to a halt for the five minutes you stand and watch her beaming up at him. He'll crouch down to take in the sight of her, speak with her, observe her showing off the day's wounds, now bandaged. He'll draw her into his arms. Time will stop almost entirely.

You've been reading about the natural history of San Francisco. You borrowed a geology book from Sutro's library months ago. You and Henry used to read it aloud to each other, chapter by chapter, on Wednesdays until nightfall, sitting outside in twilight.

You've gone ahead and finished the book without him, reading in the evenings before you turn in. You arrived at the final page alone. There was no other option. Otherwise you never would have finished the book.

May stopped by one of those nights. Sutro's ticket seller is closing in on fifty, salt-and-peppery and wide. Her loyalty disguises itself as can-

tankerousness. She and June are aware of Henry. They grasp the basic
elements of the relationship. Over the years they have seen him coming
and going. They raised no questions when you asked them to watch Blue
the week you went to Sausalito. They brought over a loaf of fresh bread
and butter after you returned early, one day after your departure, speech-
less with humiliation. They didn't pry. They fed you buttered toast.

— You know what a customer asked me today? May said the night
she stopped over. She leaned against the cottage's front door, arms
crossed, one plump hip jutting out at the angle of frustration.

You slid a marker into your geology book. — Tell me.

— He asked me: What does it feel like, being a single woman?

— What did you say to him?

— I said it feels like being a woman.

The motorman has started to pull back into motion when the conductor instructs him to brake once more, this time for two stragglers, a
girl and a woman scurrying aboard. The girl's limp slows their approach.
The woman walks with head high. Her hat is topped with a blue merle.
Whoever stuffed that bird didn't do a good job. One wing droops over
the side rim.

You return to your view out the window.

According to that geology book, two different kinds of time exist on
this planet. There is human time, and there is geologic. You read that
last part aloud to May. To humans, ten years is a long time. To a rock,
ten years is nothing. A more appropriate length of time about which a
rock might feel concerned is a million years, or twelve million.

— I can't imagine, May marveled.

I can, you almost said.

What to you seems like forever — how long Blue needs to finish a
bowl of oatmeal, for example, or how many years it's taken you to admit
you really did think Henry might leave his wife — these things occupy
no time at all from the point of view of a rock. Erosion, weathering, sub-
duction — these make up a rock's worries.

The conductor accepts his nickel fare from the late arrivals as the motorman prepares to start up the car again. The woman and girl file into
the covered interior section, the girl leading the way. She wears a brace
on one leg. She selects a seat across from you and lowers herself to the

bench with a small sigh of relief. The woman slides in beside her. You look again. It's Marilyn Plageman.

You'd know Henry's wife anywhere. You've seen her in person precisely once, the day you confronted Henry in his store and castigated him for being too sick to write, too laid up to inform you if he was living or dying. Once was enough. She has pulled her thick hair into a sophisticated twist. Her brow conveys intelligence, her eyes fatigue. You're mere feet away. You could reach out and tap the toe of her shoe with your foot if you wanted.

You try not to stare. She watches the passing landscape. She hasn't noticed you. She notices the dunes and the wet street and the empty lots. She doesn't have any reason to pay attention to you, to wonder about the woman seated across from her. No one has ever questioned her property, her right of possession. She can take for granted what's hers.

If she's going to the cemetery, she's early. If she's ahead of schedule, there's no way you can take Blue to see Henry.

You study her, trying not to be obvious. Her hands are graceful, refined, the hands of an educated woman. *She's from Gettysburg,* Henry used to say, as if that explained everything, as if you were equipped to grasp such a woman's history, the layers of genealogy, religion, class, and culture that make up a Marilyn.

You can't stop looking at her hands. They're lined but not weathered. Yours are weathered but not lined. Her hands have held your lover, comforted him, held his first child, gripped Henry in passion, and pushed him away. Because that's what finally happened. Isn't it? She pushed him away; you showed up to fill the gap. She retracted her claim; you stepped forward. You stepped too fast. Maybe she needed more time. Four years was not enough to find her footing after she lost Jack. For Henry, four years was more than he could endure. But it was not more than Marilyn could endure. Then along came you — the interloper.

Blue watches the brace-clad girl with interest. She's fascinated with young women just a few years older, compares herself to them. She stiffens on the bench, attempting to straighten her posture, trying to appear taller. You might be doing the same.

You need to get off this car.

Marilyn whispers to the girl beside her; the girl whispers back. Who is that child? Maybe Marilyn's not headed to the cemetery. Maybe she, too, is breaking a habit today. Maybe she rose from her bed this morning reciting self-admonitions. Wouldn't that be something.

She glances over, and your eyes briefly meet.

— Ma. Blue tugs at your elbow. — Will we see Ostrich before or after the snails? Will he come home with us after we go to the—

— Hush, you say and pat her shoulder.

She sighs audibly.

Again your gaze finds Marilyn's. She smiles at Blue's sigh, looking at you, mother to mother, caregiver to caregiver. And you are the vilest woman on the planet. How can she not see what's right before her? How can she not smell Henry all over you, ten years of him seeping from your pores, see the imprint of his body, his writhing, his joy, his guilt, his inability to leave her, his inability to leave you? How can she miss that history stamped all over you in the way you hold yourself, in the dress you're wearing, the same black cotton day dress he once unfastened so hurriedly he tore a seam and you had to resew it later; how can she not find the truth in your eyes, in your child, in Blue? Good Lord, how can she not see Henry in Blue?

Your daughter pokes you in the ribs. — I know I'm not supposed to talk, Mama, but I don't feel good.

I don't either, you want to say.

The two of you have shared everything two people can share without living together, without becoming lovers yourselves.

When Marilyn retreats to her bed with a chest cold, a few days later, you contract her cough. When you roast mutton on a Wednesday, she smells garlic and cloves on Henry's breath the following morning. You have plucked strands of her black hair off your sleeve, black hairs Henry came in wearing on his wool coat. Surely she has done the same in her corner of the world. Without a doubt she has plucked a blond hair from her dress after she hung it up next to Henry's jacket in the wardrobe.

Marilyn and Henry's private life, their private moments, their attempts to stay alive to each other: these are utterly unknown to you.

If Jack is moved out of the city cemetery, his disinterment will devastate Marilyn. What happens to Marilyn happens to Henry. Then he passes it to you.

—I need more time, he used to plead with you. —I need more time.

—For what?

—To find a way to be with you.

On good days you said: You already are with me.

On bad days you said: Stop lying.

—I have never lied to you, he cried.

You nodded. —That's true. You lie to yourself.

He was never going to marry you. But he's not married to Marilyn either. He's yoked to that child in the ground, that child the city wants to move.

The car has attained a respectable speed when Marilyn and the girl rise to their feet and, holding the overhead grips, cross up the aisle to the conductor. You can hear the girl asking Marilyn: Are you feeling ill again?

This isn't a scheduled stop. Something's wrong. She's bending the arc of the day.

What's the plan? you want to ask them. *Where are we heading now?*

Marilyn leans forward and murmurs something to the conductor, who nods and says something to the motorman. He guides the car to a stop. Before she steps down, Henry's wife twists around, delivering one final glance, taking in the sight of Blue. Recognition? No, but she's straining to remember if she has seen this child before. Again her eyes find yours.

Here we are, she seems to be saying, *two women marooned out here in these dunes. Two women looking after two girls.*

—Safe travels, she says to the conductor. She and the girl step off the car into the empty street.

What in God's name were you thinking?

—I need more time, Henry used to plead.

Yes. Yes, Henry, you do. You need geologic time. Human time? You're on your own.

Marilyn

HENRY WON'T KNOW WHAT TO SAY when he sees you've brought an orphan. He'll wonder why you're dragging Ida into your private catastrophe, your once-a-year mudslide.

Right now you're helping her board the streetcar. The conductor takes your fare, freeing you to follow Ida into the covered interior, where you take a seat across from a young mother missing her hat, a woman with dirty-blond hair and a square, sturdy figure. She's with a girl so bedraggled the child looks like she's been hung to dry on a clothesline. The mother's eyes meet yours. She's younger than you are, but she's wearing out faster. Her eyes look older than her face. She shifts in her seat to watch the passing streetscape.

Ida, speaking softly, begins to tell you how she wound up at Maria Kip. She tells you about her original father — that's how she refers to him, as if copies or imitations might be made — who, after losing Ida's mother to illness, relinquished Ida to charity. She was six.

— He didn't want to send me away, she recalls. — But he didn't want me to go hungry either. He didn't have sufficient means, and I was too little to keep house for him.

You pat her good knee. — And here I am, starving you too. I can hear your stomach growling.

Ida settles more comfortably into her seat. — I saw him last week. I saw my original father.

— Where?

— At the Emporium. Mrs. Wood sent me on an errand, and I saw him. He's married again. His new wife is going to have a child.

—Goodness.

The woman across the aisle glances up as her child sighs loudly. Again your eyes meet. She reminds you of the person you might have been if you'd lived this far west from day one, if you'd never known any home except the Outside Lands. She's at ease. Resilient. Fearless. She probably marches through these desolate streets without hesitation. If she has a man, if she has a husband, she doesn't *need* him. She doesn't require him for sustenance. She forfeits her life for no one.

—He was buying a needle and thread and a tin of buttons the day I saw him, Ida says.—He said his wife needed them. He said she was growing too fat for her dresses.

—Did he ask you to return home?

—No. He said he still couldn't afford my keep.

People are cruel. People are jaw-droppingly cruel, and Henry's store does not carry buttons. It carries everything but. Which you think is ridiculous.

—What kind of a store doesn't carry buttons? you taunted, baiting him, one of the few times in recent memory you have felt any genuine flood of feeling, good or bad, toward your spouse, toward anyone other than Richard.—Do you think keeping them off the shelf is going to help anyone?

Most of the time you experience only a dull possessiveness, a compulsion to check to make sure both Richard and Henry are home, inside, the door bolted; most of the time you want merely to reach out with one hand in the dark and confirm the presence of the thick-barreled body by your side. Yes, you sleep with a basset hound rather than a husband; what of it?

—What kind of a shopkeeper doesn't sell buttons? you repeated. —That's ludicrous.

Henry darkened.

—It's my decision. It's my store. It's my decision, Marilyn.

—It must be nice to decide things, you flung back.—It must be perfectly *wonderful*.

Ida bends to adjust her brace. It's too small for her.

—I didn't think I was that expensive, she says.—Do you really think

I would cost that much? He was buying an awful lot of things for his wife.

You turn to take in the street. As the rain has eased, vapor and haze have slid in from the coast, erasing the long view. That might not be a bad thing. Maybe you'll disappear in a puff of divine smoke and wake up tomorrow in a new body, with a new life. Would you like that? You might. Would you do it; would you choose to be a new woman if you could? Board a train that stays on the tracks this time. Avoid derailment.

You could be the woman across the aisle. You could stand up, change places. Start over.

—I don't decide things, Henry shouted back that day; he towered, gaunt and stiff, a headache waiting to strike you.

—I run a store, he went on. —That's all. I run a hardware store. Otherwise I wouldn't be able to feed and house us. Otherwise we'd be living on the street, Marilyn.

You didn't blink. —You practically live there now.

He laid his hand on top of yours. —Help me. Please. I'm trying here.

He pulled you into his arms. At first you weren't sure what he was doing, but he only hugged you. Contritely, you thought. Or maybe he was just sad.

Once upon a time, your husband desired you more than anything. Once upon a time he went four days without eating while summoning the nerve to ask you to marry him. That Henry no longer exists.

Ida nudges your shoulder.

—Mrs. Plageman? You've gone white again.

She's right. You're still not feeling well. You didn't notice until she said something.

—Is it your stomach?

You nod.

—The car's making you seasick. We should walk. You did better when we walked.

The only thing left in your stomach is acid, but that's enough. You'd better get off this car before you become ill a second time.

You haul yourself up and reach for the overhead grip. Ida rises too, sensing the urgency. She leads you to the front, where you ask the conductor to make an emergency stop.

— For reasons of health, you whisper.

— Of course, he swiftly says, and he turns to his motorman, delivers the request for a stop.

Maybe he has a nauseated wife back home, or a daughter whose abdomen won't stop aching. Maybe his mother suffers headaches.

As the car slows to a halt, you glance back over your shoulder. The woman across the aisle is watching your departure. Her daughter, her squirming, buzzing bee of a daughter, reminds you of somebody, you can't think whom. And the woman reminds you of someone you might have been friends with in another life.

Not in this life. In this life, your only friend is Henry.

— Want us to wait? the conductor asks. — If you only need a couple minutes, we can wait. Don't want to leave a lady stranded.

— We'll be all right, Ida says on your behalf. — We can catch another car. She needs some air.

He nods. — That's one thing your ma'll find plenty of out here.

He has a northeastern accent. Maybe Boston. It's hard to tell; you haven't been back that way in years. His face is round and sympathetic. Part of you would like to throw your arms around this conductor, say to him, *Take me out of here; take me anywhere, so long as it's east.*

You step off the car, Ida leading, holding you by the arm. The motorman eases the car back into motion. You stand marooned in the middle of the street, abandoned through your own choosing.

A woman should never push a good man away — that's the rule. A man can push a good woman away; there are others, there exists for the man a pool. But a woman cannot pick and choose. You pushed Henry away — you broke the rule. You have forgotten how to be in the same room with him, how to listen, even though half the time that's all you really want to do. Please God, let him communicate with you; let him say something. Anything.

You want him to come back; at the same time, you won't allow his return.

He withdrew. Yes, but so did you. He wandered. Yes, fair enough, but so did you. You wandered inward; Henry wandered outward. You both strayed.

The sharpest insight arrived the week you worked on the account books for his store, the week his tumble off Bailey laid him up in bed with an infection and you discovered sporadic withdrawals dating back years, modest amounts marked for petty cash, other odds and ends. This was cash the store never saw, cash Henry never used, at least not on merchandise and not on you.

Later you went back and checked, and the withdrawals had stopped.

You considered this information. You entertained the full range of scenarios. But this was Henry you were thinking about. Unshakable Henry. Steady-as-she-goes Henry. His dalliance is with the cemeteries.

You went and sat before the mirror and inspected yourself. You were trying to see what Henry saw when he looked at you. Forty-one is not nineteen, no matter what angle a woman chooses. Plucking your eyebrows, then your eyelashes, proved a disaster. Especially when he walked in on you.

That night, alone with Richard, you realized you were jealous. Of Henry. Yes, you were jealous of Henry. You would have liked to wander outward too, to roam freely, instead of this jabbing and stabbing inward, this infernal vacuum.

You still would like to wander. You'd like to smoke a cigarillo on the front porch in full view of the Chamberses. Or sail across the bay alone at sunset.

Where to? Where would you sail if you could? Portland. What would you do there? You have no idea.

— Mrs. Plageman, Ida says. — You're crying.

1:00 p.m.

Henry

— THERE SHE IS, KERR SAYS.

You're twenty paces from the entrance when Bess sidles to a halt. This path winds off Clement Street into the first row of graves. Grass and sage skirt the trail. Across the street squats a caretaker's cottage.

Neglected graves, paupers' graves, stretch far, headstones and footstones covering hillock after hillock, some listing, some toppled. Each grave once held a numbered board. Most of the numbers have faded.

Kerr clucks twice. The plants shiver with Bess's resumption of movement. Reluctantly she picks her way forward.

—Plageman? he says and raises a hand.—I had an idea.

Bess stops again, pretending the hand was meant for her.

—About the board of supervisors. About your boy.

No. Not today.

What he intends to propose—you've been thinking the same thing yourself. You've been thinking of nothing else the last quarter mile.

—My point, Kerr continues, my point is this. We could bring him with us.

You look away.

Most of this region used to be sand. The eroding Sierra Nevadas, ground down by glaciers, created the dunes. Rivers drained the mountains and carried off sediment. The sand followed a westward course. Tributaries deposited millions of grains along riverbanks from the Sierras to the coast. Wind and floods sent the sand across the exposed continental shelf, covering San Francisco and the central bay as far east as Oakland. The dunes rose up, some as high as forty feet. The same dunes before you now.

—Bring him with us, Kerr repeats.—Move him ourselves. Before anyone else lays a hand on him. Plageman. We could do it on our time, under our direction. Keep him in the hands of his father.

You cannot do this. Not today.

Kerr talks on.—He doesn't need to travel to Colma or whatever dump they'll throw them in. He can come stay with me at Odd Fellows'. I'll find him a spot. A quiet one, something with shade. We could plant him a tree.

He pauses, adds: It's the least I can do.

You try to reply, but sand rasps in your throat. Bess remains motionless, ears skimming back.

—What choice do we have? he finishes.—We can do it today, move him right now, if you want. We're here; we have the tools. You brought a shovel. Didn't you?

—I need to think. Hold on a damn minute. I need to think.

—Plageman, with all due respect, you do too much thinking.

He's right. And Marilyn's on her way.

Another gem from the *Call*:

> The winds from the ocean blow direct from this pest-breeding spot, carrying its deadly germs over all the homes of citizens, thereby endangering the lives of over 300,000 persons, the half of which has never been told. It is an appalling and fearful state of things to be allowed to exist in a civilized city like San Francisco, and should be abated at once.

Lucy would not have written such a piece. She would not have catered to fear. But Lucy will never be a real reporter. The deck's stacked against her.

Does she know it? She might. But you do not have the heart to tell her.

—We have the equipment, Kerr repeats.—And room for a coffin in back. The two of us working together won't take long. He won't be very deep buried.

You shove your hat up so your eyes meet his.

—My wife is coming. Jesus Christ. Have some sense. My wife will be here.

—I have sense. I have it aplenty. This way, you take care of him yourself. Protect him from those jackals in office. Keep him near. Keep him with his pa.

He wheezes, a hitching bray; his lungs have stalled. He turns his head and coughs spastically. The white spathes of the lilies tremble with the force of his expectoration.

You place a hand on his shoulder.—What do you need?

—New lungs, he says, panting.

He could be consumptive. You've never spent all day with him before. You had no idea how bad off he is. And his nights must be worse than his days.

The rain has pulled back, leaving a proud wind.

—Look, Kerr huskily says.—Plageman. Henry. It was just a suggestion. Nothing has to happen today. That's one thing I've learned. Nothing is an emergency in a cemetery. Whatever the emergency was, it already happened. We don't have to take your boy out now. We can do it later. Another day. Okay?

You once tried to return a souvenir card Lucy gave you from the midwinter fair. You thought she might want it for the memento box you are always encouraging her to keep.

—Why would I save this? she asked when you pressed the card into her hand.

—To remember the fair, you said.

She averted her gaze.—Why in the world would I want to do that?

She leaves the memento box under the bed to collect dust. She can't discard it, but she can't bear to look at it either. The same way she feels about you.

Kerr tries a different tack.

—Why don't I take you home, then. You can see your wife, sit her down, break the news. Hell, you can visit Chairman Hubbs too. Teach him a thing or two.

—My wife's coming *here*. I told you. To see the garden.

—So where is she, then? Kerr returns, defensive. His chest is hurting, and he's only trying to help.—When do I get to meet Mrs. Plageman?

Clammy fog dips the path in an otherworldly sheen. A figure crosses into the half-light ahead, an old man, older than Kerr, eighty, possibly. He's skeletal. He's one of the beggars no one wants to contemplate, no one wants to admit exists, the invisible citizens of the Richmond. Squinting, you follow his progress, his legs in their threadbare trousers. Maybe he's visiting a child. Maybe his son or grandson is buried in the paupers' section. Beggars have sons too, after all, and anniversaries, frozen days that refuse to release their grip. They have Marilyns, and they have Lucys, dreams they were too afraid to pursue, resignations they mistook for powerlessness.

—Where's your wife? Kerr repeats.

—On her way. I said that. She's on her way.

—Running late?

—No. She's never late.

The board of supervisors will not manage to move all the bodies. Their work will be sloppy. And those bones they do move, God knows where they'll end up. One day, rich men with gold watches will swing golf clubs on top of forgotten graves.

You have to get Jack out of here.

—She's arriving soon, you repeat numbly.—Less than an hour. We always walk to the mariners together.

—You're sure? Awful foggy out here for a lady.

—Yes. Yes. We meet at the same time and place every year.

He regards you intently.

—Date you lost him? Or date you had him?

—Both, you say.—He was turning two that day.

The foreman's face collapses.

Get to work. Plunge your hands in this soil. Work is the key; work will save you. Return these plants to the earth. Give them a chance to take root.

— Less than an hour, you repeat, still on your seat in the driver's box. — Hell, I said that already.

You need to keep talking. You, who hate talking, suddenly require conversation.

You glance over your shoulder. The shovel, solid and heavy, waits in the back of the hearse. *Just in case,* Stevens cheerfully suggested.

Kerr notices you looking at it.

— Maybe this isn't the day to do it.

— I know, you say. — But this is the day I've got.

And then you can't say any more.

The foreman's mouth tightens. He taps Bess's withers with a switch you didn't know he owned, allowing the frayed leather to graze her hip-bones. The mare jerks into a trot, her first exertion all year. She careens pell-mell into the cemetery, teeth bared, ears flattened.

Marilyn

A BLISTER HAS ERUPTED where Ida's brace chafes the tender skin behind her knee.

— You've outgrown that.

— No, ma'am.

— You have. You're wearing a brace for a girl two years shorter.

You fish in your pocket for a handkerchief, find one, and stuff it around the top of the brace.

— Does that help? We still have a little ways.

— Yes, ma'am. I'm sure it will.

— But it's not helping yet.

— I'm sure it will any minute.

Strangers in a dairy truck supplied a ride after you fled the streetcar, after you nearly fell ill a second time. Trundling by, an elderly man and woman slowed their ponies and offered to take you and Ida to your destination. You accepted their kindness. As milk bottles clattered in back, you told the old man where you were going, the city cemetery, and offered to pay him for the ride. They wouldn't take your money. They also wouldn't take you to the cemetery. Apologizing, the old man explained he'd have to drop you a few blocks from the entrance.

— There's plague in the cemetery, the old woman said.

You and Ida are hiking west now on Clement Street, Ida choosing her steps with care.

— Mrs. Plageman?

— Yes?

— I've never had such an adventure.

Is that what this is?

—I'm glad, you tell her.

But it's better for women to stay at home, to avoid adventure. It's better that women don't overexcite themselves, don't work too hard on any one cause, such as saving the cemetery, though *Henry* is right to work on saving it, though Henry *has* to work on it. His job is to ensure things stay the same. Yet you're dying for something new. This is your paralysis.

When Ida's limp worsens, you unbuckle the brace and help her slide it completely off. The handkerchief flutters to the ground.

—Can you walk without it? It was still cutting into your skin.

—I can walk. I'm sure of it.

—Are you? I don't like this, Ida. I shouldn't have brought you.

Her voice is thin.—Yes, ma'am. Please, I'm having such a lovely afternoon.

—All right. But If It starts hurting more, we're turning around.

Where to?

Women spend their youth waiting for a man to find them. They spend their middle years cheering that man on, propping him up, bearing his offspring, washing his shirts, sweeping his carpet of crumbs. They spend their waning years wearing circles into that same carpet, wondering where everyone has gone. Women outlive the men for whom they live. And sometimes the children. They revolve around unreliable suns.

Ida stumbles again. To catch herself, she grabs your skirt, clutches your waist.

—I'm sorry, she bleats.—I'll be more careful. Please don't make me go back.

—Oh, child, you say, and you set the brace down.

She flings herself into your arms, right there in the middle of Clement Street, and surrenders to a single sob. Her head presses into your chest. On the whole, she's taken well to being kidnapped. It's better than being orphaned. At least when you're kidnapped, it means someone wants you.

You have to stop calling her *child*.

—Are you all right? you say.

She nods. You two are trading the same useless questions back and forth today. Her skin smells like rain. But you're within striking distance, nearing the curvatures in the earth, the sanded peaks and valleys that mark the start of the graves. You're closing in now. Three blocks. Three unending blocks.

You pull away and search her face, woman to woman, half orphan to half wife, your hands still grasping her shoulders.

—Can you keep on? We can rest anytime.

—Yes, ma'am. I want to walk. I'm perfectly fine.

It's her first lie all day. You're surprised she held out this long.

Lucy

FINALLY. THE STREETCAR HAS PULLED into the depot by Sutro's, the same depot where you started this trek almost four hours ago, when Stone bore Blue in his arms.

She walks independently now, skipping off before the other passengers. As you step down behind her, you fight the urge to check back for Marilyn, to contemplate the empty bench where Henry's wife sat.

Blue wheels around and motions you to hurry.

— Mother! The snails.

A gated fence cordons off Sutro's stables and sheds from his public grounds. The pump station lies downhill, in another direction. No brilliant article investigating the Olympic Salt Water Company will be forthcoming today. The *Banner* editor wouldn't have printed it anyway. He thinks a woman ought to stay home and cook dinner for her husband.

What if she stays home and cooks dinner for someone else's husband?

You push open the gate and guide Blue into the estate's interior. Nearly home. She scampers ahead. She knows the route. She'll save a snail, change out of her ruined clothes. And then, quickly: the cemetery.

What about Marilyn? She disembarked in the middle of nowhere. Who knows where she went? You can't alter your plan simply because you saw her. You've spent a decade altering your plans already. If you even had them.

To the mariners. To Henry. To a habit ten years in the making and three and a half months in the breaking.

—Ma. Faster!

—I'm coming.

—We're nearly there. The snails!

—They'll be fine. The rain's letting up.

This isn't true. Great globules of water have returned, spattering earth and sand, plopping on top of Blue's head, watering your daughter, stem to roots. Nearby hulks one of the windmills that brings springwater into the estate's irrigation system. No one needs that windmill today.

Blue jumps from stone to stone, arms akimbo. Your cottage with its slanted roof lies ahead. How can she not be hurting? Her injuries are brand-new. Your daughter is twirling on formations millions of years old, serpentinite and granitic rocks that traveled from far inland. Yes, inanimate objects travel; yes, that is one reason why it takes them so long. These particular specimens probably came from the Sierra Nevadas. Give them another few million years, and who knows how far they might travel. They would get along well with Henry.

Stopping is what you needed. Or did you tell him to stop because you couldn't say what you wanted?

Stay.

Choose me.

Don't leave.

She reaches the cottage as the skies reopen. Thick drops pelt her face and shoulders. She searches, stomps from one puddle to another, poking her fingers into the glop, kneeling, soaking, peering around the front stoop, muddier and more autonomous by the minute. You'll have to scrub that sailor jacket with hot water and soap later.

She can't find her snails.

You stand, braced, waiting for her explosion. Here it comes.

—Where *are they?* she bellows, knotting her fists, raising her knuckles to the sky.— *Where are the snails?*

She speaks to the heavens, to the truculent skies. She calls the snails by name. Dear Lord, she has names for them. She has paired her snails with the U.S. presidents' names she learned at Barrington Primary. How Henry would howl with delight if you told him.

—Thomas Jefferson! John Adams! John Quincy Adams! Where are you?

The rain pounds as if delivering a curse. Is that lightning striking the ocean's surface? Lightning hardly exists in San Francisco, nor does rain of this suddenness and intensity, this bizarre, flooding release, water issuing from the skies like punishment. Normally the rain stays hesitant, nonconfrontational; it slips in and out, tiptoes in and out, much like Henry slipped in and out of his two lives, present without being present, touching without touching.

The snails have sunk to the bottom of a pool. Blue wades in. Water swirls around her calves; there go her shoes again. She reaches in, arms plunging. And there go the bandages on her legs. She digs. She produces muck and goop and snails, a handful of tiny dead creatures, fossils in the making. Are they dead? Some are. Some aren't. It's going to take a while to distinguish between the two categories. She raises her hands high. Clods of mud speckle her sleeves.

—Mama. Help!

She marches uphill and deposits her fistfuls on the cottage stoop so that they're safely out of the floodplain. You watch, enthralled. Your daughter is unreal. You must have invented her in Mr. Claude's workshop, created her out of wire and cotton batting and glue, formed the perfect specimen of the species *girl*. She's earth and shell and grit and salt, tears streaming, determined, animated, more alert than you were at that age, more alive too. Or maybe not; maybe all girls start out this way. What in the name of God happens to them?

—The rain wasn't supposed to do this!

—I'm sorry, you reply, as if you control the rain.

In her mind you do. In her mind you control the parameters of the known world. That's about to change.

Henry would want you to write about this moment. He would want you to put it in a letter. *Tell me what I'm missing,* he has written, he has begged. *Tell me. I don't want to miss her childhood.*

—I'm not a letter writer, you told him in the final throttled visits before everything ended. —And even if I were, where would I mail them?

—To the store.

—Not safe. Stevens could read them.

—I'd find a safe address, then.

—Where? you said.—Your front porch? Shall I mail them to you in care of Richard?

He excused himself and left the table.

You did not manage your anger well with Henry. Your anger toward Henry. Or toward yourself.

Blue returns to the pond and begins to scoop again; she sifts through the mud with her fingers, panning for snails.

—Hold on, you say, and you return to the cottage and come back with a metal sieve, which you hand to her.

She accepts your offering without a word. The two of you labor side by side, gardening in water, shoes squelching and sucking the base of the pool as you feel around—for what? For their sharp molluscan forms. Far below, the sea pounds, ocean foaming, licking the greywacke, salt water remaking the face of cliffs. Together, you and Blue bend and dip, sift and pan, water fountaining from the sieve; you discover sand and grime and snails, one by one and two by two; your fingers crush several; their fragility upends you. Stealing a glimpse of the top of your daughter's head, you reach down and kiss her hair, tasting rain and the soap she uses to wash with. It's the same soap you use to wash with. Your throat is all clogged up now, all stopped up with the life you have lived and the life you will not. You are full with both.

—Stop kissing me, she protests.

—Go inside and change, you say. She trembles with damp and cold. —You've saved the ones you can.

—I have not, she says.—There's more.

She's holding two new fistfuls, greedy fistfuls.

—Go inside, and I'll find the last ones. We're late, Blue. We are truly out of time.

—Promise you'll find the last ones?

—Yes. I'll do my best.

Her eyes narrow.—You have to get them *all*.

—I will.

—Promise?

—Yes! Now scoot. Dry off and put on a warmer dress. Five minutes.

She assesses you with circumspection, with an adult's weary suspicion, and trudges inside. She carries the snails with her. The front door bangs shut.

Blue

TWO SNAILS POKE THEIR ANTENNAE up from my hands. Mud drips through my fingers.

—Blue? Don't wear your good dress. Put on your navy one.

—Why?

—Just put it on, please. And hurry.

She's calling to me from outside. I'm in the bedroom. I need more time. First things first: Where to put all these snails? They need someplace safe. They've had a hard day; they need to dry out in peace and quiet. The bed. There! The mess oozes into the quilt. The snails glide everywhere. The mud seeps into the covers. They peek out from their shells to observe their new home.

—It's as fine as the Cliff House, I tell them.

Now: What to wear to see Pa? Not my good dress. Not my navy dress. Sorry, Ma. I'm of a mind to wear my cowboy costume. Pa bought it the day he and Ma took me to the fair, the same day Pa saw the man he knew and ran away. Before that happened, he bought me boy's full-legged chaps and boots and a cowboy vest. He bought me a cowboy hat too, only it wasn't small enough. A few days later, he showed up at home with everything, and he also brought a sheriff's star, of tinsel, that Ma sewed to my vest. Her dander was up because she doesn't believe in costumes.

—Pretending to be someone you're not is a poor plan, she said.

She and Pa both went quiet. To cheer them up, I tried on the costume anyway and marched around the kitchen, even though I didn't feel like being a cowboy right that second, and even though I felt a little stewy.

They clapped, but Pa's face stayed grim, and Ma's smile looked like she'd had to borrow it from someone. Pa kissed her on the side of her mouth before he left. He didn't stay as long as usual.

Ma's calling my name again, still outside.

—Blue!

I'm standing now in my underclothes, looking at myself in the mirror.—I'm coming, I say.—I'm still dressing.

—And you're hurrying. Right? I'm counting back from ten. Then I'm leaving.

That's not true, and we both know it. She would never just leave me. She's not allowed.

I didn't like that sheriff's star at first. I didn't want Ma sewing it to my vest.

—I don't care to be a sheriff, I said, talking more to Pa.—I'm of a mind to be an outlaw.

—No, you don't want that, he said.

He pulled me onto his lap. He was sitting at the table. We were eating potatoes Ma had boiled and forgotten to salt. His legs bumped the table and almost tipped my glass of milk. Ma had her back to us both. She was busy scrubbing spoons and forks, giving them a mighty scouring.

—You want to be the one who makes the rules, Blue, not breaks the rules, Pa said.

—Says who? I asked.

He reached over and plunked the cowboy hat on my head. It dropped down and covered my eyes. I tossed my head. The hat didn't move. I tossed again; nothing.

—Who turned out the lights? I said; I was trying to make him laugh. He pulled me closer, lifted up the hat, and blew his lips, *brrrzt,* against my cheek. I hate it and I love it when he does that.

—Leave her alone, Ma said, turning to glare at him.—She has a headache.

—I do not, I said.

—Ten. Nine. Blue, if you don't come out right now . . .

—You promised you would save the rest of the snails!

—I did. Eight. I'm standing right here holding the lot of them. See for yourself. Seven. Sweetheart, come on. You wanted to see your father, didn't you?

—Are you sure you found *all* of them?

—Five.

—You skipped six, Mother!

She doesn't answer. I can hear her starting to talk to someone outside, a man with a rumbling voice. Good. More time for me to find my costume. I drop to my hands and knees, push aside the bottoms of the covers, and peer under the bed slats. Three boxes and one worn-out valise live under this bed. They contain winter clothes, gloves, spare pots and pans that Pa has given Ma, that he *foisted* on her, Ma used to tell me.

—They're extras, Pa said when he heard that word.—Backups. Hand-me-downs.

Those pots have not made her cooking any better.

One box looks the right size to store a cowboy costume. I open it. No costume, but I go ahead and inspect the contents. There are souvenir cards and trinkets, a ticket stub, and a color brochure from a place called Shoobert House. A sand dollar rattles when I shake the box. There's a picture of my father, looking so young the sight of his face makes my heart hurt. A second picture is in a paper sleeve with an oval opening. It lies under the first. The paper of the first has stuck to the second. I peel the sleeves apart. The pictures are damaged. Rust has done its work. But I can tell it's Ma in the second picture.

She told me she didn't have any tintypes of herself. But here she is, alone, wearing a flat-topped hat with a ribbon. She sits with a painted backdrop of the sea and a younger Cliff House behind her. She gazes into the camera without smiling. She has freckles. Does she have them now? I've never noticed. Is the woman in the picture my mother, or is the woman outside the cottage yelling at me to hurry up my mother? The woman in the picture looks more adventurous. But I don't quite trust her.

Ma has forgotten her countdown. I peek out the window and catch sight of the master himself, Mr. Sutro. He hardly ever comes over here.

He's on his horse, and he's paunchier than ever. The poor horse has to hold all his fatness.

—I'm checking the damage from the rains, he says to Ma.—Seen any flooding?

She bends to wring out her skirt at the hem and shows him: soaked through.

The rest of this box contains letters. I rifle through them. Ma has stored things in a jumble. Totally out of order.

The letter on top is in Pa's hand. I shouldn't read it. But what have I spent all those hours learning to read for? Ma said reading is always good. She said reading is always the right thing.

February 15, 1897

L.,

I received your letter dated the twelfth. I certainly would not presume to suggest that you feel other than you do; I can only say that my sensibilities differ.

While it is true that it has been agonizing to be in this passage, it is also the one route that would make an outcome other than hopelessly harmful possible. There was an ever-darkening hollow of anger and hurt that was insufferably corrosive. So I agree with you.

With the clandestine and illicit dimension largely—albeit not completely—removed, the possibility emerges of an entirely different footing that might support something new.

So in that respect, I will not "give up"; I will have a hope that was not there before that dimensions heretofore unrealized and never brought into view will be able to manifest themselves.

H.

This is an odd letter. The sentences sound stiffer, and the words wordier, than the way Pa talks in real life. No one in real life says *heretofore*.

Outside, Ma's listening to Mr. Sutro. She can't tell *him* to hurry up; she can't force him to obey her countdown. I have time to read another one.

March 2, 1897

I am not sure that I know how to do this any better than you. But I suspect that I keep from desperate measures by disciplining myself to stay in the day. I am not at all persuaded that we are saying goodbye, any more than I think that it is genuinely possible for us to let go of one another.

I remain determined, however, that you should never experience again what you have experienced in the past days. As much as I wish that I could manage your responses, I know, of course, that I cannot. So my determination may fall wide of the mark. But it will certainly be there in full measure.

Pa didn't sign this letter. Also, he's making no sense. This letter is even more confusing than the first one.

Mr. Sutro's asking Ma how things are going at the taxidermy shop. He's talkative. He's inviting her to borrow more books from his library. He asks her about me too, how I'm doing in school.

—Second in her class, Ma says.

Another lie. I'm nowhere near second. There are too many things to do outside.

I shove the letter back into the box and slide out a third. It's from the year before I was born. My father has been writing letters to my mother longer than I've been alive.

August 2, 1888

Dear L.:

I have not been able to escape how very lovely our lunch was today. There was, above all, the probing conversation that made me rethink how I would assess what we mean when we call something providential.

Then there was the nape of your neck, and the intensity of your smile that shone so brightly.

And then the drape of your dress, beckoning my eye to your waist . . .

And then the thought of traveling with you and visiting all the places that we were talking about, and loving you by the hour. And loving you again.

And again. H.

This letter does not sound like Pa either. It sounds happy. My stomach is beginning to hurt. Do all fathers write letters? Has she written him back? Maybe he keeps a box of *her* letters under *his* bed. Where is his bed?

This thought catches me up short. What kind of father spends every single night sleeping at his store? If Pa doesn't sleep there, and he doesn't sleep here, where does he sleep?

Mr. Sutro has stopped talking. I can't put the box away. I'm hooked. This one's from when I was five:

> *June 18, 1894*
> *In the course of my days, I sometimes forget to say what a blessing you have been, what a gift you are, and how very beautiful your love is for me. I love the way you greet the world, and my days are fuller because you are in them.*

— Blue?

Ma scrapes her boots on the stoop, preparing to come inside. Mr. Sutro is leaving. He's riding off to survey the rest of his property.

— Just a minute, I call back.

I shove the letter into the box and reach for another. One more. Just one. It's short. He wrote it eight days ago. Even the ink smells new.

> *May 14, 1897*
> *By the way, if you think I don't yearn, ache, and dream of you routinely, and love you more daily, you are sadly mistaken. H.*

— Blue Christensen! How many times —

— Coming!

I return the letter to the box. Beside it is an envelope. On the back of that envelope Ma has written one line.

I'm going to die for loneliness of you.

The front door opens. I clap the lid in place, stand up, and kick the box under the bed. The snails have trailed their slime across the top of the covers.

— Ready? Ma says and enters the bedroom. — Oh, Blue. Look at you.

I stand before her, halfway undressed. My hair is snarled with tangles. Mud's all over the covers and my arms and hands. Hopefully I didn't get mud in the letters. The snails are gliding across the bed. They're dripping silt through the bed slats onto the floor. Ma's enormous eyes rest on me.

—Just what do you think you're doing, Anna Christensen, standing here like a half-naked savage, spreading sludge everywhere you move?

I feel very queer. I throw my shoulders back and say:

—If you want me to follow you around all day doing what you say, you have to help me. You have to explain things.

A shadow crosses her face. She pulls me close, crushing my ear bandage. She kisses the top of my head.

—I can't find my boots, I mumble, my nose smooshed against her bosom.—I want my cowboy costume.

She releases me and reads my face. Then she nods and, without a word, makes her way to the bureau and tugs open the bottom drawer. The costume has been waiting there all this time, in a drawer I thought she kept for herself.

She wraps fresh bandages around the cuts on my legs. She helps me dress. She ignores the mud and the snails on the quilt. She'll be madder than a wet hen about them later. She pats my sheriff's star, making sure it's sewn fast, and tells me to turn in a circle before the mirror. She eyes my costume with approval. I would have sworn she'd make me wear the navy.

—Ready? she asks.—Are we ready to be brave?

That's almost what she said this morning. Only this morning it was a sentence, and now it's a question; now I'm part of it. Together we lock eyes in the mirror.

—Ready, I say.

She places the hat on my head.—Good girl. Don't let the brim hurt your ear. Now let's hurry.

She looks hard at me, adds: Your father will be glad to see you.

We step outside. The sun wants to return. It's creeping out from the clouds. It winks at me over the old Firth Wheel, the ride Ma has never allowed me to take. I hold my head high as I walk beside her. She thinks that wheel will stop midair, trap me suspended in the sky someday.

Henry

BESS PULLS THE HEARSE into a labyrinth of quiet. Stakes and hand-made crosses mark the way, encircled by rotting fences. Scrub brush skirts the dunes.

One of the hearse's wheels strikes a rock, and the coach wobbles. Kerr pulls Bess up hard. She whinnies.

—Easy, Kerr says, sawing the reins.—She doesn't like cemeteries. Which way, Plageman?

—North.

—North. How far north?

—The master mariners' graveyard. It overlooks the strait.

He tilts his head, indicating Bess.

—She might need a short rest. She's used up what wind she had.

He could be referring to himself.

—It's not far, you say.—I'll walk her. I'll lead.

A graveled path points forward. The first rows of headstones are as crooked and stained as Kerr's teeth.

—Old girl can walk herself, the foreman says, shaking his head.

Maybe it's better this way. Maybe the vote they took will free you.

Jack's the one who needs freeing. He's earned his release. He deserves the one thing you haven't been able to grant him: time away from his parents, time to become something other than what his parents lost. Time crawls all over him; it worms through quartz and feldspar.

—Whoa, Kerr calls, tugging again.

A wind gust rattles the fence boards. These graves contain members of the Knights of Pythias. Bess rears, showing the whites of her eyes.

—She can't abide cemeteries, Kerr repeats as she lands heavily.

You climb down from the driver's box, step over to the mare, and grip her halter. Looking sidelong at you, she snorts derisively. Her muzzle's silver. She's too old to be galloping in this wind, spurred into a pace not her choosing. A body can do only one thing well on any given day. And that's on a good day.

—Which way? Kerr says again.

He misses his Odd Fellows' landmarks, the headstones he knows. To your right sprawl the rail ties that Adolph Sutro laid back when he co-opted a corner of this cemetery for his own private railroad.

Holding Bess's halter, you walk north. The mare's head bobs low against the westerly wind.

How will you tell Marilyn? Don't think about it.

Don't think about Marilyn; don't think about the neighborhood associations. Don't think about Hubbs, or Colma, or San Mateo County. Don't think about the disinterment. Either you will do it or the city will do it. Don't think about the city. Don't imagine the scrapers that will pull hundreds of skeletons up from the earth, the equipment that will drag up the deceased, plowing row after row, farmers of bone, peddlers of dust, men pinning off graves with cords, roping off coffins. Workmen wearing denim pants and cotton shirts will strain forward, staring into graves to learn what remains, what memories survived their underground purgatory. A rosary clutched in one skeletal hand. A sack of coins in another. False teeth.

They'll dig up the dead; they'll empty the cemeteries, or try to; they'll beat the sand down until it's flat and firm enough to sprout grass, to hold irrigation pipes, grow a golf course. *The dead are in the way of the living.*

—Hold up. I'm not riding if you're walking. Make me look like a useless—

Kerr leaves his sentence unfinished as he dismounts from the driver's box. He doesn't want to be carried to the edge of the continent, led like a prince on a livery. He'll walk beside you, on Bess's other side. He and his consumption will make the journey together.

The wind whips his beard, pointing it like a windsock. He claps his hat tighter and regards you.

—Ready?

You nod.—Ready.

Will you move Jack? Yes. You have to.

But put these plants in the earth first. Give something back to the earth first. This isn't grace; it's works. Marilyn's theology is finally rubbing off on you.

In January, one of your last visits to the cottage, you offered to end things with Lucy. To say goodbye for good.

—I'll stop it right now. I'll stop it for both of us, you said.

You were at your wits' end, trying to figure out what she needed. What she needed kept changing.

—How dare you abandon me, she replied with a great racking cry.

—But you told me to leave you alone, you replied, fighting back tears of your own.—You can't have it both ways.

Apparently, she can. Apparently, this is how things work. She wants to be left alone; at the same time, she will not allow you to leave her. If you heed her request and stay away, as you're currently doing, she'll conclude you've abandoned her, set her out with the trash. If you disregard her request and keep coming over, she'll tell you she's trapped, caught in secrets, not allowed to walk in the open.

—No one walks in the open, you said.—We are all ridden in the dark.

You mailed another letter to her a few days ago. Probably she hasn't yet received it. You should be taken out and shot.

No moment between us should be as conflicted as so many of ours have been, and continue to be.

I take comfort in what we know to be true, holding it fast in these growing hours of separation; it is not the separation, but the resolution of what could no longer be sustained, that matters now.

And that is an acknowledgment of the depth of what we have shared.
And an expression of hope that ours will in some time be a time without
such conflict.

She won't write you back, of course; at this point you don't expect it.
But you will keep writing her. Just as Marilyn insists that you should
keep writing Penny, keep tapping on that closed door. If you stop writing, then it truly is over. She truly is lost to you. Time will erase her,
these years, just as time has begun to erase Jack's years. And you. Time
might be starting to erase you. That last one could be a mercy.

Kerr's trying to soothe Bess. He assures her the day will end soon; he
promises her a warm blanket and sweet hay back home at Odd Fellows'.
He adores the old mare, you see this now.

—And there will be apples, he tells her.—The crispest red apples
you ever did set your eyes upon.

Fire swept over this corner of the cemetery some years back. It charred
the wooden markers. A lucky few have stones. One of the massive Chinese burial grounds lies ahead. To your left, rain has washed loose earth
downhill, has stripped so much sandy soil from the graves that in one
place you glimpse what might be exposed bone. You look away. Someone has scattered coffin handles and the fragments of an altar along the
path. You'll have to be careful not to let Bess step on them.

—This still the right way? Kerr's voice is fading.

—I'm not sure, you say, and you keep going.

That might be the story of your life: Is this the right way? Not sure;
keep going.

1:30 p.m.

Lucy

THAT LETTER YOU WROTE BACK in February asking Henry to stay away was the only true letter you've mailed him. You dropped it in the post the day after Blue's eighth birthday.

You wrote that it was over. You asked him to let go and not look back. In the last paragraph, you added:

You have been so many things to me. I think you have been more things to me than I was to you. I hope the ways we tried to care for each other will form a catch basin that holds what we have known. Thank you, whatever comes.

You've tried composing additional letters since then. They never amount to much. Your sentences falter, just like your footing falters now as you steer Blue away from the cottage, shepherd her around the standing water. Pray your daughter doesn't spot any more living things that need rescuing. Pray you don't either.

You never finish the letters you start to Henry. You never vault past the first line. The words don't land right. Then there's the never-ending matter of where you'd mail them.

The salutation is the first culprit. It does you in every time. *Dear Henry.* The phrase sounds wrong. *Dear H.* Better, but still. How about just *H.*

What to write after that? How does anyone write—or say—anything?

I'm going to die for loneliness of you. After that, what is there?

I love you, I miss you, I cannot have you; I release you.

I love you, I miss you, I cannot have you; please release me.

I need you to let go, I can't bear for you to leave me. Or Blue. What about Blue, Henry?

You never mail any of those thoughts to him, that circuitous madness. You set the attempts aside.

Blue darts ahead. You've left the estate to hike east on Point Lobos Avenue toward the turnoff for the cemetery. She barrels forward, costume intact, sheriff on the move. You'll allow her to speed forward; you'll permit her the distance, so long as she maintains her pace.

—I don't look back, you told Henry, explaining your philosophy, your worldview, your wishful thinking, when he asked once if you regretted the decision to be with him. You weren't sure *deciding* was even what you'd done. You'd stepped toward him, and then you'd taken another step, and then another. And then one day you looked up and ten years were gone.

—You don't look back? Not ever? he said.

—No. Looking back is a poor proposition.

Blue swivels around and extends her hand.

—Mama. Hurry.

Take her hand; let her think she's leading. She might be.

Henry's letters have continued to arrive. His handwriting tells you more about how he's doing than his sentences. When the penmanship resists deciphering, he's closing in on despair. When the words are pressed hard into the paper, he's angry but trying not to show it. Long looping *p*'s and *y*'s mean he misses you; he would give five years of his life for a single night with you in his bed. Or with him in your bed. These arrangements can grow confusing. You have saved the letters because what else can you do? Toss them? Someday, if you live long enough to be old (you feel old now), you will pull that memento box out from its hiding place. For what purpose are you saving his jottings? You've become a taxidermist of words, tagging and dating your collection, manipulating his letters into lifelikeness, the facsimile of a legitimate union. Then you shove everything under the bed and try to forget it.

That juvenile owl you stuffed, that first animal, a lifetime ago, after you finished with it, Mr. Claude applauded and said:

—You gave it a new soul.

You can't tolerate the sight of yourself from those years, from 1887, or '88, or '89, or '90. All those years with and without Henry. They are adding up: 1891, '92, '93, '94, '95, '96. You don't want to remember yourself young, don't want to remember the day those photographs were taken at the Pacific Ocean Beach Gallery. The smell of lacquer inside the gallery, which catered to tourists, made your eyes tear. You wanted to leave; you did not want to be documented with him; you were skittish, afraid someone would recognize him and wonder who you were.

—It's all right, Henry said.—We'll have the photographer take two pictures. One of you and one of me. We don't have to pose together. But I can't survive without a picture of you.

You relented; you allowed it; then, when the tintypes were ready, when Henry handed them back to you—because he realized he could not risk taking your likeness home, because he could not risk taking his own likeness home either, lest it spark questions—when he handed them over, preserved in their cheap paper sleeves, two discrete portraits, separate for all time, you wept.

—This is how it will be for us, you said to him.

Why would you want to remember that?

Why recall any of it? How you could not stop touching him, how your body sprang from its cage toward him, how you walked him up and down Ocean Beach under a shared umbrella after leaving the gallery near Forty-Ninth and B Streets under rain so fine it floated. Flecks of sea dust ornamented his hair.

—I should leave, he said, halfway down the beach, the flags of the Cliff House snapping behind him.—I should leave and not come back.

—No, you said; you begged.—No, don't. Don't leave me, Henry. Not yet.

Why would you want to remember so much happiness? Was it happiness? Yes. In that moment, it was. Did you recognize it as such? No. You stood on the outside. You still stand there. Having once crossed, a woman cannot go back over. And how will you look back at yourself?

You can't do it now, ten years on. How much harder will it be when you are forty, fifty, sixty if you live that long? One minute you're twenty-one and fleeing Omaha; the next you're thirty-two, assistant to a taxidermist, no husband, no money, no family beyond your mother save a dead cousin and a living daughter, your beloved, true and tried, your Blue, to whom you have lied by omission and who's about to learn the truth about her parents, whatever that means, whatever that requires her to shoulder.

She charges through sand. She tromps in those dreadful boy's boots, tips her cowboy hat back so she can see in front of her. She's lean and slight. Tall for her age. She'll have her father's height. She'll have his height, his legs, his knees, his intelligence masquerading as quiet.

—Ma? What about Mr. Stone? she asks, out of nowhere.

—What about him? you say, too curtly.

She falls silent, forgets you, forgets him, scampers forward. Ten minutes to the cemetery.

J. B. Stone is an idea. Nothing more. The idea of a man who would belong to you, and you to him. Someone to claim you. Someone you could call your own. If J. B. Stone stood before you right now, he would link arms with you and with Blue; he'd talk quietly, in a plainspoken way, eyes alive with interest. He would laugh out loud.

But Henry used to laugh sometimes too.

What would you say to J. B. Stone if he wanted to see more of you? How would you explain yourself, who you are, where you have spent your heart's blood? *I'm extricating myself.* Yes. You could say that. But if this is extrication, what does entanglement look like?

It was always and only Henry. Even now that it's not, it still is.

Marilyn

WOODEN STAKES PIERCE THE DUNES. The way north presents an obstacle course of leaning fences, fallen crosses, thistles and thorns.

Find Henry.

Catch your husband putting in the plants this year. He won't want to be caught. It will serve as the equivalent of him stumbling upon you doing something highly personal, like what happened last week.

He barged in while you were examining an itching mole on your left shoulder. You had unbuttoned your dress and pulled your arms out of the muttonchop sleeves. After yanking the material past your corset, nearly to the waist, you positioned yourself so you could study the worrisome spot in the mirror. Henry breezed in looking for his reading glasses. He took one look at your bare breasts in the mirror and walked out, closing the door behind him.

— I'll come back, he said. — Sorry.

— Wait, you said to the shutting door. You felt a whisper of cold air across your breasts. You almost said it twice. *Wait. Wait.* But pride shushed you. Henry feigned not hearing. Either that, or he really didn't hear. His footsteps faded as he retreated to the parlor. His eyeglasses stayed on the shelf.

You tried to return to inspecting the mole. You could hear him opening and shutting desk drawers, hunting for stationery, tapping the lid of his inkwell. He was unsettled. You looked at your breasts in the mirror. Used to be, they were quite something.

Ida has chewed her bottom lip raw.

—You ought to stop doing that, you tell her.—You'll tear the skin.

—I'm sorry.

—No need to say you're sorry. Do you think you can make it to the mariners?

—Yes, ma'am. Who are they?

Beneath the Maria Kip uniform, Ida's own breasts have started to develop. You notice such things out here in the middle of nowhere, notice them without wanting to notice, without trying, out here where no life exists except what a person brings in, what she carries. The girl's slim frame is regal and steady. Despite her physical challenges, she enjoys flawless posture. You could balance all of Luther's dogmatics on top of this girl's head and she wouldn't drop them; she wouldn't lose a page.

—The mariners are buried at the northern end of the cemetery. It's still a little ways away, you say.

—I can do it, she vows.

How? On her leg that doesn't work right? On stubbornness? On youthfulness? Yes.

You reach out a hand to steady her.

—I'm fine, she bleats, flinging out an arm to keep you away.

She's frustrated now; she caught that from you. And she's tough, tougher than Mrs. Wood knew. She'll leave that orphanage one day. She'll make it out, to work in a factory, most likely. A sewing shop. She has the hands. Look at them: long fingers. She won't marry. She'll slide into spinsterhood sewing pockets into trousers and seams into shirtwaists. She'll return to her boarding house each night to a cat and a cup of soup as outside her window, downtown streetlamps flicker on at sunset. That might not be the end of the world. It might not be bad at all.

She'll stay awake. She won't fall asleep to her life.

Two days ago you accidentally found a letter Henry had left in the far corner of the third drawer of his desk. You thought it was one of his updates to Penny, so you picked it up. You kept reading even after you realized he didn't intend it for your sister.

Dear One:

Let me try this again. What I try to say gets lost because we have an obligatory dance that I hope one day will disappear. Anything that gets said is a potential for misunderstanding because both of us are on edge. But perhaps time helps.

I recall your acknowledgment that you miss me, and my confirmation of that for myself about you. Somewhere I hope we will begin to relax to the point of just talking, and possibly even hearing each other. How I miss the conversation, the movement of you as you walk across the room, the warmth of your touch. You reprise the role of the one who is always alone, even as I sit saying that that is not really necessarily so. And so it winds up being a lot for a single conversation.

Did you tell him you missed him? You must have. You can't remember when, but you must have said it, or he wouldn't have written it down. Also, by saying *wait* during your self-inspection of that mole on your shoulder, you were admitting you missed him. Weren't you? Though not in so many words. By calling out to that closing door, you were saying, *Come back.*

Then again, he hasn't actually given you the letter. Maybe he's saving it for the right moment. Is he shy? No. Romantic? No. Reserved, preoccupied, occasionally pedantic? Yes. Did he write the letter for you? Or for someone else?

You looked up from the page.

You sat in silence. You studied your hands.

There were those petty-cash withdrawals. Those Wednesdays working late. But the lateness was regular. It never varied. For ten years. Like a metronome. Who has relations at the exact same time once a week for ten years? That's not an affair. That's a marriage.

Besides, only you understand this back-and-forth your husband's epistle described, this push-pull, this alone-and-not. Only you grasp how he can be both present and absent, how he stores up great paragraphs of fealty and ferocity only to shove those sentiments back in the desk drawer, unfinished.

The last part of his letter took your breath away.

*If I forgot to say how stunning your hair was, or your eyes, or the way you
walked across the room the last time I saw you, it was a simple sign of my
paralysis in the face of your presence. Of course, that is what I would have
said, had I been able to speak.*

Fourteen years have passed since you made love to Henry. Fourteen
years ago today, if you don't count the three attempts that landed you
at the hypnotist's doorstep. You hardly think of him as a man anymore.
He's more of a dining-room table: functional, load-bearing, requiring
sporadic cleaning, occasional upkeep. He's like Richard, needing to be
let out, needing affection (yes, you give Henry affection; no, he doesn't
recognize it as such), needing food, water, time outdoors. But you no
longer touch him.

That day of the white curtains was the last. Jack lay sleeping in the nursery next door.
    Henry kissed you under a canopy of bedding. His eyes held curiosity,
surprise, lust. You touched him, took him in hand; your fingers felt as
if they belonged to some other woman. He clutched your arms, slid on
top of you, rolled on top before you could think, before you could utter
a word. It was a relief. Him entering you was a relief.
    When he spent himself, it was like bands of rain pounding a harbor
in a storm. The outer bands arrived light and inconsequential, but the
squall at the center engulfed you both, like so much rain, you could not
see your hand in front of your face, like so much rain, you were sight-
less. When it was over you heard a lonesome sound like water dripping
off the eaves, only it was not rain you heard but Henry. Rarely does he
weep. He covered his face with his hands.
    You curled up against him, pressed your palms again his chest, drag-
ging the sheet with you.
    —Hush, you whispered, listening to his galloping heart.—Don't
cry.
    —I love you, he said.—I just love you.
    —Will you look in on Jack?
    —Yes, he said.—Yes. Absolutely.

And you both plummeted to sleep. Bliss knocked you both out.

Fifteen minutes later, light pouring through the window, burnishing the bedposts, you awoke and you knew. What had opened was closed. And there is punishment.

You sprang from the bed as if the sheets were boiling.

— *No,* you cried, swallowing your awareness. You gagged, fought the urge to regurgitate. The awareness fought back. You aspirated it. Awareness flooded your lungs, your chest cavity. You flew to the door, naked, abject, still gagging, sunshine grabbing your breasts, your legs, buttocks. Henry, startled awake, sat up, feverish, blinking.

— What? he said. — What? What happened? What's wrong?

He saw you; he apprehended the nightmare through you; he saw its silhouette. You moved by instinct. A mother knows. Something was wrong. The house was too still. You tugged at the door to the nursery. Henry leaped to join. The handle is old and it sticks. You pulled again, hair unbound, brushing the base of your spine, your nakedness exposed, breasts swaying, the wooden floor inert under your feet, the floor unearthly; you could not feel your toes.

— Move, Henry shouted, pushing you out of the way, taking on the door himself; he yanked at the handle; nothing. He attacked it again; still nothing.

— Goddamn it. He blew, stepped back, and threw his shoulder into it, trying to shock the hinges loose. He hurled himself into the wood. His shoulder would wear a bruise. The hinges squealed; the bedroom door sang open. He rocked back. You heard sounds coming from your mother's mouth. Wait, they were not coming from your mother's mouth, they were coming from your mouth — you and your mother had fused. Henry, recovering, staggered forward. By now you both knew. Before you saw the cradle, you grasped the truth. God must have told you. God riding His mule.

Your son choked on a button. Your son worked a red button off its thread, off his quilt, a brand-new blue-and-white quilt you had pieced together as a present for his second birthday and laid over him for the first time an hour before. That tiny button lodged itself in his windpipe while you and Henry lay milking each other in the next room, two beasts plagued with thirst. And then here came God, swaggering into the sunlight, saying:

—Here is your son, your offering. Fools.

Ida hobbles to the far side of the path. The trail curves toward one of the Chinese grounds. An abandoned tunic covers one of the graves, its sleeves flapping as the wind returns. Someone has come and gone and left behind a set of scraping tools.

Recently you read that the Chinese do not want the bones of women and children under the age of ten to be removed once they have been consigned to the earth. The discussion appeared within a *Call* article debating the cemetery's fate. You turned the page, but not before you had taken in the editorialist's ill-informed claim, his argument about ancient traditions unknown to him.

The Chinese believe a woman loses her identity and therefore her usefulness once she departs for the unknown, the writer maintained. And their tradition holds that a child's death is a punishment or affliction for some crime the parents committed. As a consequence, the unoffending babe is "hurriedly got rid of" immediately after death.

—The *Call* is no expert in anything other than good old-fashioned ignorance, Henry scoffed when you reported this information. But the description stayed with you.

After you read that letter from Henry, that letter he hasn't given you, the front door opened and shut; you heard him uttering something to Richard as the two of them shuffled into the kitchen. Your husband performs the same ritual daily. He stands before the stove, fills it with coke, lights it, puts water in the kettle, and sets it on the stove. He readies the percolator, scoops in grounds for coffee, and waits for the water to boil. He keeps vigil, slump-shouldered, fair hair falling into his eyes, the slightest hint of a potbelly protruding when his carriage is poor, his age showing in the hard light of late afternoon. He watches over that kettle until it sings, and then he pours the water into the percolator, retrieves two cups from the cupboard, and waits again. He excels at waiting. He can stand unmoving for fifteen minutes, fifteen years, if no one interrupts him.

You slipped the letter into the pocket of your skirt and ducked into the kitchen, where you rested your head against the door frame and watched him without speaking. The slope of your husband's shoulders affected you, pained your heart. His shoulders never used to slump. They used to be broad. They used to be thrown wide with music. They used to carry you.

You recalled his dogged good cheer, the way he insists, even now, at some personal cost, on the goodness of this life, a grace he continues to believe will spring forth, is springing forth.

You asked him about it. The words slipped out before you could stop them.

—From which desert? you said.

He turned from the stove. —What's that?

Normally you are not so opaque nor so desperate. But you wanted an answer to the question.

—From which desert do you believe that the goodness of life will spring forth, Henry?

He misunderstood. He wasn't listening. Or he was. —There are springs everywhere, he said. —Under Golden Gate Park there are sub-terranean springs. There's water all over the Outside Lands, if you know where to look. We could go on a walking tour. I could show you.

—I know where to look, you said, shaking your head. —And we live in the middle of a sand dune.

The kettle began to sing. He took it off the stove and let it sit. He needed you to understand his point of view.

—The dunes have water. Think about how much it rains, Marilyn. Rainwater drains from the highest hills westward and collects in the springs for us to use.

—Drains to where? you said. —And you're not answering the question.

Really, enough was enough. If you cannot see water, if no visible sign of water exists, then there should not be any water. Right? Your husband should stop claiming water's existence where there is none.

He left the kitchen to pull out a map of the Richmond from the bookshelf. Returning, he began trying to explain the topography to you.

—Since when did you start caring about rocks? you said.

—See here? Rainwater drains from the slopes of Lone Mountain, *here*. And from the heights of Mount Sutro. And the tallest point at Lands End, and Strawberry Hill, and the lake in the park. All of them drain to Lobos Creek and Mountain Lake — he jabbed at the spot — *here*. You've been there. We've been there together. Haven't we?

He lifted his eyes helplessly.

— I don't remember, you said, just as helplessly.

You might love him because of those shoulders, not because they are strapping and protective but because they once were and now are not. His shoulders and his hope both upend you.

— Mrs. Plageman? Ida asks. — Why is your husband in the cemetery?

— He's gardening. I told you.

You've already explained the plan to her. Everything repeats itself on May 22.

She nods, but she wants to know *why* he's gardening. Everyone wants to hear that tale. People want to know what happened. How he died. How Jack died. And if you grant them one morsel, they snatch for another. As soon as someone hears the Plagemans lost a child, their first question is always: How? People want the cause of death spelled out. They want to ensure the same misfortune will not strike their house. They want to imagine the death and feel better, smarter, luckier, whatever their God allows, that their family has not suffered the same fate, that their baby is safe at home batting a silver mobile over his head.

Their second question is always: How old?

And their third is: Who found him? By which they also mean: Whose fault?

Since that day, you have lost the capacity to make love to your husband. As soon as you sense Henry's hunger, less for sex than for touch, less for touch than for solace, and less for solace than for someone simply to stand beside him, facing the silence of years, whenever you sense that famishment, that loneliness, you remember Henry's buttocks shining in the Sunday-afternoon light, your husband's naked buttocks clenching as he bent and lifted his burden from the cradle, swung his burden in a sunlit circle, the child he had promised to check, promised and then forgot, walloped by sleep, and you remember him begging the heavens for help, saying, *Oh God, please don't let this be happening, please don't do this to us,* as if movement alone could heal, as if all any of us requires in the end is a whirl, a whorl, a push of love, and we will reanimate, resuscitate; we will claim that promise that says God knows His plans for us; God wants to look kindly on us in our latter end.

Henry was a pastor. Do you see your dilemma now? He was a pastor. He has since quit. But his eyes stay old.

Henry

THIS QUADRANT OF THE CEMETERY is so dry that the rain can't dampen the ground for long. The wind electrifies the sand. It moves. It's alive. It twines around Bess's legs, tendrils snaking, caking the back of your trousers. It streams up the footpath, curves north. Welcome to San Francisco, where those beneath the earth remain as segregated as those who walk on land.

You can recite the names of the associations that will be affected by the closing: *Improved Order of Red Men. Christian Chinese Society. Slavonic Mutual Benevolent Society. Greek Russian Slavonian Benevolent Society.*

The poorest of the poor lie scattered in every direction, mounds of the indigent on all sides, crammed in corners. Sand travels through hollows and dead grasses.

German Benevolent Society. Scandinavian Society. French Benevolent Society. Congregation Schaarai Zedek. Italian Benevolent Society.

Bess lightly leans against your shoulder, eyes closed. She does not like gusting sand.

A voice calls out to Kerr. The voice is yours.

—Get me a plant, will you?

A verse from the Old Testament springs to mind. *For I know the thoughts that I think toward you,* said the Lord to Jeremiah, the weeping prophet. *Thoughts of peace and not of evil, to give you hope in your latter end.* But look how Jeremiah's life turned out.

Bess pauses in the middle of the path, encircled by graves. She nibbles at your collar. You repeat your request.

Kerr leaves her other side and returns to the driver's box, where he
retrieves one of the lilies. He returns and sets the plant in its small pot
on the ground at your feet. He crosses his arms and waits. Bess, too, observes with equanimity.

Your throat is dry as you reach for the plant.

— Now I need the trowel.

The foreman nods and makes his way to the rear of the hearse, leaving the shovel untouched. He retrieves the trowel and hands it silently
to you. Overhead fly two brown pelicans. You're holding Bess's halter
with your free hand.

*Congregation Beth Israel. St. Andrew's Society and Caledonian Club.
Qui Son Tong Company. Hop Wo Association. Ning Yung Association.*

— What are you doing? he asks. — This isn't the right place. These
are the paupers. This isn't your son's burial ground.

How does he know where you are buried? Where Jack is buried? The
skin is but one organ; the earth is but one surface. A man can exsangui-
nate from a single cut in the base of his foot. You can plant a lily here
amid the unnamed. Who says a man should mourn only the ones who
belonged to him? Are you not permitted to mourn the ones who didn't
belong to you, to grieve the lives you missed? What else did you bury
Jack here for, if not this?

— Plageman. Henry. Look. You're not doing anyone any good here.
My friend, this isn't why we came.

The day is tilting off its axis. Kerr's starting to grasp this fact.

You release Bess and he snatches her halter. You cross to the closest
of the paupers' graves. You set the plant down, reach for the trowel, and
dig. Penniless grit swirls in your face.

Don't hit anything. Don't dig too deep. Dig wide. Always dig twice as
wide as you think the roots need.

That's the last lesson.

You pull the lily from its clay pot and nestle it in the hole. You cup
the sand and pour it back in. It flies up. More flies up then down. The
grains dance.

— Water, you call out. — I need water.

Kerr finds the water jug in the rear of the hearse and brings it over.
Bess looks on impassively. You take a swig. That's better. You pour some

into the soil. It glugs into the sand, the plant greedily absorbing. You toggle the plant until it's firmly in place. It tilts. Retilt it. Tip it right. Get those roots in. One grave down, a thousand to go. You're planting memorials at the wrong end of the cemetery, memorializing the wrong child, the wrong family, the wrong tribe and nation.

Is this the right thing to be doing? Not sure; keep going.

What about Blue? Don't think about her. Don't think about how much you loved her. The thought of Blue is absolutely unbearable.

—Get me another, you command, coughing, your throat shuttered. You sound like Kerr now; that's what they say an hour in the city cemetery will accomplish.

Chuc Sen Tong Company. Ladies' Seamen's Friend Society. Societa Cosmopolita Italiana d'Mutua Beneficenza. Grand Army of the Republic. Knights of Pythias. Society of Old Friends.

Maybe that last one is where you and Lucy belong. Maybe that's where you'll wind up one day, if you're fortunate: the Society of Old Friends.

Maybe all this straining and striving and coming apart boils down to friendship. She is your friend. Your only friend, if you're honest, if by *friend* you mean someone from whom you do not have to hide your true life. If that is the definition of *friendship*, if that is the requirement, then yes, you possess one; and you will never have more than one, because even if you stop seeing her, even though you *have* stopped seeing her, even though she has stoppered up her heart with a precision and savagery you do not possess, you will not share the truth, these past ten years, with anyone. You will box the tale up, lock it away, secure it underground, beneath those wretched water pipes she's always writing about. You'll remain standing long after that box is buried. You'll endure as half a man, half a person.

It's not that unusual.

You plant four more lilies in the wrong place before Kerr takes you by the arm and forces you to your feet.

—Enough, he says, and points down the path.—Plageman, someone's coming.

A woman.

Marilyn

IDA PUSHES HER BRAIDS back from her face.

— Are we heading the right way, Mrs. Plageman?

— Of course.

Maps are not required in the city cemetery. Familiarity with subterranean springs is not required. You've been here enough times.

You lean into the wind. It pushes against your chest. You're climbing uphill, rounding the second Chinese field, nearing one of the paupers' enclaves.

There is still the letter to consider. Yes, you still have that letter. Did Henry intend it for you?

You'll find out when you see him. You'll read it in his expression. You'll know the truth within the first five seconds.

— Mrs. Plageman. Look!

Ida points.

There, up ahead, near the crest of the hill, crouches the man himself, your husband, aswim in a sea of beggars' graves. There he is, and an old man and a vile hearse besides.

He's on his knees, tugging a plant from a pot. A trowel and a water jug flank him. Wilting calla lilies surround him. Yes, that's your Henry, marooned in the wrong burial ground, digging the wrong memorial. Planting in the wrong place.

You leave Ida and start running.

2:00 p.m.

Henry

NEVER BEFORE HAVE YOU SEEN your wife run. With one hand, she steadies the merle topping her hat; with the other, she clutches her skirts.

A girl trails behind, clad in a cheap frock and pinafore, courtesy of the grand new Maria Kip. The headmistress forces those girls to wear those uniforms to deliver a lesson, telling them to be grateful, reminding the children that were it not for charity, for the wealthy, they would be homeless. But gratitude is not grace.

Lilies tipping from clay pots encircle the nearest graves. The four you've planted raise their thin heads high. Their leaves droop from the shock of transplant.

You haven't made it to the mariners, haven't reached Jack yet. Marilyn will ask what in God's name you're doing, allowing yourself to be sidetracked. The words are forming; the question's bubbling; it's a matter of seconds; she's within chastising distance. Her eyes reflect the gilded light. She's lovely, flushed; running has stolen her breath.

You set the trowel aside and rise to meet her. You're a mess; wiping your hands on your trousers only makes things worse. You're filthy, covered with grime, a catastrophe.

Behind Bess, as he leans against the side of the hearse, Kerr relights his pipe, asks:

—That the missus?

She's nearly upon you.

You nod. Don't answer Kerr; don't answer Marilyn. Don't answer anyone, not today, not anymore. You don't have any more explanations to distribute. You're out of stock. Best to dig a trench and crawl in it; burrow into the earth's magma. Or maybe sleep. There's a thought. Sleep for a day, or two, or a year. You haven't slept soundly, truly soundly, in fourteen years, if you're honest. You've worn yourself out, worn your life out, shuffling between worlds, between cottages, learning two vocabularies, two dialects, two histories, a bifurcation of your own making, all because you could not find a way to release Lucy. Or Blue. Or Marilyn. Or Jack. What kind of man says: *I am enough for two women. I can juggle. I can satisfy both.* Is that what you said? No. Did you ever say it? Possibly the first ten seconds. And now? You can't satisfy one woman, let alone two. Both Marilyn and Lucy have assessed your capacities and found you wanting.

Marilyn weaves through the half-buried headstones and the footboards that have reverted to driftwood. Her dark hair tips her head back with its weight. As she crosses the sand, she looks straight at you.

Behind her, the orphan girl stops at the gate and wrinkles her nose, inhaling incense and smoke from the Chinese burial grounds. The girl's eyes hold fear. Tunics flap and snap in the wind, tunics held to those faraway graves with stones, like pale birds pinned under detritus after a storm.

— Henry, Marilyn says. — You're planting in the wrong place.

Blue

— WALK WITH ME, Ma says. — Don't race so far ahead.

— It's not my fault you're slow, I say.

— Listen to me. Blue, I need to explain something before we reach your father. I need to tell you something.

We're making a beeline for the turnoff to the cemetery, which is where Pa takes me to play. Or where he used to take me. Hardly anything but loons and gulls live this far west.

— Where is he? I ask. — Where's Pa?

— A little farther. We'll reach him in a few minutes. Sweetheart, you can't listen when your back is to me. Come here.

— You told me to hurry. You told me to walk as fast as I can. I'm obeying!

— And now I'm telling you to slow down. I'm only asking once.

Actually, this makes twice. I stomp to a halt. Sand has found its way into my cowboy chaps. I put my hands on my hips, just the way Ma's doing. My hat slides off; it's still too big. Her eyes rake over me.

— What's wrong now? she asks as she stoops to pick up my hat.

— Nothing. You told me to walk fast.

— You know what I mean. Something upset you back at the cottage while I was outside. What?

— Nothing! My bandages are hurting.

— Give it time, pumpkin.

— Don't call me pumpkin!

I snatch the hat from her hands and beat it against my leg in the exact way a real cowboy would do. I start walking again. We're close. I can almost see the cemetery entrance.

—Hold on, Ma says, and she comes up to me, wraps her arms around me, hugs me hard.—Sweetheart. Blue. I know today has been a hard day.

Her eyes meet mine.

—It's okay. I shrug, a little shy.—It's been a hard day for you too.

A heron perches on a dead branch up the street. Its head swivels to listen to me. Its unblinking eyes look into mine. It's begging to be chased.

I'll race you, I think. *I'll race you to the entrance.* I leave Ma and sprint ahead toward the cemetery. The heron soars up, wings beating.

Lucy

YOU'VE PROVEN YOU CAN GIVE HIM UP. You've done it every day for almost four months.

And here you are now, hurtling up the path after him.

A few weeks ago Blue asked you for a photograph, a picture of her mother she could keep for herself after you're gone.

— I'm never gone, you told her.

She wouldn't meet your gaze. — Pa's gone.

— He still visits.

— Hardly ever. And not with you.

— Well, you don't have to worry about me going anywhere, you told her. — You're stuck with me. We're a twosome. We're glued at the hip until you peel away from me someday.

Suddenly you thought of your own mother, what she must have felt years ago, watching her only child, her daughter, walking as fast as her legs would take her to that train station, focused on only one thing: getting away.

— I still want a picture, Blue said.

— Well, I don't have one right now. I'll have to have one taken.

But you do have a picture. It lives in the box under your bed.

Worse than looking at your own tintype is looking at Henry's. You can't bear it now; how will you manage when you're old, when you're older than Henry is today? You don't want to rediscover his face years hence and realize he was still young when all this time he has seemed so old.

None of the things you'd actually *want* in a memento box can be put in it. His walk. You'd like to box that. Or his hands. Henry's veined hands turning the page of your geology book by lamplight. Hooking the back of your dress. Or unhooking. Massaging the nape of your neck. Who is going to rub the back of your neck when you are old?

Blue darts into a ray of sunshine. Light whitens the sand leading into the cemetery. As the rain has peeled back, fog and sun are taking turns.

More than once you've run into a drunkard here in the Outside Lands, some stinking soul staggering through the hinterland, whiskers rancid with spat tobacco. To the north sprawls a corner of cemetery property the U.S. government annexed. Officials went ahead and took a chunk of that land, tore it off with federal teeth. They have built nothing on it. But it's theirs if they want it. The first human need might be possession.

Two months ago you took Blue to see loggers in one of the great redwood forests. Paired men in plaid shirts worked with a whipsaw to take down giants in the Santa Cruz Mountains. One logger pushed. The other pulled. Then they changed roles. They toppled the redwood; they took it down near the base of the trunk.

This is Henry too: felled by a two-handled saw. It's not a contest between love and duty. It's between love and love, between duty and duty. Together you and Marilyn have nearly sawed him through.

Someone has abandoned a pitchfork on the side of the road.

Unbidden, you recall J. B. Stone, with his red hair, his overalls, his alert, searching expression. He wanted to protect you. He meant well. He's too young to comprehend the true dangers.

Maybe you are too.

What does *J. B.* stand for? Hopefully his Christian name is John. That's a fine name. James would be nice as well. He mentioned his father's name was Jimmy. J. B. Stone knows nothing about you, not a scrap of your history. He thinks you're free; he assumes a woman of the Outside Lands can come and go almost as she chooses.

Blue sprints ahead, chasing a heron to the cemetery entrance. The great long-necked bird starts up, agitated, its rest disturbed.

Age should not be measured in years, should not be measured in time. Age is an epistemological quality. We are as old as we know.

Henry

AND NOW YOUR WIFE IS UPON YOU.

The skin above Marilyn's lip shines with perspiration. She reaches out and plants her right palm on your chest. She never does that. She never just comes out and touches you.

Her hand remains.

She presses your heart as if measuring the anatomic distance between souls. This close, you can smell a hint of sickness, combined with the rosewater she splashed on herself after she rose from her bed this morning alone.

She stands before you. Her eyes hold a question.

—You're here, she murmurs.

—I'm here, you say.

Her fingers sear through your shirt. Gently you remove her hand from your chest and return her arm to her side, where it belongs.

She turns her head. Recoils as if struck. The wind stills.

What have you done? You removed her hand. It burned. It burned, and you wanted to keep planting. You wanted to stay in the day, to return these plants to the earth. To focus on what still has a chance of taking root.

She steps away. She appraises the lilies, considering one plant, then another. Inspecting their fragile petals allows her to avoid your eyes.

—You're planting in the wrong place, Henry, she says again.

She speaks as if you have lost your hearing and not just your reason. Her voice is stony.

—This is the wrong graveyard. This isn't Jack's corner.

You start to speak, but she raises a hand and cuts you off.

—Please don't.

She surveys the perimeter. She paces. She surveys the beggars' graves, the numbered footboards, shards of pots, the stray vessels and glass beads left by visitors or forgotten by vagrants who needed a place to stay, a moment of safety. She's so intent on her analysis she doesn't see Kerr and bumps into him.

He doffs his hat, steadying her, before stepping aside with a gentlemanly bow. Bess whinnies.

—Ma'am, he says, casting a glance your way. He's well aware of the storms wives bring.—Thomas Kerr at your service.

—Mr. Kerr. My husband thinks the graves of strangers require the full sum of his attention. What do you say?

He glances from Marilyn to you and back again. This is not his argument, not his marriage.

—He's tired, you say.—You want to quarrel, do it with me.

—This isn't a quarrel. If I wanted to quarrel, you would know it, Henry.

Let her have her say. Let her castigate. You removed her hand. You declined her overture. It's not often she reaches out. She never reaches out. Not that way. Not in fourteen years. What were you thinking? She laid her hand on you. She offered, and you declined. You didn't think. You reacted. Or didn't react.

That's the real truth, isn't it? Your body didn't respond. Your body politely declined. You and your body together have lost the will to keep trying.

But be grateful for what you're allowed.

And if a fourteen-year gap occurs between the last time your wife placed her hand on your chest and now, so be it. You're the husband. You're supposed to be patient. To be present. To wait. Waiting's your job. You are not very good at it. You didn't wait long enough. You surrendered after four years, after drying to kindling. All it took was a match.

Marilyn treads in a circle, the hem of her skirt trailing in sand. She threads her way through the graves.

—Why did you come here? she asks.—This land isn't ours.

—But that's the point. That was the whole point, you say.—Remember?

—The point of what?

She shakes her head. She doesn't want to hear your answer, your philosophies. Not today. This is your wife: a woman who will sprint in your direction so fast she practically knocks over an orphan, only to balk once she's within forgiving distance. Unlike you, Marilyn can travel in reverse. It might be her preferred direction.

—This land isn't ours, she says again.

—It never was, you say.—Not even the garden.

You shouldn't have said it like that. The words just popped out. She glances at you, squints into the amber light.

—What? What are you implying?

—Plageman . . . Kerr warns.

She hears something in the foreman's voice.

—What? What is it?

—Marilyn, it's all right.

You reach for her hands and hold them. You take back the hand you released a moment before. She shakes her head, wants to pull away. You hold on.

—Marilyn, listen to me.

She wrenches away. She is beginning to comprehend. She hears in your voice the outcome of this long neighborhood contest, this failed fight.

—Listen to me, please, you say again.—We can fight to keep him here. We will keep trying.

—No. Don't! I don't want to hear it. I don't want to hear another word.

—Shh, you say and pull her close. She resists, twisting away, and in the process she delivers an elbow to your gut, unintended, maybe, but hard enough you double over. Kerr masks a sympathetic groan with a cough.

—Let go of me, Henry, she says, even though you're no longer holding her.

You straighten.—You have to understand. Please, Marilyn. We spent last night locked in the park station.

Her face is ashen. — I told you to handle the cemeteries. You said you would take care of it. That's all I asked. I asked you for one thing only. I let you do everything else you want.

She takes a breath; she's not finished.

— I never asked you any questions, Henry. I never asked you for a single thing. All these years. Only this. So don't say it. Don't say anything. Don't even try.

She swipes at her eyes, adds:

— You don't deserve it.

She knows.

Almost four months ago, Lucy wrote and asked you to stay away from her, to take care of things at home. To mend what you could. Did you obey? Yes to staying away from her. No to taking care of things at home. No to mending what you could.

— Marilyn, you say. — Hear me. Please. I need to explain what happened. While Kerr and I were locked up, Hubbs had the Richmond group take a vote.

She shakes her head. — What did I —

— They voted without us. We tried. We did everything we could do. But they voted to shut this place down.

Kerr nods.

Her fists press against her mouth, grinding into her lips.

— They're going to move him. They'll move our Jack?

— Yes, you say.

— They're going to dig him up?

She sags. Her knees find the sand first, and the rest of her follows. You step forward, but she motions you back. She's about to be sick. The skin under her jaw, visible as she heaves, as her spine spasms and her stomach expels nothing, has begun to show the slackness of middle age.

Kerr claps a hand on your back.

— Tell her, he rasps. — Plageman, tell her the plan.

Bring him back up? You will not; you cannot; you must. Otherwise some other man will put a hand on him. Whoever digs up a child should know that child's name. That ought to be in the Bible.

You look up at the sky and search for a single sign of life in the firmament.

Kerr returns his pipe to his mouth and steps back as you crouch next to her. Kneeling on the sand, you're side by side, heads bowed, as if facing an altar. Her mouth is slightly parted.

— When? she breathes.

— We don't know. He might not be moved for a while. Or it could happen soon. It's up to the supervisors.

— But it's coming.

— Yes.

— Mr. Kerr, she calls out. — Is it coming?

She does not lift her head to look at the foreman.

— Yes, ma'am, he calls back. — I am truly sorry to say.

Think of something else, and you might make it through this day. Shut your eyes. What will you see? A wooden box. It will hold nothing but rest within.

Lucy asked you to stay away. She asked you to give her up. You did what she asked. But you would have liked the chance to say goodbye to her.

Here, then, is your duty. It's in the ground. Your duty is to dig. This is the day that the Lord hath made. Let us rejoice and be glad. Go ahead. Choke on it, Henry Plageman. Choke on the gifts of the day.

Blue

THESE BUSHES ARE REACHING OUT with their sharp arms to grab me and my costume. Ma pushes a branch out of my way. It snags her sleeve and tears it.

I stop along the path to free her.

—Hold on, Mama, I say.

We're passing one of the burial grounds for people with no families. She nods but stays quiet. Her calm way fills me with pride. I can't talk about it. But my heart feels what I mean. And my bandaged ear won't quit throbbing.

When Pa comes over—when he used to come over—the time for talking always went by too fast. There was never enough time to tell him what was on my mind. He'd listen until his ears gave out, and then he'd put me to bed. Next it became Ma's turn to tell him everything she was thinking about. One time I peeked around the door and spied them sitting side by side at the table. Ma was all talked out. They weren't saying a word. They just sat there next to each other, holding hands and staying quiet. Ma's head was resting on his shoulder.

The trail has come to a fork. Ma stops and looks at me.

—There's something I have to tell you, she says.—I need to tell you before we reach the mariners. Before you see your pa.

There's something she needs to tell me, or there's something I need to hear? There's a difference. I think I'd rather not hear whatever she wants to say. Not with that scrunched-up face she's wearing.

—Remember a few months ago, she says, the day you walked with me across the estate to mail a letter? I promised then I would explain everything to you.

—My ear hurts, I fling back and keep walking. Overhead four gulls fly, racing to reach the highest dune.

—Sweetheart, this is important. It's about your father. It's about why you can't see him as much as you'd like. It's about why he doesn't live with us. I need you to listen to me.

She catches me by the shoulder and crouches, so the two of us are at eye level.

—Please hear me out.

—Don't talk to me. I want to see Pa!

—We're about to see him. We'll be with him in just a minute. That's why I need to—

—I don't want any more stories, Mama. Stop it. My ear's hurting!

She reaches out to take my hand. I pull away. She grabs me a second time, clamps my wrist with her cold fingers. She's trying to trap me. I pull back, hard. Her eyes are bigger and sadder than I've ever seen them.

—Today would have been Jack Plageman's sixteenth birthday, Blue.

—Whose birthday?

—A boy named Jack. The boy in the story I need to tell you.

—No. No, that makes my ear hurt. I want Pa!

—This is about Pa. I need you to understand whom he's visiting.

—I'm not feeling well. I may be sick.

—*Might.* You *might* be sick.

—Ma!

She squints at me. It is not a nice squint.—You'll feel a lot worse if you don't listen when I tell you to.

—Stop that. You're hurting me!

She pumps my arm.

—Why don't you ever do what I ask? she splutters.

She's making a wreck of this day, and she knows it. But she can't stop herself; she can't push her wheels out of that ditch. Too late. She pumps my arm again. This time it hurts.

I cry out and plunk myself down in the middle of the footpath. I won't say another word. That'll show her. I'll be a rock. A boulder. Good luck now, Mother.

—Blue? she says. Her voice sounds like someone else's. —The boy Jack. It's his grave your father's going to see. Jack was your half brother.

Henry

HERE'S WHAT SURVIVES: The tides. The spiked yerba buena, once used as a tonic for good health. The coast aster, thought capable of charming away evil. The seaside daisy, whose Greek name means "old man in the spring."

The ghosts of the Ohlone people endure too, specters chasing game along the footpaths. Elsewhere along the bay, the Ohlone shell mounds constitute the original cemeteries of San Francisco.

Marilyn watches the path that leads to the mariners. You and Kerr stand on either side, flanking her.

— Move him, she says, addressing you.

Over her head, Kerr glances your way.

She continues. — I said, move him. Move our son. Do it, Henry. That's what you're planning anyway, isn't it? That's what you were going to suggest. So go and do it. Move him before they tear this place to shreds. Before they turn this godforsaken place inside out.

— Ma'am? Kerr says. — We don't have to take on anything today —

She turns. Her voice rises, hard as glass, and as shattered:

— You drove a hearse here, Mr. Kerr, didn't you? It appears my husband finally thought a plan through. And Henry, you brought a shovel, I presume?

You nod, feeling as if you've committed a crime. Her eyes return to you. Those eyes convey an entreaty, a gasping need.

But she will never just say it. She will never just come out and say it.

— Then that's just fine, she finally says. — That's fine, both of you. Move him. Do it. Do what you came here to do.

Kerr vigorously nods.

—That's exactly it. That's exactly what I suggested to your husband. Do it first. Do it ourselves. Don't let the city get anywhere near your poor boy. Beat them at their game.

She raises her eyebrows.—This isn't a game, Mr. Kerr.

Is she awake? Yes. Is it the awakening you wanted, you once begged her to claim? No. But a man doesn't get to choose.

Kerr, humbled, says:

—We'll find a place for him at Odd Fellows'. I can promise you, Mrs. Plageman. It's not this view. But it's still the Richmond. Still the Outside Lands.

—You think that helps me?

A clogged gasp, a half laugh, escapes her. She turns her back to you, bows her head, and prays silently. Her Catholic sensibilities are rising up, demanding their place, telling her the only thing left to do is pray to a woman, to a mother. There are no other gods left for her.

You shouldn't have told her. But what you said was so much less than what you could have said, what you ought to say, what you are overdue to tell her. What you said was hardly anything, if one takes the long view.

That might be the only view you can bear.

The orphan has crossed the gate and stands ready to lend her aid, a sentry at her post. She catches your eye and briefly lifts her chin. She will not reside long at Maria Kip. That much you can ascertain without her uttering a word. This girl will take the next step of life on her own.

Marilyn twists around so she faces you. She raises her eyes to yours and nods slightly. She'll allow you to gather her in now, for the briefest of moments; she'll permit you to enfold her in the tree of mourning— the union she knows.

She's stiff; her joints are showing signs of arthritis. You tuck a stray hair behind her ear. She's starting to silver at the temples. Paupers' graves surround you both.

—Marilyn.

—Don't, she whispers, and closes her eyes.—Henry. Just don't.

There are children laid to rest all over this cemetery. She could be kneeling on one now.

— Sweetheart.

You fold her into your arms; slowly her body slackens against your chest.

— It's time.

— I know what time it is, she cries.

— Let's go wish him happy birthday, you say, embracing her as tight as you can, as close as your lives will allow. Kerr looks away as she forcefully sinks against you. She sobs. Her head crushes your shoulder. This is parenthood pared to the bone.

— Maybe he'll be relieved, you say into her ear. — Maybe we've started to embarrass him, living so close, living just up the street.

You kiss her hair, her forehead. You taste old grains, filaments from the sea, and briefly the vault of memory opens: Marilyn, young, in her yellow dressing gown, hair falling to her waist, smiling as you entered the nursery, her finger to her mouth signaling *shh* as she rocked your newborn son in her arms.

— He would be turning sixteen, you whisper. — And you know what that means.

— What? she whispers back, barely audible.

— It's the age when a young man wants to see less of his parents.

And then you can't say any more. Your lips brush the top of her head.

Kerr's unable to keep his pipe lit, it seems; his shoulders shake. He tries one match, tries another, keeps his back to you both.

— You were supposed to take care of him, Marilyn says, her voice muffled. — You were supposed to protect him.

— I know, you say. — I will carry it always.

You take her arm, rise, and help her to the hearse.

2:30 p.m.

Blue

WHAT SHE SAID DOESN'T MAKE SENSE. What would half a brother look like?

—Wait for me, I tell her.—I need to use the toilet.

I don't have to go too badly. But I need to get away from her. I need to think.

—Use the bushes. Ma tersely points.—Watch out for poison oak. And hurry.

I hike up a hill of sand. Scrub brush and sage cover these dunes. I choose my hiding place, squat in a thicket, and pull down my cowboy trousers. The branches scratch my hindquarters.

While I'm relieving myself, I look up. Past the sage, the graves spread wide. From here I can see clear to the Golden Gate. The water is emerald and swirls. The moving air fills my lungs. It tickles the weeds over the graves. A gull swoops low over the headstones. Far away, almost falling off the horizon, a steamer with a black-and-white smokestack churns toward its landing.

I love this place. I will love it my whole life.

And there he is. Finally! I see him. There is my papa.

I stand and pull up my trousers. Pushing past the sage, I stare as hard as I can. Yes. That's him. That's definitely Pa. Though he's far away, and he looks thinner and more rumpled than the last time I saw him.

He's stepping down from a black coach, the same coach I saw back his store. He stands with his hands behind his back. The graves arou him are tacked with sailcloth. The canvases snap and flap. Those must be the mariners he told me about. Seamen buried under blankets of sails.

He walks around to the rear of the coach and pulls something out of the back. It's a shovel. He's about to dig in the sand. What else would those tools be for? Wait. He's not alone. I should have seen that before. Three people are climbing down from the coach after him. They had only one horse to pull them, one old gray mare, the same one I wanted to pet earlier. She's too old to pull three people at once.

Pa crosses over to a stone angel that's standing in the sand. He crouches beside the angel and looks at it. Probably he wishes the other people around him would go away. He and I have something in common today. We'd rather be left alone.

An old man with a scraggly beard has stepped down from the coach and lights a pipe. A tall girl in a uniform steps down after him. She sticks close to the mare. She speaks in her ear. The mare lowers her head to listen. The girl is older than me. Whatever she's saying is for the horse and only the horse, whose head drops low. She must be thirsty. The girl better water her.

The last passenger is a woman. She's the same lady who rode the streetcar on the way home. So is the girl, now that I see the two of them together. The woman takes the longest to leave the coach. She has black hair. She's pretty. She's presentable. She looks like a newspaper advertisement for a tonic promising a women's cure.

She faces the strait. She stands apart from the others and stares very hard at that water. Her hair must be so long. Ma's never grows that long.

Pa scoops up sand. He's crouching down. He weighs and tests the sand. He says something, but the woman doesn't say anything back. He's talking to himself now.

He places a hand on the head of the angel. He tries to lift the angel. It must be heavy. It doesn't want to be pried up. I bet it weighs more than the pretend statues in Mr. Sutro's gardens. This one's real.

He tries again. He tips up one corner, but the other side stays in the sand.

The old man with the beard walks over to him. Together they bring the angel. They tear the stone up from the ground, up from clods of

sand and dirt. They're making a mess. Ma would have a fit if I were doing that. Pa carries the statue over to the hearse. He comes back and his
hands are empty.

I look behind me. Ma's twenty feet down the dune's other side; she's
still waiting for me to finish my business. Half of me wants to return to
her. The other half of me wants to help Pa. Which half should win? Pa
needs me more. But Ma has the temper.

Pa's in trouble. How, I can't quite figure. I need more information.
That's the answer. Now's the time. The sheriff is on the move.

Pushing aside the branches, I call for him through the brush.

—Ostrich?

The clouds have rolled back, and so has the fog; the sun clobbers my
eyes.

—Ostrich!

Another gull beats its wings and flies up, annoyed with me, startled
high. A garter snake shoots through the bushes. Every living creature on
this dune hears me. Everyone except my father.

But my mother hears. My mother is coming.

She breathes up behind me. She slips and crashes through the brush.
She pushes through the thicket. Now she can see what I see. She can see
all the way to the strait. And to Pa.

I skip toward the far side of the dune. Away from her, toward him.
Toward the clearing.

—No, Ma breathes. —No. No. No. We're too late.

She moves. She sprints. She's fast. Faster than she's been all day. Her
talons reach out and grab my neck. She's dragging me back, jerking me
away from that side of the dune. She's not about to free me. Not about
to let me take a single step in Pa's direction. Her nails sink deep into my
arm.

—No, she says again. —Don't. Blue. Don't do this.

—Let go!

I reel backward. She's jabbing at me on all sides, pecking at me until
I lose my footing. She snatches me from behind. She's trying to hide me
away. To take me back to her side of the dune.

—No, she says again. —No. We're too late. She's already here. I cannot do this.

But she already did. Didn't she? Yes. She started this stone rolling. She pushed it down the hill. She wanted to see him. She wanted him to see me. She wanted us to be together again. All three.

—Let me go, I bellow, pushing her away.—Ostrich!

I break for the clearing.

Lucy

STOP RUNNING, CHILD. Stop racing toward the open. Don't make the mistake of thinking the open is something you deserve.

Sailcloth ripples over the headstones. She flies toward the mariners, her spurs sparkling in the sunlight. She darts around scrub brush. She dodges sage. That cowboy hat keeps falling into her eyes. It'll be her downfall.

And there he is. There is your Henry. And there is Marilyn.

You're too late. What were you thinking? How long did you think you could let the world slide?

Marilyn landed here first, with history behind her. History filled her sails. And you arrived second. You showed up too early for your life and too late for Henry's.

He stands before Jack's grave. Marilyn observes the moving waters of the strait. He grips a shovel. He is gardener, caretaker, gravedigger. She is overseer, landlord, owner. She owns him. She owns this day; she is legitimate. She wears his name by law, by sacrament. She has earned her place at his side through fidelity, childbirth, a quantity of sorrow. But so have you.

Two truths can subsist together. Two loves can too. Your daughter will succeed where you have failed. She will reach the clearing.

Blue doesn't need you to tell her the truth, to spring some revelation on her. She *is* the truth. She is the story her parents don't want to tell. She is your second person.

———

Marilyn faces the water. The curve of her waist and hips, the hint of sway beneath her gown, compels your stare, your admiration, this grand dame who daily claims Henry, who nightly takes him for granted, who listens to him scrubbing his teeth before he sleeps. She is beautiful. Not even for her age. Just beautiful. She moves modestly, with grace; she conserves her movements. She's not the kind of woman who trips over a Raggedy Ann doll while reaching for a whiskey bottle. Not the kind of woman who takes a ten-year detour into another woman's husband.

Blue, throwing a glance back at you, sticks out her tongue. She's taunting you now; she's slippery, faster than you, even with her bandages, and she knows it. You race forward, grab for her collar, trying to avoid her ear, trying to avoid inflicting more damage.

—Get back here, you snap.

She sprints away. You chase again, hitching up your skirts.

When you and Henry disagree, Marilyn catches the tail end of your quarrel. She receives your ambivalence, your loneliness, filtered by way of Henry. She hands them back to you through him as resignation, detachment—all that goes unspoken. Henry is the carrier, the broker, the go-between. The real marriage, the real affair in this tale, is between you and Marilyn.

Only you're not dueling over a man. Henry is the stand-in. For what?

Autonomy. A key to unlock the right door.

Marilyn will notice Blue any moment. All she needs to do is turn.

Knowing what you do now, would you do it all over again? No. But you still love him.

Henry's within range, a straight shot down a slope of pocked sand.

—Ostrich!

He doesn't hear his child. He hears the wind. He hears the day.

Marilyn paces, her eyes fixed on the waters. Henry gestures, calls out something to her, you can't hear what. She doesn't respond. She won the right to ignore him. She inherited that right when Jack passed. And you solidified it. You polished and hung that right for her, turned it into a looking glass.

You seize Blue's sleeve. Her cowboy hat slides off yet again. Let it go. She heaves away, pulling out of your arms a final time, darts across the 's flank. She flings out her arms as Pacific loons waltz overhead on their way to the strait. You feign a left and lunge right. At last you have her. Barely, but you have her.

She writhes and screws up her face; you have her by the arms.

—Let me go, she says, seething.—I want Ostrich.

Yes, child, this is a tale of birds. Blue is a sparrow. Marilyn is a crow, a raven. Glittering, black-haired, she will never relinquish him.

And you; what are you? That juvenile horned owl back on the taxidermist's table, molting as if its life depended on it.

He hears Blue calling. He looks up; the shovel slips from his hand. He loosens his tie. He's haggard, out of breath. His neck's damp, no doubt, where he always used to sweat, right there, that smoothness at the base of his throat. That hollow in the flesh.

Dig your nails into Blue's shoulders. Stop her from feeling. Every woman has to learn that skill some time. Does Henry love his daughter? Yes. Of course. But love can take one hundred different forms. Blue rescuing her snails is love. J. B. Stone paying for your hospital bill might be love also. A different form. But still. Something shines through.

Blue escapes your arms a final time. She surges free.

—You wanted to take me to the cemetery, she says, black with fury.

—Blue—

—You wanted me to see my father. And now I will see him. You are not allowed to change the plan midcourse!

She dashes for the open, flies down the dune's rim, between hollows of sand. She spouts joy, a plume of it.

—Ostrich! she calls.—Ostrich, wait till you hear what happened to me. I fell into a well and it tried to swallow me!

He turns toward her. At last he sees. She will tell him everything he has missed. She's fifty yards out when she stumbles.

Blue

I'M CLOSING IN ON PA when a broken fence post trips me. It's hiding in the sand and shows up out of nowhere. I'm running down the dune so fast I can't avoid it, a wooden spike with nasty splinters. I fly forward. Most of me makes a safe landing in sand, but my hand smacks the top of the post. Two splinters spear the skin between my thumb and my first finger.

One of the splinters lodges so deep, the sting runs all the way up my arm.

I pull my hand off the wood. First nothing happens. Then a white patch appears in my skin. Blood wells up. It dribbles down my hand. It trickles. It will soak my sleeve.

And Pa sees me. At last! He goes absolutely still. The woman beside him sees me too. She covers her mouth.

The girl standing by the old horse watches also. I look up at her. She's pretty far away, and I'm still on my hands and knees. She looks steady and thoughtful. She looks like the kind of girl who would not cause things to get any worse.

But now my mother is upon me.

Lucy

HE'S FIFTY YARDS AWAY. He takes two forward steps before he stops; he's standing over Jack's grave. He looks at Marilyn, a few feet to his right, and then he looks down. His feet have planted themselves wide, over his son. And your feet will plant themselves wide too, over your daughter, your child who has fallen but will get up; your Blue, who possesses the full sum of courage that this life is going to require of her.

Henry seizes your gaze. *Yes, we are both parents,* he seems to be saying; *yes, there is this much desert between us.*

His hand lifts in greeting. His hand refuses to stay at his side. It's been too long.

Do you still miss me?

Every goddamn centimeter.

Happy birthday, Jack Plageman. You can count the years right along with Marilyn and Henry. Across the expanse of sand, you stand and face this campus of dead seamen. Sunlight hollows Henry's countenance. Behind him lie the churning waters of the strait. Beside him, Marilyn looks straight at you, a question on her lips, a question she will ask.

— Henry? she says. — Who is that?

He bows his head.

Here you are, the last ten years in your throat. And here is Henry and his peacefulness, his calm, his hope — yes, even here, in this awful moment, because finally, everyone he loves is with him at the same time. He is not missing anyone. Jack is here. You are here. Blue is too. Blue, though bruised, is pushing up from the sand, as she prepares to address you, and her father, the both of you, *why* and *how come* stamped acros her face. Or are those your questions? You taught them to her. And Marilyn is here too. For the first time, Henry Plageman is not missing part of his life. He is not split in two.

There you are. He lifts his head. Across the divide, his eyes lock with yours. *There you are. I was hoping you'd come.*

I'm here.

He smiles.

—Henry? Marilyn says.

He speaks not a word. You'll speak in his stead as you stanch the blood flowing from Blue's hand. You'll speak by breathing. That's the only voice a person has some days. You reach for your petticoat, tear a corner off, ripping the cloth with your teeth, listening to Blue sob once and no more than once, listening to the sound of her becoming an adult; you tear off a strip of that cloth and wrap it around her hand, tight. Breathing is enough; your individual inhalations and exhalations will reach him. They are the code, the transmittal across the wire. And Marilyn has seen you; Marilyn has asked who you are. You cannot allow her to find out; you cannot allow her to be hurt. But she is already hurt. From what, then, are you protecting her? You're not capable of changing her life any more than it has already been changed. Marilyn's life right now *is* her life with you in it.

You're having trouble with your vision. Look at Blue. She's your sharp relief. Look at her, and then one last time at Henry as, blindly, Marilyn reaches for his hand.

Henry, your eyes say to him as he takes his wife's hand. *Tell me you'll miss me. Tell me you'll not forget me. Even when you're old. I know you're already old, but even when you're very old, far older than you are now.*

He reads your countenance.

Sweetheart, your eyes go on. *One day you will die, and I will not be allowed to be with you. I will not be allowed to sit beside your bed. The angel of propriety will take you.*

Silently he replies:

Be gentle. Be gentle with your heart. Give thanks for what we were allowed.

And you: *But we were allowed nothing.*

Henry: *Not true. We were given everything two people can be given.*

And you: *Does Marilyn know she is holding the hand of my husband?*
Henry: *She knows.*
You: *Why didn't you ever stay? Why didn't you ever once stay?*
Henry: *I never left. I'm still standing on your front step, Lucy.*
You: *What are we going to do now?*
Henry: *Pray.*
You: *But you don't pray anymore.*
Henry: *Oh, Lucy. I pray every single day.*

You can bear his eyes no longer. Marilyn drops his hand. Blue's alert but not speaking. You check the cloth tied around her thumb and palm. An endless day of bandaging and unraveling and rebandaging. She does not emit a sound.

Yours remains an odd power. You have the power to send love away, to close the door. You do not have the power to invite it inside. Is this true? You're no longer certain. It's the doctrine you have believed, the creed you have assumed.

You don't want the rest of your life to follow the same course.

Then pray, he silently urges you across the dune. *With or without me, pray.*

He will remain standing. For he has two loves and two duties, not one love and one duty. And an afternoon and evening lie ahead, a transit through a starred night, the lamp of the moon above him. He swore an oath stronger than stone, older than the gravel time has ground, dust the current blows into lungs, dust a sick man tries to expel. The remnants of old mountains oxygenate our blood.

Blue reaches up and strokes your hair. It's a tender gesture, and unexpected.

—Mama, she says. —I'm ready to go home.

You pull her into your arms and cradle her head in your lap. She emits a single sigh. She lies very still.

—You're a good girl, you whisper. —You are an absolute wonder.

She nods. You will not hear her call him Ostrich again.

—Henry? Marilyn says a final time. —Who are they?

Count your breath. Count the hairs on Blue's head. Wait for it.

—Henry?

The anguish in her voice is unbearable.

Leave before he answers her, before she utters his name again. You stand, help Blue to her feet, and lift her into your arms.

But he's calling after you, calling without a sound: *Don't make me do this. Please. Lucy. Don't make me choose.*

I didn't.

And then—a word. A name. He utters the name of the child who remains. Every fiber, every living cell in him roars it.

—*Blue.*

It lasts less than a second. But before it shuts off, before he swallows his daughter's name, his cry begs you to come back, to come home.

—Papa? Blue shouts, twisting around in your arms.

Home where? Carry her. Carry her and keep moving.

Marilyn

THE WOMAN AND THE GIRL stagger up the dune's bank. They disappear into whatever crevasse out of which they crawled.

In the back of the hearse, the stone angel waits.

The mariners' burial ground has changed. The light trails off, forgets its last thought. The wind has quieted. Past the lighthouse at Point Bonita, the Marin headlands have dissolved into indigo silhouette. To the east, Lone Mountain absorbs the rays of the sun. Odd Fellows' Cemetery lies at the foot of that hill. That's where your son will be moved; east of here. A new direction on the compass.

Henry has changed too. His mouth forms a word, a single syllable. His eyes contain the dark sea. He watches the dune's summit, the path the woman and child followed.

And here you are too, a mother on her son's birthday, asking him not to leave, not to abandon his parents. Your son is finally giving you an opportunity for regular motherhood, an experience regular mothers can fathom, a loss to which they can relate. To parent is to be left behind in stages. It is not that different from the rest of life, then.

You will not stay for what has to be done. Henry will stay. Henry will do it.

You walk to the hearse, pausing to brush sand from the top of a calla lily, still in its clay pot. It's just as well your husband didn't get around to planting most of them this year. Nothing lasts in this soil. He can try again next year, start over in a new cemetery. He can create the world anew. He can try. Lob another set of planets into the sorry sky.

A new garden in a new location.

Maybe someday.

You try to think of something to say to him, but nothing's coming. You straighten and cross the sand toward Ida.

Henry picks up the shovel. His intake of air is audible as he prepares to speak.

— Don't, you say, not looking at him. — Please don't.

— You're leaving?

— Yes.

— I thought you were going to stay.

The shovel is waiting.

— No, you say. — No, Henry, I'm not staying.

— Marilyn, he begs. — Please. I cannot do this alone.

— Yes, you say. — You can.

The letter was not to you.

Kerr walks over to him, rests his age-old hand on Henry's age-old shoulder. Kerr will stay with him. Kerr will become the helpmeet.

Ida stands by the mare and speaks softly to her. She gives her words to a creature who cares only for tone and lilt and timbre. Her gaze as she contemplates the horse is benevolent. The wind has untied her green ribbons. In the glinting afternoon light, this girl contains the promise of beauty. It's not here yet. But it's coming.

Henry lifts the shovel. It might weigh more than he does. His breath issues forth, hard, deliberate, labored. Every inhalation pierces. His exhalations are jagged, catching in his throat. They hold all he has learned to accept, all he will carry.

— Henry, Kerr says, and he reaches for the shovel. — Give it to me. I'll do it.

— No.

Your husband's eyes are bloodshot. He shakes his head. This duty is his. This love was his. He will bear them both.

The mare shoulders Ida meaningfully, deliberately, the friend Ida always wanted. She lowers her muzzle to Ida's hair, finds a section of ribbon, and tugs at it. Ida laughs.

This is the part of the tale that counts, the part that will stay standing five years from now.

— Let's go home, you tell her.

— Home where? Ida asks.

It's a good question. You can't answer yet. But when you offer your hand, she takes it. Together you leave the cemetery.

3:00 p.m.

Henry

IT'S JUST A SMALL WOODEN BOX, covered with earth. Cobwebs dust the hinges. The lid remains fast. The box will not be opened.

Will you travel to see him at Odd Fellows'? Of course. You'll visit wherever he goes. But Odd Fellows' is not the land of the forgotten. You will not dwell just a few blocks away; you will not peer out the window, stretching awake, on a Monday in June and say, *It's damp and drizzling today, therefore Jack is cold.* On a Saturday in September, you will not say, *The horned larks are out, fighting over the rights to the telephone wire, therefore the sun shines on him.* You will not smell the same rain.

Jack Plageman, when you used to sing him to sleep at night; you would sit in the wicker chair that later moved to its exile on the front porch. Your son would collapse against your chest, fists grabbing your shirt, head heavy. You would warble hymns, gazing down at him, and his eyes would fasten to yours, wise, filled with amusement, older than you, older than anyone alive. Joy comes along but once or twice in a life, and when it does, a man must take hold.

You and Kerr are sliding the coffin into the back of the hearse when you smell the fire. The Chinese have lit another one of their bonfires. Great licking flames push heat in this direction. The fire crackles. You look at the old man with the dying lungs. He looks back at you and waits.

Every hour, every week that has passed without seeing her, you leak from a thousand holes. But you must not show it. You may not lay a stone at the head of that loss or place a board at the foot. You may not plant a lily in her honor or beg a plot of earth from the mariners.

—I have to go, you say to Kerr.

He listens. He has said not a word about all that he has just witnessed.

—I have to, you repeat.

He nods, replies:

—I'll drive him over to Odd Fellows', then. We'll find him a place. I'll get the work started. Meet you over there in a couple of hours?

—Yes. A couple of hours.

Just not yet.

—Henry? he says.—Safe travels.

Speaking carefully, he adds:

—Mrs. Plageman went thataway.

But you're not walking thataway. And he knows it. You're taking the shortcut. The path Lucy used. It's the same path you taught her to take during the ten years she spent helping you tend the garden, the ten years she spent helping you stay married.

You clap Kerr on both shoulders.—Thank you.

He lowers his head.

You run. You run through dunes. They were the first inhabitants. After them came plants, hardy varieties that stabilized the sand. Lupine, dune tansies, beach sagewort, coyote bush. Later came hunters and gatherers, and later still came settlers, who moved across San Francisco. They leveled hills, carted sand to Yerba Buena Cove and Mission Bay, filled in marshland and estuaries, created dry land out of standing ponds, out of black interdune pools. They cut out one section of the land and grafted it onto another. They became surgeons of earth.

The wind is working against you. Your legs are working against you too. You're gasping for air, just like Kerr's been doing.

At the Clement Street entrance, you stop, doubled over once more. Never have you run like a fool after someone; never have you ridden your own horse as opposed to being God's or the devil's. You should have been a fool a long time ago. You should have been the fool to end all fools, the protester to end all protests.

What would it have done to Marilyn? It nearly would have killed her. But what has your staying done?

You peer past the gate. At the far end of the street, sunlight stripes the path. And at the outer reaches of your vision, you see her.

There's a horse and gig, and inside, three riders. Blue. And Lucy. A stranger is driving them. A stranger, a man, giving them a lift. Lucy sits on his left with that stiffness she always displays when she's trying too hard to be at ease with someone.

You raise your hand. You prepare to shout, to call out. Prepare to chase after them. You can catch up with a horse. You've done worse.

Lucy shifts in her seat. And even this far away, you glimpse it, the way she carries herself, adjusting her position so she's no longer side by side but halfway facing him. Her body relaxes. Her body orients toward him. You know the posture. She once held herself the same way for you in the front row of the Women's Memorial Church, the day you stood at the podium and uttered your final sermon.

The horse veers onto a side street. They're taking a different route from the one you would have taken. They're leaving your line of vision. In half a minute, in twenty seconds, she and Blue will be gone.

Remain where you are standing.

The day spreads wide and long.

Blue

SHE WALKS ME SOUTH, past the Grand Order of This and That, groups with strange names, groups that make sense to people who belong to them. Twice she stops to inspect my hand. The second time, she reaches down and tears off another section of her petticoat. Her hands are steady. She ties the cloth around me where the splinter went in and tells me to keep walking. The way out is downhill.

—Are you scared? she asks.

I shake my head. When people ask if you're scared, it's a good bet that they're scared themselves.

—Because I'll take care of you. I will.

Yes. She'll sure try.

People in general take care of their own. They guard their families. They lock their doors. They watch over their horses and their vegetables. They feed their children. But wild things need saving too.

Ma strides with a sure long gait. The sun is hard and hot and shows the lines at her eyes. I don't mind them. I'd take her face over anyone's.

She will not go back to the cemetery.

My hand hurts more than ever. This sheriff's costume is a sweat trap. Sand grits the inside of my chaps.

The snails at the cottage are crossing the floor by now, exploring under the bed, sliding in and out of Ma's box of letters.

The sun beats down on her head and neck. It glares at the sand, and the sand glares back.

—It's too bright, she says, and darts a glance my way. I keep walking.

———

Near the gate exiting onto Clement Street, she stops short. I stop too, behind her, and peek around.

There's the street, which climbs uphill to the west, and across the lane sprawls a field, the start of a newcomer's farm, with two bony cows by the caretaker's shed, cows studying us with curiosity. And someone is here. Someone is at the cemetery gate, waiting under the wide sky. No one ever waits for us. The wind blows Ma's hair into her face. She walks forward.

The man leans against the gate. His hands are tucked into his armpits. His jacket is unbuttoned. His hat rests at an angle. He watches Ma with a good deal of concentration. The only moving part of him is his mouth, chewing a piece of grass.

Ma stops.

—Oh, she says, to me, sort of, but also to the air. To the day.

She takes one more step toward the gate. And stops again.

She needs to say something. She needs to stop looking like she just swallowed a spoonful of sand.

So I poke her in the side. Pinch her, actually.

—Mother, I say.—Wake up.

She walks forward. She makes her way to the gate, holding my good hand.

—You, she says to him.—You're here.

I stick close to her side. I am the sheriff. I will always be the sheriff where my mother is concerned.

—Course I'm here, Mr. Stone says.

He uncrosses his arms and attends to me first. He reaches for my hurt hand. He studies it first one way, then the other. His eyes never stray.

—You're a true troublemaker, little one, he says to me.—A genuine outlaw.

He reaches into his pocket and pulls out a handkerchief, then wraps it around the cloth Ma tied on earlier. After knotting it, he studies me with a good deal of seriousness. I am now triple bandaged. Ma keeps looking at that handkerchief.

He turns and regards her. His smile slowly fades. His eyes rest on her. And for the first time in I can't remember how long, she stays totally quiet.

—Ready? he says, and he clears his throat, softer all of a sudden, and gentler.

Then I see a horse and gig. I was so caught up with everything, I missed the beauteous creature across the street, nosing for greens. J. B. Stone has a chestnut horse with a black mane and a white star on its forehead.

Ma glances over her shoulder. She looks back at the graveyards. She looks for a long time. No one is coming after her. No one is following her out.

—Mother, I say.—Turn around.

A Note About San Francisco History

On May 22 and May 23, 1897, the *San Francisco Call* included coverage of three local events deemed newsworthy—a child's fall through a skylight, a Richmond district neighborhood meeting about the city cemetery, and an orphanage's grand opening. I borrowed from these three unrelated events to launch the stories of Blue and Lucy, Henry, and Marilyn.

Historical records also tell us that a man named Thomas Kerr was the foreman of Odd Fellows' Cemetery. Kerr disrupted the Richmond neighborhood meeting along with several other foremen by shouting "Amen" multiple times. A man named Henry Plagemann (spelled with two *n*'s) was a locally well-known quartet singer. He is listed as a party to a lawsuit against the city regarding the cemeteries, a case that went all the way to the U.S. Supreme Court, which ruled in favor of the city in September 1903. The parties against the cemetery ordinance included the Masonic Cemetery, the Odd Fellows' Cemetery, and Plagemann, who was reportedly the owner of a lot in one of the graveyards.

Catherine Wood was the incoming vice president of the board of managers for the Maria Kip Orphanage. Adolph Sutro was a celebrity in his day, the former mayor of San Francisco and a wealthy tycoon and collector. He is best remembered now for the various landmarks and locations in San Francisco that bear his name. His daughter Emma Sutro Merritt was a physician—an unusual accomplishment for a woman in the late nineteenth century.

The debate over the closure of San Francisco's city cemetery began well before May 22, 1897, and continued long afterward.

1908: San Francisco coroner Thomas B. W. Leland, MD, finally initiates a plan to remove the bodies from Golden Gate cemetery (the city cemetery). The *Call* observes: "It has been more than 10 years since interments were permitted, and the park has suffered from neglect. Fire swept over the place a few years ago and destroyed headstones."

1908 to 1921: The *Call* falls largely silent on the subject of disinterment. When it does report on the city cemetery, attention focuses on the plan for the new Lincoln Park, the new "scenic driveway" for the city, and the new golf course. In 1913 the *Call* notes that the twenty-five acres in San Mateo purchased by the city to hold the occupants previously relocated from the city cemetery have not been utilized. "Nothing but money has been buried in the property," the article declares. And seven of the twenty-five acres have been washed away due to erosion.

December 23, 1921: During the construction of a memorial to the war dead in Lincoln Park (what will become the Palace of the Legion of Honor), a reporter from the *Daily News* finds crews scraping up bodies and coffins from the ground. The foreman estimates they have "taken up" about fifteen hundred bodies so far. The article scandalizes San Francisco with its graphic report of disinterred corpses scattered across the parkland:

> The site of the $250,000 memorial to the dead was once a cemetery. It still is, but the bones are now scattered. In the excavation work for the memorial workmen have uncovered about 1500 skeleton-filled coffins. No provision was made for the reburying of the bodies. Workmen have cut down about nine or 10 feet in their work. Sometimes as many as four or five bodies have been pulled out in an hour . . . Just as I arrived one large and two small skeletons were ripped out of one grave. In the grave were household utensils. Besides the skeletons lay the coffin boards. Wrapped about them were the shrouds. Workmen steered clear of the mess . . . Here was the bottom end of a coffin sticking out of the sand bluff. Further along the bluff the head of the coffin. A skull there. The coffins poked out all along that cliff. At night, after the workmen have gone, small boys of the neighborhood kick their toes into the dirt. Why? One said that $35 had been found

in one of the coffins. An expensive ring in another, he said. And the skulls—sometimes students at the Affiliated colleges bought them.

Summer 1993: During an expansion of the California Palace of the Legion of Honor, bodies are again accidentally unearthed. Researchers arrive to investigate, and approximately nine hundred additional corpses are recovered. The *Los Angeles Times* reports that two of the corpses still clutched rosaries; others were wearing dentures.

The *Times* interviews an expert who claims that thousands more bodies might well lie underneath the museum grounds. Remains and artifacts are turned over to the coroner's office.

The team of archaeologists called in suggest doing an extensive dig. Museum officials decline. The lead scientist working on the site is Phillip Walker. In collaboration with Walker, Michele Buzon (as well as Susan Kerr and Francine Drayer) conducts a project involving the analysis of paleopathological data collected from the bodies. Their resulting report, "Health and Disease in 19th Century San Francisco: Skeletal Evidence from a Forgotten Cemetery," appears in *Historical Archaeology* in 2005. To date, it is the only peer-reviewed academic article examining forgotten remains from the former city cemetery.

The research of this team suggests that these individuals were interred in the city cemetery between 1868 and about 1906. The research further indicates that they were most likely "poor, working-class people of European ancestry" as well as persons of Chinese descent.

Visitors to the Legion of Honor museum today will find no information about the discovery of the cemetery's overlooked remains. The golf course holds just two reminders that a cemetery once occupied this land: an obelisk presented to the Ladies' Seaman's Friends Society and a modest monument honoring the old Chinese graves. But surrounding a tree near the seamen's memorial are large granite pieces from the old cemetery plots.

Acknowledgments

I would like to thank Nicole Angeloro, Michele Buzon, Pilar Garcia-Brown, Hannah Harlow, Brooks Holifield, Jenna Johnson, Mark Kasprow, John Martini, Maggi McKay, Liza Nelson, Tracy Roe, Doris Sloan, and Erika West. I'm also grateful to the members of my Emory Medicine writing group; to my parents, Gordon and Marion Brown; and to my sister, Candace Brown. A generous residency at the Hambidge Center allowed me to begin writing this novel. The members of the Western Neighborhoods Project in San Francisco provided superb advice and resources.

Special thanks to Henry Dunow, agent and friend, and to John Freeman, teacher and historian. John generously shared a treasure-trove of knowledge about the Outside Lands of the city and county of San Francisco.

This book is dedicated to Mark Joseph Pelletier.

Reading Group Guide

1. The novel takes place over the course of one day—May 22, 1897—and any events that occurred prior to that date are depicted through recollection. What effect does this compression of time have on the narrative? What is the relationship between time and memory?

2. The vast majority of the novel is told via second-person narration. What does this mode of narration achieve that first and third person do not?

   a. Unlike Marilyn, Lucy, and Henry, Blue delivers her narration in first person. Considering Blue's role within the novel, why do you think Pelletier made this choice?

3. "The city cemetery is the largest and the poorest, the most dilapidated. It's a potter's field, a burial ground for the immigrant, the indigent, the homeless, the nameless, the outsider" (5). The novel is framed by Henry's struggle to prevent the San Francisco government from closing the cemetery where his son is buried. Consider the personal and political stakes involved in this conflict. Is the city's fight to exhume these graves and deposit the human remains outside the city borders symbolic in any way?

4. On page 22, the narrator says, "Marriage is a series of carefully managed letdowns." What do you make of this statement? Discuss in relation to the novel as a whole.

5. Faith, or loss thereof, plays a critical role in the novel, particularly for Henry, an ex-Lutheran minister. What unique relationships do

Henry, Marilyn, and Lucy each have with religion? How do notions of virtue and sin factor into each character's personal morality? In your opinion, is any character beyond redemption?

6. "Two truths can subsist together. Two loves can too" (304). Do you agree? Upon what factors is truth contingent? Upon what factors is love contingent?

7. Near the end of the novel, when Lucy encounters Henry and Marilyn at Jack's graveside, the narrator writes, "The real marriage, the real affair in this tale, is between you [Lucy] and Marilyn" (306). What do you make of this insight? What is the nature of Lucy and Marilyn's dynamic? In what ways do they mirror one another?

8. Discuss the ending. Did you find it hopeful, or do you doubt that the characters will ever find closure? Why do you think Pelletier chose to conclude the novel with Blue's perspective?

9. As Pelletier describes in "A Note About San Francisco History" (325), the novel was inspired by real events discovered in historical documents. What do you make of historical research as a mode of weaving together a narrative? How has the novel shaped your understanding of San Francisco in this era?

Q&A with Stacia Pelletier

What was the inspiration for The Half Wives?

Relationships conducted in secret fascinate me. A few years ago I was walking my dogs through a cemetery and saw a gravestone for a man flanked by two smaller gravestones. One was clearly marked as his wife, and the other was neither a daughter nor a second wife but some unidentified woman who did not share the family name. I began to imagine a story in which a man tried to provide for two families—one legitimate, the other kept secret. I wanted to know how the two women involved would experience that kind of situation if it took place over a considerable number of years. What would happen if they met each other? *The Half Wives* is the result.

Why did you decide to set the novel in nineteenth-century San Francisco?

I lived in San Francisco for a couple of years in the 1990s and fell in love with the city and its geographical history. I became obsessed with a political fight that erupted in the late nineteenth century when developers and neighborhood groups began advocating for the closure of the city cemetery so that they could repurpose the land for their own uses. This was a fight between the forces of economic progress and the voices of the marginalized—the poor, the outsider, the immigrant—who did not want their dead to be disinterred. I wanted to explore the story of Henry and his two families against this broader backdrop. Unfortunately, the city cemetery was eventually closed and a golf course was built on top of it.

You have graduate degrees in religion and historical theology. How did this impact you when writing about Henry, a former minister?

When I was in my first year at seminary a very old German professor with a long, white beard sat beside me one day at lunch and announced to me: "Man is a mule forever being ridden either by God or by the devil!" He was so adamant in his declaration—I later learned that he was paraphrasing Martin Luther—that his image of man-as-mule stayed with me through the next nine years of graduate school. It's entirely possible I could have skipped the next nine years and just held on to that image. I find it compelling for a variety of reasons, particularly relating to how we do—or do not—take responsibility for our lives and our decisions. In *The Half Wives,* Henry has stepped away from the formal practice of his faith because, in the aftermath of losing his son, he can no longer answer the questions his congregation members pose. But the teachings and the difficult beauty of Lutheranism continue to haunt him.

Your first novel, Accidents of Providence, *also dealt with themes of motherhood, fidelity, and women's autonomy. What draws you to these subjects?*

I'm interested in who "counts" as a mother, in part because I do not have biological children of my own, though I do have stepdaughters. I'm interested in what counts as faithfulness in a relationship, probably because I think we pay lip service to the notion of monogamy and uphold it as an ideal, but rarely talk about the challenges that significant loss or stress can bring to even the most faithful couples. And I'm interested in autonomy because without it, you pretty much have nothing, but with it, if you turn it into an end in itself, it can sometimes overtake your capacity to be vulnerable to another in a positive sense. Without that type of vulnerability, that type of trust, you don't have the possibility of a truly mutual love. We've all been hurt. The question is: what do you do the day after?